Sophie

The
Schoolhouse

Sophie Ward is an actor and writer who has worked in film and television since her feature film debut in *Young Sherlock Holmes*, and in theater, most notably with the Citizens Theatre in Glasgow. Sophie has been an active campaigner for LGBTQ rights, and her nonfiction book, *A Marriage Proposal*, was published by Guardian Shorts in 2014. Her first novel, *Love and Other Thought Experiments*, was longlisted for the Booker Prize in 2020.

Also by Sophie Ward

Love and Other Thought Experiments

The
Schoolhouse

The Schoolhouse

Sophie Ward

VINTAGE BOOKS

A Division of Penguin Random House LLC

New York

A VINTAGE BOOKS ORIGINAL 2023

The Library of Congress has cataloged the Hachette edition as follows:
Name: Ward, Sophie, [date] author.
Title: The schoolhouse / Sophie Ward.
Description: First edition. | London : Corsair, 2022.
Identifiers: LCCN 2020478959
Subjects: LCSH: London (England)—Fiction.
Classification: LCC PR6123.A725 S36 2022 | DDC 823.92—dc23
LC record available at https://lccn.loc.gov/2020478959

Vintage Books Trade Paperback ISBN: 978-0-593-46926-2
eBook ISBN: 978-0-593-46927-9

vintagebooks.com

Printed in the United States of America
10 9 8 7 6 5 4 3 2 1

For Nat and Josh

Let the children be free; encourage them; let them run outside when it is raining; let them remove their shoes when they find a puddle of water; and, when the grass of the meadows is wet with dew, let them run on it and trample it with their bare feet; let them rest peacefully when a tree invites them to sleep beneath its shade; let them shout and laugh when the sun wakes them in the morning.

MARIA MONTESSORI,
The Discovery of the Child

Contents

December 1990

Friday

1

The university library was housed in an unimposing corner of North London, halfway up the Holloway Road. A small campus occupied the grounds of a former landfill site and seagulls still circled overhead, drawn by the scent of waste. When Isobel walked back from lunch the shadows of the birds followed her in the winter sunlight.

From the safety of her desk, she flinched at the thought of the gulls' swollen bodies. Across the room in the study area, two children sat in modular chairs and read books they had brought with them. The children distracted her. She was used to the research students and teaching staff using the library but visitors had to be registered with the university. The children must belong to one of the faculty. Isobel watched them from her workstation.

The library stood at the back of the campus, a liver-bricked cube with a wide staircase leading from the entrance to the road below. Inside, the books were arranged over two levels. Isobel's station was placed in the middle of the ground floor. From there, she could see everyone who entered. If she turned, she had a clear view between the rows of shelving behind her and Periodicals on her left. It was among the newspapers and magazines that the children sat. They didn't speak to each other.

The only activity came from Melanie Harris at the front desk, stamping books and stacking them onto the metal trolleys. Isobel imagined that Melanie must stamp books in her sleep.

She shared her desk with Jenny. Since Isobel was not a qualified librarian, she was responsible for the maintenance of the books and some of the filing while Jenny took care of all research enquiries. The senior librarians worked in their offices upstairs, visiting the ground floor when they had specific requests. They were always smartly dressed, the two male librarians in suits, while the women wore silky blouses and woollen skirts. Isobel enjoyed the busy periods at the end of term, when everyone worked on the shelves. The jewel colours of the women's clothes shone out against the sea of student denim. Isobel did not care to shine, but she admired the confidence of those who did.

She took a sip of coffee from the Thermos she kept on the shelf under the countertop. Jenny was making a fresh pot in the staffroom but Isobel preferred the way they made it in the university canteen. The liquid was cold now, but she drank it while she watched the children.

The two girls sat with their hair hanging loose, shoulders rounded as they bent over their books. They looked alike, thin bodies in flared jeans and polo neck jumpers, with the floury faces and shadowed eyes of city children in winter. It had been so long since Isobel had spent any time with children. They were young to be on their own in the library, but they knew how to behave. Nine, maybe? Ten? They each turned the page they were reading and glanced up at each other. She could almost read their lips from where she stood.

'No,' one of the girls seemed to say, 'family.'

Isobel looked away.

When Jenny returned from her break, Isobel got her

coat and scarf and went outside. Clouds drooped over the campus square. A few students leaned against benches, eating chips and smoking. A solitary Christmas star in gold tinsel shimmered from a lamp post. Isobel walked across the icy concrete, feeling the cold spread through the soles of her shoes up into her toes, and letting her breath condense in the wool under her chin. She went back to the library as the last streetlight flickered on. The children were gone.

Dalston Echo

18 December 1974

NEW PREMISES FOR CHARITY SCHOOL

The Christmas spirit has helped provide a new building for the plucky children at the Schoolhouse. The charity-funded school has been searching for a site large enough to accommodate the different needs of its pupils, some of whom are handicapped. This month, the Society for Children's Learning signed the lease on a Victorian warehouse behind Graham Road.

'This is great news for all our children,' Schoolhouse headmaster Colin Sanders told the *Echo*. 'We were growing out of the old building and it was time for us to expand. The new site has a lot of potential. The Society for Children's Learning has been our Christmas angel.'

Children from the Schoolhouse can be seen singing Christmas hymns at Smithfield's meat market this Saturday lunchtime.

Thursday

It was the first day of term today but we didn't have to learn anything because we moved into the new building and we helped unpack. The school used to be a house in a street but now it is in a big building with an outdoors that will be a playground one day. All of us are still in one room, except for the kindergarten classes upstairs, and the Maths room. There is a basement called the undercroft and Mr Dickens said it will be the art room one day but I said it's so dusty that you can't breathe. Mr Dickens said, 'You can clean it, Izzy.'

The headmaster Mr Sanders has an office and he has put in loudspeakers called a Tannoy all over the school, even in the toilets. He has plans for the building and he wants to show us that it is 'an exciting new venture'. He asked Christopher to walk in front of us all. I have never seen Christopher walk but Mr Sanders said he practised. We stood in the main hall and watched while he wheeled Christopher into position.

'This is a very exciting day. Let's show Christopher we care!' Mr Sanders started clapping. We were supposed to clap as well. It's just pretending. I didn't say anything though, I just clapped.

Christopher pushed himself up so he was standing against

the chair. Miss Spill went to hold his arm but Mr Sanders waved her away.

Christopher moved one foot forward and then he leaned over and dragged his other foot. He wobbled for a bit and then he took another step.

Mr Sanders stamped his feet from side to side to show Christopher how to do it.

Christopher took another step but he had to use his hands to carry his back leg and he lost his balance and fell over. Mr Sanders started clapping even harder.

No one was allowed to help Christopher get in his wheelchair.

I was hungry in the afternoon and I didn't have any money for sweets but I had some of my candy necklace in my pocket. It was fluffy from my coat because I licked it yesterday but I washed it under the tap in the loos and sucked it on the way home and I didn't feel hungry any more.

Monday

I got the early bus into school. Mum and Dad were still in bed. Lucy gave me this diary for my birthday. She is deaf so she can't hear, but she can talk and she can read. Sometimes she wears a hearing aid but she doesn't like it. There are other children at school who can't hear, one boy who is still in kindergarten and a girl who hurt her head when she was born. Lucy taught me some words from sign language so we can talk to each other.

Lucy has her own diary and we can write in our diaries all day. The girls have a gang like the boys now. We are all eleven, Kathy Binks, Lucy and me. Kathy is new from last term, I think she was expelled from her old school. Loads of people get expelled from school. You can't be expelled from the Schoolhouse though; Mr Sanders says it is a refuge.

Wednesday

There are two caffs the teachers take us to for lunch because there isn't a kitchen in the new school yet. The girls go to one caff and the boys go to the other and we swap the next day. Luigi's is best. There are yellow tables and you can have an ice cream float to drink. I always choose cream soda because then I can pretend I am an American girl like Anne of Green Gables. All the food here is from the meat market where we sing at Christmas. I cut it up into small pieces and put it at the side of the plate and it looks like I have eaten some.

Tuesday

The school guinea pig died today. I used to bring him home at the weekends and once we had to smoke him out because he got stuck under the shed in the garden. I think he would have come out if we talked to him but Dad made a fire before I had the chance. You can still see the burn marks where the grass used to be.

At school Kathy and I went to clean his cage and when I touched him he was hard under his fur like a flannel when you leave it on the side of the bath. Kathy pushed him and he didn't move. Kathy said he was dead.

Angie stood in the pet area, watching us. She said, 'I want to hug'. 'Fuck,' Kathy said, 'the fucking thing's dead.' I didn't know what to say. 'I really want to hug,' said Angie. 'You can't hug it. It's d-e-a-d.'

The guinea pig was called Bartholomew.

Friday

I was late after school because I walked to Kathy's house first and we ate an avocado pear. When I got home Mum was on the phone. She waved at me and her bracelets jangled but she kept talking. She told her friend I was so independent because of the Schoolhouse.

I do like exploring but I don't see what it's got to do with school. The Schoolhouse has about a hundred children in it. We don't have lessons like in other schools and I don't think they teach us anything. When Mum and Dad sent me there they said it was important to go to a mixed school. They went to strict schools and they didn't like them and Mum's always telling her friends how much the Schoolhouse does for disadvantaged children. She thinks we are different kinds of people. But it's not like that. They don't listen when I try to tell them what it is like. So I will write this diary and then they will see.

2

Leabrook police station was a forty-minute walk from Palmerston Housing Estate. Detective Sergeant Sally Carter had noted it that morning while she waited for Susan Thompson. It took less than ten minutes to drive, avoiding the High Street and the one-way system, but no one in the Thompson residence had a car.

The woman had reported her daughter missing the previous night and PC Rebecca Hill had taken the statement. The report was on Carter's desk. Ten-year-old Caitlin Thompson had not come home from school the day before. Her parents had searched the estate, been to her local friends and called everyone in their family. Only when they had run out of options did they consider the police. It was late by the time they called.

Hill had checked in with the local hospitals and phoned the contact numbers Susan Thompson had given. Two uniforms searched the estate. There was no news of Caitlin by the time Carter arrived for work on Friday morning, and the girl's father had already called several times. His wife was on her way, he said, they couldn't sit at home and do nothing.

Carter did not know the estate well, she had served her beat years a few miles away in Islington, and when she looked at the missing child's mother that morning, she felt her lack of local experience. It wasn't the geography, she'd worked in Leabrook long enough to understand the streets and what connected them, but she was not yet part of the community, and Susan Thompson could tell.

'Where's Rebecca?' The woman looked around the reception area.

'She's not here this morning, Mrs Thompson.' Carter stopped herself from adding 'I'm sorry', although she was.

Carter got Susan Thompson a cup of tea and took Hill's report to her DI's office.

Detective Inspector Brecon glanced at the case and agreed Carter should take Mrs Thompson home. Missing children were always a headache. They usually turned out to be nothing, a waste of time and money, but the possibility of a serious crime had to be considered. There was a protocol, but it didn't matter if you'd stuck to the rules if the case was an abduction, abuse, or worse. Brecon would let Carter carry that particular weight for now.

Carter took PC Dawson to accompany her in the car with Susan Thompson, and asked Dawson's beat partner, PC Marshall, to join them on the estate. The mother stared out the window for the journey, twisting round for a better look whenever a child came into view. She answered Carter's careful questions without elaborating on her earlier state-ment. When Carter tried to get a sense of the missing girl, Thompson closed her eyes and leaned back against the seat, her mouth set in a tense ridge. Whether to prevent herself from talking or crying, Carter was not sure.

Probably both, she decided as they walked up the two flights of exterior steps to the Thompson household, a two-bedroom flat in the middle of one of the larger low-rise housing estates in Leabrook. The Right to Buy schemes of the past decade hadn't reached Palmerston. It was a type of community Carter recognised from her own early childhood, but she didn't make the mistake of thinking that gave her any special insight into the residents.

David Thompson was waiting for them. At his feet, a grey-and-white dog stood to attention. Carter saw the father's expectant look turn to worry and anger as he stared at the police standing in his living room.

'Well? Where is she?' The man's thin face tightened.

Carter detected guilt as well, but there were plenty of things for parents to feel guilty about once a child had gone. She went through the events that led to Caitlin's disappearance. The Thompsons were at work when their daughter should have been home. David Thompson got back around 6 p.m. Usually his wife was there before him but on Thursday he knew she'd gone to her sister's. When he saw Caitlin wasn't in her room, he called his wife at her sister's place but she was already on her way back. The sister hadn't seen Caitlin. Susan stopped to get some shopping and it was after seven by the time she got home. By then, David had done a search of the estate. The Thompsons had clearly argued about whether to call the police. 'I told you they wouldn't do anything,' David said now, more than once, as they went over the night's events.

Once she had seen the girl's bedroom, Carter asked the Thompsons to walk round the estate with her. The dog pushed between them.

'Don't mind Spencer,' Susan Thompson bent to stroke the wiry coat, 'he's missing her too.'

'Seems like an old-fashioned neighbourhood,' Carter said, 'where you can count on each other.'

'It is,' Susan Thompson nodded. 'They're a decent lot.'

'That's what we thought.' David kept his eyes on the ground in front of him.

Carter left Dawson at the flat and followed the Thompsons along the walkways that linked each three-storey unit. The dog didn't leave their side. At each corner the bitter wind attacked from a new direction. The units had a row of flats on every floor and all the hallways were external, the front doors visible to the flats opposite. Over five hundred homes and more than a thousand residents.

'You think Caitlin might be with someone on the estate?'

David shrugged. 'I don't know what to think.'

They stopped at the next walkway and the dog took a desultory pee against the wall. Even from the second floor it was hard to see beyond the concrete buildings. Carter scanned the landscape. In the middle of the estate a pair of teenagers kicked a ball round a tarmac rectangle. Kids on bikes circled parked cars. Carter frowned. They were too young to be out of school.

'Was there anywhere she liked to go with her friends?' Carter turned to the parents. 'There was nothing to do when I was a kid, except the park or our house. It's different now though, isn't it?'

Susan Thompson stared at her, petite and sharp-featured with wide-set eyes.

'Caitlin isn't a truant. She's never done anything like this before. She goes to school every day. You can check the register.'

'How about after school, though?' Carter took a cigarette from a pack of Marlboro Lights in her jacket pocket and offered one to the Thompsons. She had stopped smoking two years ago but she hadn't come up with anything better for encouraging people to talk. David looked away, but Susan nodded and Carter saw how her hand shook as she drew a cigarette from the pack.

'You're both at work,' Carter continued.

'She comes home with her friend Ruby.' Susan cupped her hand round the lighter Carter held out. 'Caitlin's got keys.'

'But she didn't see Ruby last night and no one saw her come home?'

The Thompsons exchanged glances.

'She goes to the pool,' David said.

'On her own?'

'She doesn't swim.' The father shook his head. 'She just hangs out there. It's warm, there's a caff.'

Susan's lips pursed. 'She's allowed to go out as long as she comes home first and gets back for tea. It's only an hour.'

'Except on Thursdays?' Carter kept the question neutral but she caught Susan's glance at David.

'I go over to help out at my sister's place. She's on her own with three kids and she has to take her eldest to hospital on Thursdays.' Susan coughed into the hand that held her cigarette, scattering ash onto Carter's shoulder.

'So, when Caitlin wasn't . . . '

David jumped in before Carter had finished the sentence. 'I thought she was with Susie. When her sister said Caitlin wasn't with her, I went out to look.'

Susan Thompson took a step towards her husband and held on to his arm. 'We should be looking for her now. You,' she turned to Carter, 'you'll help us won't you? They should be out there, looking for her.'

'We are, Mrs Thompson. We're in touch with the school and Caitlin is registered as a missing person.'

'She's ten.' The mother shivered.

'A missing child, yes.' Carter stubbed out her cigarette before she could finish it. 'This friend, Ruby? Any idea why she didn't say at the time that Caitlin hadn't turned up?'

Susan's eyes closed for a moment. 'She didn't want to get Cait in trouble. At that age, they get other friends and . . .' Her voice broke. 'Where is she? Where's my baby?' Tears slicked down her grey face. From the corner of the walkway, the dog stared back at them, head to one side. Carter took a deep breath as her thoughts connected.

'What about your dog? Spencer. Where was Spencer when you were all out?'

David Thompson shook his head. 'What?'

'With me,' said Susan, a catch in her throat. 'He always comes with me. I take him to the laundrette when I'm at work and he comes to my sister's. Always. You can't leave a dog on its own all day. You can't.'

Her voice trailed to a sob as her husband put a hand on her back, and the couple bent into each other. Carter watched them, the wind grazing her eyes in the darkening December light. She had grown up here. Somewhere like this. A smaller estate, less than an hour east of this place, with her own family and a dog, and the chill that seeped into your blood. But that family hadn't held one another. That dog hadn't gone out. And no one looked for you when you didn't come home.

Carter followed Susan Thompson's directions for the route to Leabrook South Primary School. The building was at the end of a cul-de-sac off the High Street, and looked about twenty years old. Carter could see the amputated terraced houses that the council must have carved up to build the new school. She guessed most of those councillors had retired on profits from their property companies. There was no borough that was too broke not to have the unscrupulous break it some more.

She asked to speak to the headmaster, Mr Fry, and Caitlin's friend Ruby before a general search and questioning of the pupils. In Carter's experience, a school full of disrupted children was about as easy to control as a prison riot and a lot more unpredictable. The children were already overexcited in the weeks before Christmas.

Ruby Siltmore was six months younger than Caitlin and in the class below her. Since the new school year, Ruby and Caitlin had been allowed to walk home together, an arrangement Susan Thompson said she liked because it was good for Caitlin to 'keep an eye on a younger one'.

Carter was shown to the dining room to wait for Ruby and her form teacher, Miss Davies. The girl was tiny. Skinny arms and legs in the school uniform of bottle-green jumper and polo shirt, green tights with a band of grey fabric at the top that passed for a skirt. Carter thought of Caitlin's school photo she'd removed from on top of the telly in the Thompsons' living room, the girl's scrubbed face full of sulky bravado.

'Ruby?' Carter smiled and nodded. 'I'm Sally Carter. I'm a police officer. Do you know why I'm here?'

The girl shrank back.

'It's OK.' Carter checked with Miss Davies that she should continue.

'Cait?' Ruby ventured.

'Yes. She's not been home and no one has seen her since school yesterday. Her mum says you walk home together?'

The girl stared at her, eyes wide.

'Did you walk home with Caitlin yesterday?'

A shake of the head.

'But you waited for her at the gates.'

An imperceptible nod. Carter got out her notebook.

'It would really help us, Ruby, if you could tell me what happened after school. Anything you remember that was different from normal.'

Ruby looked at the notepad and back at her teacher.

'You waited for Caitlin, like you usually do, because you get out five minutes earlier. Is that right?' Carter tried looking at the pad instead of the child.

'Ruby?' The teacher's voice was calm but insistent.

'Cait didn't come.'

'So you had to walk home alone? Why didn't you tell your mum?'

The child wailed, the sound of a feral cat.

'Ruby?'

Miss Davies ignored the girl's sobs. 'It's OK, Ruby. You can tell the truth.'

'It wasn't my fault. I thought she'd gone to the pool with her friends, I . . . I didn't want to tell on her . . . ' Ruby hung her head as the thin shoulders heaved.

Carter put her notepad away and left the teacher to comfort Ruby. She had no technique for dealing with the situation. Ten-year-old girls were only part of her life as truants or victims. They were rarely good witnesses.

There were few security procedures at the school. Visitors came and went without registering but everyone was obliged to enter by the main entrance, which was locked during the day. A receptionist buzzed people in and out. Miss Traynor. When it was quiet she had a good view of all the visitors but during busy periods she admitted it became too hectic to see much except a wave of children streaming past her desk. She was young, mid-twenties, and hadn't worked at the school for long.

'She ran off?'

'We're not sure. She could be with a friend or have got lost or be in trouble with her family. We're asking everyone to think about when they last saw Caitlin and if they can remember anything unusual about her behaviour recently.'

Miss Traynor sucked on her lips while she thought.

'I saw her yesterday. She borrowed a hairband for gym. She was always needing a hairband. Seemed fine.'

'Her friend Ruby was waiting for her outside after school but Caitlin didn't turn up. Her form teacher confirmed she was in class all day, but could she have left early?'

'Not before the bell. Door's locked.'

'It's busy though, when the bell does go? You wouldn't know who was coming in or going out?'

The receptionist shrugged her shoulders.

'Thing is, if Caitlin didn't leave with the rest of her class, and Ruby says she didn't, then either she was still in the school or she left on her own and no one saw her, or possibly . . . ' Carter spoke over Miss Traynor's objection, 'she left with someone else that you'd let in.'

It took thirty minutes to get the names of those visitors she could remember between Caitlin's gym class after lunch and the bell at 3.20. A few parents and a couple of deliveries. There was no reason to think any of them was connected to Caitlin, though she would ask the Thompsons, and none of them had been seen leaving with her. Carter radioed a request for Detective Sergeant Lafferty to attend with two uniformed officers to assist with the search while she talked to a few more of the staff. She made a note to ask Lafferty to check the leisure centre and find out if anyone had seen Caitlin.

The headmaster oversaw the search of the premises while answering questions. Carter was surprised that he was able to discuss Caitlin Thompson in some detail.

'We're a small school, Sergeant. Caitlin has been here for five years. She's not in any trouble is she?'

Carter frowned. 'What sort of trouble could she be in, Mr Fry?'

'Oh, you hear such things.'

'About Caitlin?'

'No, no. She's a good girl. Not exactly academic,' Fry smiled, 'but bright enough.'

Academic? Carter wondered how men like Fry ended up running schools in hard-pressed London boroughs.

'In all likelihood she's at a friend's house.' Carter put her notebook away. 'But we need to be alert to all possibilities. She is only ten.'

'Quite.' Fry pressed his palms together. 'That's what your Detective Inspector said.'

Carter shouldn't have been surprised but she wished Brecon had talked to her first. Fry had the confidence of a man who felt he had the upper hand and now Carter had to work out how she could turn that to her advantage. She made a point to thank him for his cooperation as the search progressed.

All the kids stood in noisy crocodiles in the front yard while their classrooms were checked. They dangled legs and arms through the front railings and howled like a many-limbed beast when Carter left the premises.

The police radio crackled to life.

'That's a negative at the swimming pool. Couple of the kids know her but no one saw her yesterday. Dawson and Marshall are bringing the Thompsons in.'

Carter watched the children being ushered back into the building for lunch. The familiar damp cloth scent of school dinners hung in the afternoon air and she felt grateful for the bacon sandwich she could buy on the way back to the station. She was hungry, and she needed a break. She wished she could share the time with Rebecca Hill. She still hadn't had a chance to go over Hill's first impression of the case from the night before, and she valued her insight.

Susan and David Thompson had been called in for formal interviews. The Thompsons had no police record and were visibly desperate, but for Brecon they were the main suspects. It was going to take more than a well-loved dog to convince him otherwise.

In the six months since Carter had been a Detective Sergeant at Leabrook, she had seen more than a dozen cases where primary school children had run away or been taken out of the country or kept off school. In every instance the parents had known why the children were absent and where they had gone.

She sat in her office at Leabrook Station with the door open. She hadn't always recognised that most parents were trying their best. During her training at Hendon Police College she had been taught to nurture her suspicions. In truth, if it hadn't been for her boss when she started in Islington, she wouldn't have lasted on patrol. Sergeant Finch made a point of seeing cases through to the end, and he encouraged Carter to go even further while she finished her qualification. That meant following up on the people who it turned out hadn't stolen anything or hit anyone, the people who had found what or who they had lost. It meant more phone calls and paperwork, but after a while Carter understood. Most people were doing their best. She no longer laid the wreaths of fear and anger at the feet of each encounter, but it didn't hurt that she knew both well.

It was early Friday evening. Nearly twenty-four hours since Caitlin was reported missing, a few more since she had failed to meet her friend after school. Only one day. But now it was a timeline.

Carter had spoken to Hill and listened to the recording of the Thompsons' interviews. The couple came in on a 'voluntary' basis. Carter would have been content to talk to the parents at Palmerston again, but Brecon was keen to put more pressure on them. Brecon and Lafferty remained perfectly civil and offered every sympathy throughout the conversation. But Carter, who had met the parents at reception and later escorted them back to their car, knew how quickly an interview could become an interrogation, and a subject become a suspect. The only legal nicety needed was a formal caution, and on the tape she could hear Brecon's friendly tone sharpen several times as he considered this option.

Brecon didn't make the arrest but he hadn't broadened the search yet either. It wouldn't be long before DCI Atherton took over as Senior Investigating Officer, and Carter saw the hours ahead as wasted time. It didn't matter whether the case turned out to be a dead end; her job was to deal with the facts as reported and work from there. The rest was politics.

She pressed her head into her palms. She remembered one case of child abduction by a stranger during her time in Islington. A thirteen-year-old girl went missing for a week. It was early in Carter's career, so she was only involved in some of the legwork. Senior officers changed the investigation from a missing person to a possible body search after five days. That moment had stayed with her, the sense of failure and frustration. The child had been traced, but the public celebration when she was found alive soon turned to criticism. The girl couldn't provide any evidence. Six months later she was dead.

For the first time she felt that police work really could make the difference between life and death, and that she, Sally Carter, had not made that difference. The case was sealed and Carter went back to her regular beat, but that was the year she decided to be a Detective Sergeant.

Caitlin Thompson's case had the advantage that her school and home were in the same borough. It made life a lot simpler. Not just the investigation, and the paperwork, but the bodies on the job. In Islington, she'd been sent over to the missing child's school some miles away, and it was hard to connect information between the two forces, as a junior PC and an outsider. She couldn't remember why they had sent her, and not a local uniform. It might have been Sergeant Finch's idea.

She stared at the notes in front of her. The collator who put the information together at the station had found two registered paedophiles from the List 99 check, living in Leabrook. Neither man had a long criminal history or any reported parole violations. Both had volunteered to attend the station later that evening, accompanied by their solicitors.

'I've sent that one home.' A finger tapped the photo on the desk and Carter glanced up to see her boss.

'Alibi checks out.' DI Brecon sniffed Carter's hair. 'Cigarettes?'

Carter pulled her head away. 'They both have alibis.'

'Well, this bloke was in a meeting on the building site

where he works, over twenty witnesses. But this one,'
Brecon moved his finger to the other mug shot, 'was at home
with his mum. WPC Hill checked it out.'

Karl Moffatt was an overweight white male in his forties.
He had been arrested three times for indecent exposure in
parks and playgrounds and served time on the third charge
because of the intention to expose to a minor.

'Bit of a step up for a flasher, sir.'

'Is it? Anything on the home search? Why did it take so
long for them to report their daughter missing?'

'Dad was at work. Mum was at her sister's and got home
late. They both ran around looking for her before they
called it in.'

'Who's with them now?'

'I left Dawson there. Marshall to join. They're on their
way.' Carter took the paperwork and got up. The two of
them stood at roughly the same height but Carter wouldn't
bet on herself in a fight; Brecon could dodge anything that
was thrown at him. Not that she wanted to hit Brecon, he
was one of the better ones, it was more a question of plan-
ning. As long as you were ready, it didn't matter who threw
the first punch.

'Search and Recovery have been alerted.'

Brecon snorted. 'No search teams until we have the all-
clear. We're focusing on the family.'

'And this guy?'

'General suspect. Costs nothing to check him out.'

'Our lucky day, then.' Carter turned away.

'How's that?'

'All the nonces in Leabrook and our suspect is one of the
two we have an address for.' The Sergeant moved to leave.
'I'd call that lucky.' She waited for Brecon to follow her.

'It's part of the investigation. This is routine, Sally. Face it, if the girl's come to harm, someone's guilty.'

'And it might as well be Moffatt?'

Brecon stopped at the incident room. They both stared at the map. Carter had filled in places of interest around the school and the housing estate. The girl's life revolved around a handful of local addresses.

'I rate the dad. But Moffatt's in the frame. Your choice.' Brecon tapped the map.

'My choice is that we widen the search now.'

'It's day one, Carter. Let's make sure the girl is missing.'

'DCI Atherton?'

'He's been informed. See how you get on with Moffatt.'

Carter tightened her grip on the notes and headed to the interview room.

3

In the fifteen years since she had left primary school, Isobel had not travelled far. Her mother liked to say that eleven was young to finish an education and since Isobel had been denied the rest of her childhood, she would never fully grow up. She said it to Isobel's face, which was one good thing about her mother. There wasn't anything so dreadful that she wouldn't say it in front of you. As for Isobel's development, it would have suited her mother better if they had moved out of London together. Living so close to the family's old home, her mother said, and to all the places associated with her accident, would only serve to hold her back. Isobel wanted to stay behind. She longed to be left alone.

'Until you can move out, Isobel, you cannot move on.'

She knew her mother would consider a move to Brighton a true recovery, being the place in which Clare herself had chosen to live, but Isobel had no desire to leave London. She had forged a new life in a part of North London that was far enough away from all that had gone before while being close enough to feel familiar.

The house on Bowman Road was divided into two flats with a narrow communal hallway on the ground floor. Isobel lived in the top one. She liked the way all the rooms were separate, though it meant they were small. Dan, who lived in the flat below, had knocked down the wall between the kitchen and the sitting room. Isobel went there for a Christmas drink once and was surprised by his American-style breakfast bar and the gas fire with a single flame shuddering in a glass bowl. Her own fireplace was plastered over and the melamine kitchen units were shabby when she'd bought the place five years ago. But after an hour of Dan's open-plan entertaining Isobel was glad to return upstairs and eat her dinner at the foldaway table by the oven, every door in the four-room flat shut tight.

She kept her home warm, setting the timer so the radiators would be hot long before she got back from work in the evening. Heavy curtains hung from poles in all the windows, helping to retain the heat. Isobel did not open the curtains, preferring only the amount of daylight that leaked between the wide loops at the top of the fabric. At the library, the natural light came from a glass dome in the ceiling and onto the stairwell, showing prisms of dust whenever the sun shone. There was plenty to clean in the flat without worrying about dust in the air. She took care with the few books she owned, and tried not to collect them, though she kept a favourite by her bed. She could borrow as many as she liked at work.

The day the two children visited the library Isobel went to the supermarket after work. She bought a bottle of wine and a chicken breast, a potato, broccoli, and added a small bar of dark chocolate as she approached the checkout. She did not need to count calories but she disliked the feeling of food waiting to be digested in her stomach. She laid the objects in her basket as she would on a plate, each without touching the other.

She watched the strangers in front of her pile their purchases on the counter.

The lights were on in the flat downstairs when Isobel got home and she grabbed her mail from the shelf in the hall-way without sorting through it. Dan sometimes came out when she turned her key in the front door and there was an awkward interval while he tried to make conversation. This evening he had the television turned up so loudly that she could feel the vibrations through the floorboards outside his flat but she still rushed upstairs in case he heard her. Isobel knew he was trying to be kind and she was always polite to him when they did meet, but the thought of the friendship was enough; she told herself she didn't need the real thing.

She dropped the post on the kitchen counter, annoyed by the amount of junk mail in the pile. In her home most of all, she avoided the intrusion of the outside world. She owned a television, but rarely turned it on, and the minicom phone was for emergencies only.

She waited until she had unpacked the groceries before looking through the envelopes. A couple of Christmas cards, one from her mother, the other from Whittington Park. A bank statement, a water bill, and one typewritten letter with no return address on the envelope. She was expecting a training application from the university. She took the letter with her and went to run a bath.

1–3 Railway Cottages
Walthamstow E17 8EQ
18 December 1990

Dear Isobel,

    You may not remember me, it has been many years since we last met and you were very young. I can understand if you have chosen to forget the

circumstances or, at any rate, my involvement in
them. I hope you do not think it too much of an
intrusion that I write to you now, and that you will
read this letter and act upon it.

I will stick to the facts. We were notified that
Jason Ryall was being released from prison, and I
wanted you to know. I spoke to your mother, but
I thought I should tell you myself. Although I have
kept in touch with her since the trial, we never speak
about your accident, or what happened to Angela.
I think she prefers not to be reminded. As, perhaps, do you.

I am living now near the canal, in private accommodation, as guardian to Mary Mason. The house
belongs to Mary but she can't stay here alone. Mrs
Mason died in August. That must be how you
remember her, as Mrs Mason, but Patricia was a good
friend to me and I stayed with her and Mary for over
a year while I was on the council waiting list.

I would like you to visit us. Is that too much to
ask? I do not want to rake over the past. This is about
the future, for Mary and for you. You can write back
to me at the above address. Please give this your
consideration.

Yours,
Agnes (Miss Spill)

The page fell from Isobel's fingers, landing in a perfect N
on the bathroom floor. Isobel stared at the neat folds. The
envelope was still in her hand, Isobel's address on the front,
not forwarded, postmarked yesterday. Agnes Spill knew

where she lived. Isobel turned off the tap and backed out of the room. She stood in the hallway, trying to stop the words forcing their way into her head.

The protection of her new life had been violated in a moment. Isobel went into the kitchen and stared at the food laid on the counter. Jason was out of prison. She was supposed to cook her supper and read her book and go to bed. She was supposed to be alone. Now Agnes Spill had found her and she couldn't think of anything else. Two minutes later, she left the flat.

Bowman Road was deserted. Isobel locked the front door and hurried past the rows of identical houses. Hard droplets of rain stung her face as she walked. She needed to block out her thoughts. At the turn in the road she could see people walking along the crowded High Street, heads bent against the night. Christmas lights threw crimson puddles onto the wet pavement. Isobel slowed down. She saw the noise in front of her. In her flat, the silence had seemed too vast, a lure for memories of Agnes Spill and the Mason family, but Isobel now regretted her rush to escape. She could cope with ghosts on her own territory. She had done it for years. Outside, the intruders were made flesh and they pushed back. She walked the last steps to the High Street and forced herself to join the evening shoppers and office parties, ending and starting their nights.

She approached the shelter of the newsagent's that delivered the only magazine she read that she couldn't get at the library. The glimmer of the cigarette display was visible through the gated door. She didn't usually go in because there was only one till and the customer display never worked. Isobel paused. Maybe the daughter would be working today. She was always helpful. She took a breath and collided with a body at the door.

The man she walked into grabbed her as he steadied himself. Isobel pulled free, sounding out an apology.

'Sorry,' she said and the word stuck in her mouth. 'Sorry.'

She started back for the door of the shop but the man had her by the shoulder and spun her round. He wore a look of mock astonishment and his mouth hung open. Isobel apologised again. He looked middle-aged, thinning scalp, and an unzipped fleece with his bare chest exposed underneath. He held his arms out as if expecting an embrace. His lips were moving but Isobel didn't want to look. She shrugged and tried to move away.

The man dodged round in front of her. He was calling out now, shouting to someone behind her. She turned to see two of his friends making their way towards them. All three men were talking now, their mouths opening in long bursts as they surrounded Isobel.

The first man cocked his head to one side and stared at her. She felt the shock of his scrutiny, a jolt in her memory. He smiled, asked her something. Isobel kept her hands down, her fingers moving against her leg. She took a step forward and he blocked her. His friends joined in, tapped their heads with closed fists and puckered their lips. The man's scalp glistened. He wasn't anyone, she told herself. No one at all.

She pushed hard past them. They jumped around, thrilled with themselves, as Isobel marched up the road towards a side street that could lead her home. Hands in her pockets, keys held tight. Before she rounded the corner she looked back. They were dancing now, faces tilted to the night, their breath pluming in the starless sky.

When the bald man glanced up, she ran.

Wednesday

We had a surprise trip to the countryside with school. We went to a hill outside London where there was snow. Miss Spill brought some sleds and trays. It was cold and I didn't have a coat. I wanted to wait at the bottom with Kathy and see if we could find a sweet shop to buy some Fruit Salads for half a pence. I had two half pences and I said Kathy could have one but Mr Dickens paired us up with other kids and I got Angie and Kathy got Drew.

Kathy and Mr Dickens stayed at the bottom of the hill holding onto a rope with Drew because he is blind. Angie wanted to climb the hill. She stood at the top of the slope in her pink bobble hat and pink trousers. All the rest of us had to wear our uniform, which is blue and yellow which do not go together. I had to say the names of the people that she pointed to. If she liked them she said 'Hug'. She hugged nearly everyone, even Mr Dickens. Angie is happy almost all the time but when she saw Steven she stopped talking.

Steven ran up with a tray. I knew Angie didn't want to slide down the hill. She sits in the shallow end at the swimming baths with her armbands on even though she's older than me. When we go on the trampoline, Angie lies down and we bounce it for her.

I looked for a teacher. Mr Dickens was busy with the kids on a rope and Miss Spill had taken Lucy to write sums in the snow. Steven stood there at the top of the hill with his hands on his hips, daring me. I didn't stop him. He pushed Angie over and on to the plastic tray and gave her a shove and the tray tipped over the edge really quickly and slid down the hill. Her legs stuck out like sausages and I got scared in case one of them broke and she told on me. She got faster and faster but she stayed on all the way to the bottom and fell off where the snow was slushy. Steven was laughing. She didn't move and I felt sick. I saw Mr Dickens say something to her and to Drew. Angie put her arms in the air as if she'd won some big race. She didn't look at me even though I was shouting her name. Steven had gone. I went down by the steps.

Saturday

I was at Aunt Sasha's house for tea. She is Dad's sister but they argue all the time. If I had a sister we would have adventures together and she would be my friend. I have two cousins, Emily and Joe. They wanted to play schools but they do it wrong. They make the children sit at desks and do work, like they do in old books. I told them children should be allowed to run about and learn when they want to and they said that was because I was at a school for stupid people. I said she didn't know what she was talking about but Emily said I should be going to a normal school. She said her mum thinks my mum is a hippy and my dad can't say no to her.

On the way home I asked Mum what a hippy was and she told me it was a person who cared about the world. I don't think children can be hippies.

Tuesday

We did police club again today. It is a quiz where you have to learn about all the things to do with the police like the Green Cross Code and the Highway Code. If you get chosen to be in the team you go to the police station for the competition. I was on the team with Lucy and Kathy and Christopher.

The questions are hard, and so are all the driving rules. You sit at a table with another school and if you win you get a badge. We didn't win but I like doing the quiz and the police gave us sweets.

Friday

Because it's Valentine's Day, we had a game of kiss chase with Steven in the yard. We ran around for ages. I think Steven likes Kathy. Kathy wears a bra. Drew walked right into the middle of the game and tripped Lucy up with his stick, but Miss Spill thought it was our fault and banged on the windows.

The gravel in the yard is the worst kind to fall on, you cut yourself and the cut goes all sticky. Mr Dickens spat on my cut knee once. He said the spit would make it clean but I think he just wanted to spit on me.

Steven was chasing Kathy and Patrick joined in. Patrick shouts all the time and he is fifteen and if you get in his way, he pulls your hair. Kathy started singing, 'Izzy loves Patrick', and he grabbed my skirt and pulled it down. Everyone was laughing so I said, 'Patrick wants to kiss me.'

He was really close and I closed my eyes. All I could hear was laughing and when I opened my eyes Patrick was just looking at me. I wanted to go home.

I said, 'Patrick smells like gravy.'

4

'My client has demonstrated his innocence.' The solicitor addressed Brecon directly.

The four of them had sat in the small room together for the best part of two hours and the solicitor had barely acknowledged Carter. She noticed the lapel on the solicitor's suit had drooped, revealing a tiny Def Leppard badge. 'As you have no grounds on which to charge him, and if there is nothing further, I think we are done here.' She put her papers in a file and stood while Moffatt looked around the room. 'Mr Moffatt?'

'Is that it? I won't be . . . called in again? You won't come back round to my house?'

'Your solicitor will advise you of any further enquiries, Mr Moffatt. This is a continuing investigation.' Brecon remained seated. They had nothing on the man but it was worth a few more minutes to see him flustered. You never knew.

'Karl?' The solicitor's tone softened. 'We can go now.'

Carter wondered if she lay awake at night wishing she could set everyone free.

It was evening by the time Karl Moffatt and his solicitor walked out of Leabrook police station. Carter escorted them to the front steps and watched as they made their way through the press photographers who had assembled on the pavement. Moffatt's bulk slowed him down. It was hard to imagine he could have taken Caitlin Thompson from the school without being seen.

Carter checked her watch and headed back into the station. Susan and David Thompson were waiting to be interviewed, but Brecon had asked for Lafferty. 'Let's have a fresh pair of eyes on them.' Carter agreed with the theory, but not the practice of the arrangement. She already had opinions about the Thompsons, and an objective formal interview would be helpful, but she was always going to be second choice for Brecon, and Lafferty's grin was familiar and tiring.

'Should have kept him in overnight.' Brecon stared at the hunched figures of the press from the safety of the lobby. 'He'd be putty in the morning.'

'Check in on the Thompsons, will you? I'm not sure they're going to say much to Lafferty.'

She didn't think they'd be any more open to Brecon, but it was worth letting him know where they all stood. Carter pulled the glass door closed behind her and kept on walking through reception. She had become a Detective so that she could choose where she should look and for how long. In her experience this was rarely at the people or in the places you were told to. Dawson and Marshall had been through Moffatt's house, talked to the mother and returned empty-handed. Brecon had made one concession to sensitivity and assigned Hill to watch the Thompsons' place that night. These were the only suspects and so far there wasn't another thread to pull on. Carter was glad Hill was at Palmerston. She'd give her a call when she was off the job and they'd catch up properly.

She grabbed her jacket and the half-eaten bag of chips left over from her tea. If the girl wasn't found soon, it would be front page and television news. The weeks before Christmas were the perfect time to feature a missing child and the higher-ups would feel the pressure. The publicity might bring some benefits, with any luck the calls would start coming in. But it would also bring DCI Atherton as their Senior Investigating Officer. Brecon's main focus was on the parents and if Carter couldn't give Atherton anything else, the DCI would guide the red tops to that story.

She checked her watch. The school would be closed but for now the building was the closest thing she had to a last witness.

It was nearly seven o'clock when she pulled up to the cul-de-sac that ended with Leabrook South. She sat in the car regarding the dark outline of the school ahead, the street lamps wrapped in mist. At this time of year, children walked home at dusk. Ruby Siltmore would have waited for her friend and searched for her face among the crowd pouring out of the gates, but she might not have waited long if it was nearly dark. After a few minutes Carter got out of the car and walked towards the school.

There was no access to the small playground behind the building from this end of the street. Solid brick walls with thick railings at intervals book-ended the property. Staff and pupils entered and left through the gates at the front. Carter noted down the number plates of the half-dozen vehicles in the street.

Carter pulled at the tie she was still wearing from the press conference and glanced up at the council signpost. It didn't matter how far away you got from these buildings, they held on to you. All those years being ferried between school and the children's home, she'd served her time in institutions. And still gone on to join another one. Her thoughts pushed up against a memory of the other missing girl, the disabled one from Islington all those years before. She had been to a special school, a charity school, that had been implicated in some way. It was one of the schools on the Police in Education Programme, a competition for primary school kids to help with community outreach. Carter peered at the ordinary modern primary beyond the railings. A different time, a different kind of school, but what had changed?

One of the gates was open and a row of lights shone through the wire-enforced windows on the right-hand corridor of the ground floor. Carter hadn't phoned ahead. She pushed at the gate and walked through the playground veering to the right of the reception area. Fluorescent pools lit up wet patches of tarmac. She reached the corner of the school and looked back. The wall to the side of the building cast a deep shadow but from where she stood she had a clear view of the gates and some of the street beyond. Turning back, she pulled a torch from her pocket.

There was a bicycle hangar in this front yard, built along the wall at the side. The corrugated roof was supported by metal posts at each corner. The frame of a bike lay across the floor, one crooked wheel jammed at an angle, but in the middle of the hangar, neatly padlocked, stood an expensive bike in perfect condition. Carter shone her torch around the structure, running the light several times over the shadow where the roof of the hangar met the wall of the yard. There was a gap.

'Can I help you?'

Carter's hand jerked back. She recognised the headmaster.

'DS Carter, Mr . . . ' Carter pointed the torch away and reached for the notebook in her jacket. The headmaster waited while Carter made a show of peering at the pages.

'Sorry. Mr Fry. DS Carter. We met this morning. About Caitlin . . . '

'Thompson. Yes. She's not in the bike shed, I'm afraid.'

'What? Oh, no.' Carter attempted a smile. 'I just noticed the space behind it. I'm trying to establish if Caitlin could have left the school by any other exit without being seen.'

She pointed the torch ahead of them and the headmaster walked to the back. Metal bicycle clips around his ankles caught in the beam.

'There is a gate here, actually. We blocked it off with the shed to stop the children using it. We keep it pad-locked as well.'

The two of them peered behind the hangar. There was a shoulder-width gap between the shed and the wall. Carter squeezed into the space and found the gate. It was shut and bolted from the inside. There was no padlock. The light picked up some drinks cans and sweet wrappers on the ground. Carter pulled on her gloves and undid the bolt, careful to cover as little of the handle as possible. She shook the gate. It opened inwards and was stiff from lack of use.

'You'll have to speak to the caretaker. This whole area is out of bounds. And, as I said, the gate should be padlocked.'

Carter couldn't get out of the gate from where she stood. She pushed it closed, moved along a few feet and opened it again. The thickness of the gate and the difficulty of pulling it from the wrong side prevented her from opening it more than a few inches. She could see an alleyway ahead and the gardens belonging to the row of houses next to the school. She shut the gate and made her way back to Fry.

'Looks like the kids have been using it as a den. Is the caretaker on site? Can I speak to him?'

'He'll be here on Monday. He starts early, we all do.' The headmaster looked at his watch. 'Can we arrange a meeting for then? It's been a long week, Detective. I'm not sure we can achieve anything in the dark, so to speak.'

'Monday?' Carter gestured to the school and they started walking back. 'There're a couple of things I'll need as soon as possible. The building plans for the school. The register of all the pupils for yesterday and today. And a list of staff number plates.'

Fry nodded. 'Yes, of course. The register is no problem.'

'I'll have someone collect them in the morning.'

'There won't be anyone here over the weekend. And the school closes for the Christmas break on Wednesday. Two more full days for all of us and they will be extremely busy.'

Carter stopped and turned to the headmaster.

'Mr Fry. Do you understand that a child, one of your pupils, is missing and may very well have been abducted?'

'Abducted? I have spoken to your Detective Inspector and he assured me that your colleagues saw this as a domestic matter.'

'The last known sighting of Caitlin was on school premises.'

Fry continued to walk back towards the school.

'The caretaker has access to the building if you need anything further. I believe you have everybody's contact details.'

'And the number plates?' Carter followed him.

'There is no database. We would have to ask each member of staff individually.'

At the school entrance, Carter stopped several paces away from Fry and put her notebook and torch away.

'Very well.' She turned towards the street, checked herself and looked back at Fry. 'We may still need to contact you over the weekend.'

By the time Carter reached her car, the school was dark. She drove around the corner and pulled in behind a van on the far side of the street. It was ten minutes before another car pulled out of the close. She wrote Fry's name beside one of the number plates she had recorded earlier and stared at the list. Carter had expected the headmaster to be on a bicycle.

She had been on duty since eight o'clock that morning. It was now eight o'clock on a Friday night, and she'd get little help at the station until Brecon decided to pull the ban on overtime. Friday night in Leabrook meant drunks and drugs and home thefts, joy riders and visits to A & E. There wouldn't be many bodies left on duty.

Carter knew that by noon tomorrow, Brecon would have co-ordinated with DCI Atherton and officers would be recalled. That gave her twelve hours to see what unravelled overnight without any backup from the station or permission to be on the case. She could ask a favour and run a few plates but she needed the list of staff vehicles she had requested from the school to make any sense of the information. Then she could match up staff with the cars parked in the street last night and find out whose car Fry was driving, if it wasn't his own.

She was the first point of contact for the parents and there was no reason she couldn't visit them for a chat. It was eight o'clock, not too late. Rebecca was on watch at the Palmerston Estate. Any other Friday night and they would have got a takeaway and gone back to Carter's. Seeing her would be better than a phone call. She helped herself to the rest of the cold chips and headed for the Thompsons'.

5

Isobel's hands were shaking when she got back to Bowman Road. She tried to turn the key in the lock several times before giving up. The rain was falling steadily and her face was numb with cold. She stood in the street with her fingers pressed to her lips, waiting for her breath to slow.

She was still standing on the front step when Dan opened the door five minutes later.

His face registered concern more than surprise. He spoke too carefully and Isobel found it difficult to read him by the shadow of the hallway light. She was reminded of the way her speech therapists had insisted she practise talking. 'You mustn't forget how to make the shapes and sounds, Isobel.' All the coaches at the rehab unit had agreed. But not Isobel. She never wanted to speak again.

She shook her head and pointed at the bunch of wet keys hanging from the lock.

'Come inside,' Dan said. She stepped past him into the hallway as Dan pulled at the keys in the door.

'You really jammed them in.' He handed her the keys and smiled in acknowledgement of her strength.

A small pool of water was forming at Isobel's feet and her coat smelled of wet dog. She wanted to be on her own, to lie in a hot bath and put her head under the water until all she could think about was needing to breathe. But she made no attempt to go upstairs.

'You'd better come in,' Dan pushed open the door which led directly into his living room. The gas fire was burning in its glass bowl and strings of white lights and red ribbons were threaded through the branches of an overgrown potted plant. The effect was glamorous, a Hollywood Christmas.

'I know, I know,' Dan was laughing. 'Do you think it's over the top?'

Isobel shook her head. She pointed to the room and signed *like*. Dan looked pleased. Had he learned some signs?

'I'll get you a towel.' Dan disappeared and emerged a minute later. 'Aren't you freezing?' He handed her the towel.

The adrenalin from her encounter outside the newsagents had faded and she could feel the chill of the night under her skin. She started to rub at her hair with the heavy towel. She imagined taking her coat off and lying on the leather sofa in front of the fire.

'I must go.' Isobel felt the hard pressure of her tongue forcing air around her mouth like a pebble.

'Sure,' he said. 'No problem.' Neither of them moved. 'Do you want to get something to eat? I know a great place, Indian food. Not like my aunt's, but good enough, and you won't have to give your life story. We could drive, if you like.'

Isobel studied his face while he talked. His features were expressive and she understood most of what he said. There was a light in his eyes when he spoke to her.

'If you like,' he repeated and made the sign for *like* that Isobel had made earlier. He hadn't been studying after all.

I like, she signed. Then, *If you like,* which was actually, *You want?*

'Different.' The pebble rolled to the back of her teeth.

Dan copied her signs clumsily.

'I'm not very good, am I?'

OK, Isobel signed.

'Yeah? It's difficult, isn't it? I want to mime things instead. You know? Like charades.' He drew a pair of curtains in the air then tapped his fingers on his arm. Isobel moved one hand in a cutting motion and pushed the 'fork' into her mouth.

Dan smiled. 'Oh, right. Dinner. Great. Wait right there.' Dan left the room.

What was she doing? The thought of spending the next few hours trying to communicate in public with a hearing man who couldn't sign was unbearable. Why hadn't she just gone up to her flat? She still could. An image of the bald man flashed into her mind.

'Ready?' Dan stood in front of her in a moleskin jacket. He'd done something to his hair and a scent of citrus sweetness filled the room. Isobel nodded.

It had stopped raining. They walked in silence along the pavement, Dan throwing and catching his car keys as though practising a magic trick. It was something boys liked to do, she'd noticed, demonstrate an obscure skill in idle moments. The boys at school had palmed coins or dislocated their shoulders for effect. Drew used to take his eyes out. She didn't suppose many guys used that as a dating technique. She felt so tired. She didn't want to think about her school days. She didn't want this to be a date.

OK? Dan mimicked Isobel's earlier thumbs up sign. They had reached the car, and he was opening her door for her in the dark. The car was low to the ground, sporty. She leaned against the roof while Dan went around to the driver's side.

Isobel watched him through the windscreen searching a bunch of cassettes for the tape he wanted. At the far end of the street, someone else was getting into a car, turning on lights. Isobel swung down beside Dan just in time to see him shoving his music collection onto the back seat. Isobel busied herself with the belt.

'Is Indian food all right with you?' The interior light of the car threw shadows on his face that made it even harder to read his lips.

'Indian?' He repeated. Isobel had never eaten at an Indian restaurant. She had an idea that the food was mixed together. She felt safer with Chinese food; her parents had often taken her to Chinatown when she was a child. They ordered baskets of dim sum and Isobel used chopsticks and drank Jasmine tea. That was all before though. She might as well go somewhere Dan knew.

All right.

'Great,' Dan started the engine and Isobel felt the low vibration beneath her seat when the car gasped to life. He turned to smile at her as they pulled out of the parking space.

Full-beam headlights from a car behind them flashed across the dashboard.

Dan held his hand to the back window and mouthed at the other car. 'Sorry, mate!'

The lights on the other car flashed off and on. Isobel saw Dan mutter something to himself in the rear-view mirror as they drove away. 'Giraffe' she thought he said. The car's undimmed lights followed them until they reached the roundabout.

The restaurant was in Highgate, tucked into an alleyway behind the shops and pubs of the main street. The smell of cloves drifted down the lane towards them. Through the window, they could see a few people standing at the bar, waiting for a table.

'It's always busy. But they should squeeze us in.' Dan held the door open for her and a blanket of warm air wrapped itself around Isobel's damp body. The room was full, any semblance of order abandoned. Several tables were pushed together along the walls to make room for larger parties and extra chairs had been added to the centre tables. Waiters sidled between the gaps with trays and steaming bowls. All the food was served in brightly coloured sauces, red and yellow and pink. Like dishes of hot paint.

She felt Dan's hand on her shoulder. 'There's a table for two just about ready.' Dan pointed to a middle-aged couple studying their bill. 'The food here is great. Vegetarian.' Isobel could see he was shouting, trying to make himself heard above the obvious din. It took a while for the hearing to comprehend that they didn't need to vocalise. The idea of a vegetarian restaurant appealed to her, removing some of the butcher-shop horror of the kitchen. She found herself study-ing the vermillion lumps being spooned from bowl to plate.

Dan and Isobel were shown to the table by a waiter who managed to squeeze between the other customers, clear the plates and remove the top tablecloth in the time it took them both to sit down. From his aproned waistband he produced two menus and waited for their drink orders. Dan pointed to his glass and looked at Isobel.

'Beer?' He smiled when Isobel nodded. Was he hoping she wouldn't embarrass him? That was ridiculous, he had asked her out, had obviously given it some thought beforehand. Why would he take her out if he was worried she would show him up? She stared at the menu and tried to focus on the Italic print. Could she just have rice? Were the lumps available without sauces?

On the other side of the table, Dan rummaged through his jacket pocket. His hair had broken loose from the gel he smoothed on it earlier and the separated dark waves framed his face. Lowering her menu, Isobel noticed a chicken pox scar at the top of his cheekbone and, along his temple, a deeper scar, pale stitch marks. She thought about her own scars, the patchwork of lines at the back of her scalp. Her father used to stroke her head when he visited her in hospital, as if he could smooth the accident away. After a few months she took to wearing hats.

Dan brandished a small notepad and the stub of a pencil, holding them in the air with the same questioning expression he had used for the beer. This time, she raised her own eyebrows in return. She had communicated on paper for years, stopping when she realised that the notebooks removed an advantage of not hearing. It was hard to misunderstand a message that had been written down for her.

The drinks arrived and Isobel took a gulp from hers. Dan scribbled and slid the pad and pencil across the table to her. **Do you want to write or talk? I wish I could sign.** Isobel almost admired his bold approach. It appealed to a good nature she wasn't sure she had, but for now it was easier to play along with Dan's relaxed idea of deaf communication than to tell him the truth. Let him think it was all a bit of a game. He could order her food while he was at it.

You talk, I'll watch, she signed.

Dan understood.

'I'm used to talking about myself,' he said, 'I thought last time, when you came over to see the flat, maybe I talked too much. I want to know about you.'

She picked up the pencil. She could write it all down, tell him her life story. She could go home and get out the spiral- bound notebook they had given her at the care home. **My name is Isobel. I am d/Deaf**. That would keep it all simple wouldn't it? She put the pencil back on the table. Appealing to her good nature wasn't working after all.

Dan shrugged.

'It's fine, you know, if you don't want to talk? I've got plenty to say.' He laughed. 'I'm an actor; I do it for a living.'

She wrote **I like to watch you talk**. She had forgotten he was an actor but perhaps that was what illuminated his face when he spoke, the desire to communicate. She hadn't felt that need for a long time, but she remembered it. Remembered wanting to let everyone know exactly what she thought. Dan probably assumed she didn't speak because she couldn't hear, but that wasn't the reason. It was true that on days away from the rehab unit, she'd been thrown out of bars and cafés with the deaf students for unmodulated conversations. But that didn't stop them. When she was a child, her friend Lucy had plenty to say and always told you what she was feeling. Sometimes with words but other times it was more a connectivity. You had to pay attention in a different way. Isobel shook her head. She didn't want to think about Lucy.

'Can you hear anything?' He pointed to his ear.

Isobel shook her head.

'But you don't wear a hearing aid.'

Isobel nodded.

'Well, stop me if I go too fast,' Dan peered at her. 'I love the sound of my own voice. Oh,' he smiled, 'well, you know what I mean. My own thoughts, really.'

Shameless. But she could read most of the words and was

grateful not to have to explain her deafness again. Profound. That usually covered it, but you never knew. She'd answered more questions from strangers about what she could not hear than she had from the numerous specialists she had seen. I can't hear you, she would say, but I can understand you perfectly. It usually shut them up.

'So, where have we got to? I'm Dan . . . Nash, you know that. I'm 32, I'm an actor.' He shook his head. 'Sorry, that sounds a bit . . . I do get some work, mostly commercials in Europe, which pay well, and theatre in the provinces, which does not. You don't like commercials?' Isobel's mouth had turned down at the corners and Dan smiled. 'I know, I know. You work in a library, don't you? Now that's a proper job. I worked in a bookshop for a while. Never took home any money though, I was always buying books. Right,' the waiter was standing behind Isobel. 'What would you like?'

In the end, the ordering, and the meal, proved much simpler than Isobel had thought. There was the plain rice, and fried cauliflower, and a hot cheese that did not have sauce on it, only some spices that were quite pleasant. There was also spinach, but she thought it looked like something had been added to it, so she put a small amount on her plate when she had nearly finished, to show willing. The waiter understood when she asked for 'no sauce' and she liked the way that all the food came in separate dishes, so that you could help yourself. She wished they had chopsticks, it was harder to rub a fork clean on a napkin, but other than that, she enjoyed it all.

Dan hadn't been exaggerating about his ability or his enthusiasm to speak at length. He made her laugh more than once, and she read most of what he said. Now she was sitting alone at the table watching him make his way back to her from the toilet. He was grinning and shaking his head.

'Well,' he sat back in his seat. 'I've aged, Isobel. Bloke in the toilet thought we'd gone to school together. Must have been five years older than me.' He finished his coffee in one gulp and started to put his jacket on.

Isobel's coat was still damp. She plucked her purse out of the pocket and offered Dan some money.

'I've paid the bill,' Dan tapped his wallet on the table. 'I asked you out, it's only fair.'

Thank you, Isobel signed. She put the purse away.

It was after eleven by the time they left the restaurant and the wet pavement was starting to ice over. Isobel shivered. She had to concentrate on placing her feet as they walked towards the car. It wasn't until she reached the relative safety of a dry patch of concrete that she noticed Dan was still outside the restaurant, chatting to a heavyset man who was smoking a cigarette. Dan waved and started to cross over, blocking her view of the alleyway.

When he reached her he took off his jacket, put it over Isobel's shoulders and ran his fingers through his hair. 'He's got to have a few years on me anyway.'

On the drive to Bowman Road, Isobel checked in the mirrors a couple of times to see if they were being followed. The incident at the newsagents had thrown her. And the letter. It would still be there when she got in. She felt Dan touch her lightly on the shoulder.

OK? he signed, smiling.

She smiled back. She was OK. It was just a letter.

In the hallway, Isobel went straight to her door while Dan locked up at the front.

'See you over the weekend,' he said when Isobel turned to mouth goodbye. 'Let's go to the park or something.'

She nodded and went to close her door but Dan took a step towards her.

'Night then.' He smiled and held her gaze.

Isobel stared back at him. In fifteen years, she had not stood by her door for a kiss. Not since school. Dan's face swam in front of her, kind and open. He was not who she had run from. She put a hand out to steady herself and Dan took it.

'Easy,' he said, 'you're a cheap date.'

She looked down at his hand, how it held hers.

'No,' she said, with a small breath behind the mouthed word, 'not really.'

With a squeeze of his fingers, she let go, took a step back and shut the door.

March 1975

Wednesday

Dad drove me to school today. The first thing I did was go on the rope swing in the main hall. Patrick was standing around and he started screaming when he saw me. I swung over to the history area to sit with Kathy. 'He just wants some sex,' she said. I said that was disgusting. She looked at me funny. 'Maybe with Patrick it is.'

My chart book this year looks better. We were given new ones when we moved buildings, and I have tried to get it all filled in. The subjects we do are written down with boxes for each week, and the teacher puts their initials in the box when you have finished a lesson. If you get it full, then you can go to any subject you like.

We sat on the mats for half an hour but when we asked Miss Peden to sign our chart book, she said we hadn't done any work. I have five history boxes every week and I never have enough initials in them.

'Get out the Tudor timeline.' Miss Peden has shiny blue shoes with gold buckles. When you are crawling around on the floor with her timeline, she stands over you and taps the cards with her blue shoe if they are wrong.

The only sessions that are always filled in my chart book are Maths and English. I can sit and write stories or read for as long as I like if I bring my own book. We don't have a library at school because the books got torn.

For Maths we go into another room and there are tables. The teacher is called Miss Spill. She has scabs on her hands and she smells old but she is a good teacher. She can look at you sometimes like it is a test to see what you are like. Dad says she has a 'heart of gold' but Mum says he feels sorry for her because she is homeless. There is another Maths teacher called Miss Coburn and I think Dad likes her more.

Thursday

I felt ill when I woke up this morning. My throat hurt and Mum said I didn't have to go to school. She tried to take me to the doctor's but they are on strike so we couldn't get an appointment. Dad let me stay with him in the office while he drew his buildings. I wanted to tell him about Patrick and the other boys but I didn't know how to say it.

Monday

In the middle of the morning, Mr Sanders made a Tannoy announcement. He said, 'Isobel Williams is a weed.' He said it because I missed two days of school. We were sitting in the English area and Kathy and Lucy were laughing. Lucy can sometimes read your lips as long as you look at her when you speak. Mark and Steven ran past shouting 'Weeeed'.

I said that Mr Sanders doesn't even know why I missed school and that I'd been on an aeroplane to a special funfair.

Kathy laughed but Lucy just nodded and I felt bad because it was a made-up story.

I asked Lucy to show me some of her language and we

went to the art room and practised. Kathy didn't come because she said she can already speak English. Mr Dickens signed our chart books after. I told him they should teach deaf language to all the children but he said Mr Sanders wants everyone to be able to fit in with the world when they have left the Schoolhouse.

Thursday

Mr Sanders called me into his office at lunch. I didn't want to go because sometimes he smacks us but Kathy said if he did and I cried then he would give me Smarties. Mr Sanders didn't smack me and I didn't get any Smarties but he said I had to eat when we went to lunch or I would keep getting sick. 'You are always missing school. Your chart book is not filled in. If you don't eat more you will have to stay in my office at lunch and eat on the floor with Lois.'

I don't want to eat on the floor with Lois; she has spit all round her face. She is a St Bernard.

Friday

In the hall, there is a drawing of how Mr Sanders wants the new school to look if they get the money. The whole building is painted in rainbow colours and there are proper classrooms. The yard has grass and a pet farm and a play-ground. But the best thing about the picture is the giant slide that goes all the way from the top floor into an outdoor swimming pool. I can't wait until they build that slide. I will go on the slide all day and when it is lunchtime I will hide underwater so they can't make me eat anything.

Monday

My parents came into school to talk to Mr Sanders about me eating with the dog. I told them at the weekend and they thought I was joking. Mum says they sent me to the Schoolhouse because she went to boarding school when she was seven. They said that Mr Sanders was doing a wonderful job at the school and I shouldn't get jealous if he gives the other children more attention. Dad said he hated his school days and he always hoped it would be different for me at a new kind of school. I don't like it when Dad looks sad so I said I was happy at the Schoolhouse, I just don't want to eat with Lois.

When we got to school, Mr Sanders told my parents I had won a prize for my writing and he was going to put my story in the school magazine. Dad was pleased and we didn't talk about eating on the floor. My story is called 'The Irises'. It is about a duck that lives on the riverbank near our house. She sits on her eggs in the iris leaves until they hatch. Even if it is freezing cold she does not leave the eggs on their own.

On the way out, we looked at the school plans. Dad laughed when he saw the slide and Mum and Dad held hands. 'It is extraordinary what we can achieve if we put our minds to it,' Mum said. She works for the prison service and listens to the problems of the criminals. My mother thinks that prisoners should be better cared for.

Dad gave Mr Sanders a cheque for the building fund.

I didn't know we had a school magazine.

December 1990

Saturday

6

The Silver Spoon opened at 7 a.m., and on Saturday morning Carter was one of the first customers. She looked around in case Hill had decided to drop by. Rebecca had worked late but they often met up here at the weekends. Carter wondered again if she should give Hill a set of keys to her place. She tried to imagine what it would be like. She hadn't lived with anyone since she'd left care and finished her training but it wasn't just about giving up her space.

Rebecca was not in the caff. Carter stopped at the counter, ordered a full English breakfast and sat in the corner at her usual table.

Brecon hadn't called her in, but it was only a matter of hours. There was no news on Caitlin Thompson and her parents had spent the evening with neighbours calling her name round the estate. Carter had left after an hour and promised to return the next day with reinforcements.

She opened her notebook to the list of number plates she had seen outside the school and the question beside them: bicycle clips? Fry had been ready to cycle home but something Carter said had changed his mind. She'd asked for a list of staff cars, and Fry had then removed a car from the premises. Would you keep a car and a bicycle at work? And if the car wasn't his, why did he have the keys and why was he worried about moving it?

Her breakfast arrived. Sex, thought Carter, dousing the eggs with ketchup. Fry could be having an affair with a member of staff. He would certainly want to keep that quiet, but it might have nothing to do with Caitlin's disappearance. Or it could mean he had an accomplice. If Caitlin had left with a stranger after school, the receptionist would have noticed them. But if the girl had left with another member of staff or been met by one outside? That was how it had worked in her day. The girls weren't as young as Caitlin Thompson but they went voluntarily.

She drank her tea and considered the layout of the school buildings. The front door was locked during school hours, you had to be buzzed in and out, and the children played in the walled playground at the back of the school during breaks. Her form teacher had said Caitlin was in class all day. None of the children had access to the gate behind the bicycle shed except when they were coming into school and when they were leaving. Some of the kids were clearly using it as a makeshift den during those times. Whether Caitlin left through the side gate or the main entrance, no one had come forward to say they saw her leave at all.

Carter made a note of the staff she needed to talk to at the school. She had been warned not to be heavy-handed. Start a rumour in a school and the consequences soon became political. Newspapers loved stories about schools. She supposed their readers did too.

The suspects that Brecon wanted her to concentrate on were more convenient. Susan and David Thompson and their immediate family and neighbours could have their homes and lives scrutinised. Any objection to helping police with their enquiries would seem suspicious. They could also search Karl Moffatt's house again and bring him in on the slightest excuse as soon as Brecon or Atherton scaled up the investigation. She looked at her watch. The swimming pool where the kids hung out would be open.

She paid the bill and bought a couple of Fantas for the car. Orange flavour. They reminded her of the orange carton drinks you used to get at the cinema. 'We all adora Kia Ora.' We sure do, she thought, and shoved the Fantas in the glove compartment.

The Mandela Leisure Centre was on her way to the Thompsons'. DS Lafferty had drawn a blank when he visited the previous afternoon, but Saturdays were busy even at this time of the morning. There might be more kids around who knew Caitlin and if there were security cameras she could hand over Thursday's tapes to Lafferty when they both got called in.

A wall of heat hit Carter as she pushed through the swing doors of the swimming pool. Red and gold tinsel trees shivered in the draught and Christmas muzak echoed around the concrete hallway. Carter made a note of the position of the cameras but she couldn't find a name for the security company. At the desk, the staff were friendly but unhelpful.

'You can go to Loungers and ask there,' a girl in a navy-blue shell suit offered. 'Only you'll have to wait for the manager.'

The manager was a tall young man who seemed uncomfortable in a jacket. Given the subtropical temperature of the building, Carter couldn't blame him.

'Security footage?' The manager frowned. 'I'll check with the firm that handles the system. They're not employed by the leisure centre itself you see, outsourced to a different company. I can't give out that information without senior management approval,' he added in reply to Carter's unasked question. 'And it's the weekend.'

'If you could get someone on the phone. It is fairly urgent.' Carter continued as she saw the man hesitate.

'Of course. And Nicola said you wanted to interview people in Loungers? There was a nice policeman here yesterday, I don't think he came up with much.'

'No, sir. That's why I'm here today.'

'It's just I don't want to cause any alarm, with the parents. It's Swim with Tim today and the juniors will all be in the pool.'

'Caitlin Thompson has been missing since Thursday. If we don't find her soon, there will be every reason to be alarmed.'

The manager focused on a point somewhere in the middle distance and sucked in his cheeks. Carter watched him thinking. She took back the benefit of the doubt about the suit. This bloke was on the make.

After a moment he seemed to recollect why Carter was there. 'I'll come with you, if you don't mind. To reassure people.'

'And the security footage?'

'Right. Should I be asking for a search warrant or something?'

'I don't think you should, sir, no. Think of it more as a request.'

The man nodded.

'I'll see you down there.'

In the small café, the wet heat circulated on a tide of chlorine fumes. Several parents sat with babies and toddlers and watched their older children through the glass panels that formed one wall of the room. Carter glanced at the group of six-year-olds lined up by the pool. An attractive woman in a bright red swimming costume was handing out floats. Carter wondered if she was Tim or if everyone had got lucky today.

At the back of the café, five teenagers shared a plate of toast and played a game involving bottle tops and an empty crisp packet. Carter reassessed her comments to the Thompsons about kids having more to do these days.

She took out her badge and held it up to the room. 'Detective Sergeant Carter. A ten-year-old local girl from Leabrook South Primary has been reported missing and I'm asking for any information about her in the last two days. Her name is Caitlin and she comes to the baths after school.'

The reaction was muted. Two of the teenagers had a small coughing fit at the word 'baths' and one of the mothers wrapped her arms tighter around her son.

'She would be in school uniform. Green and grey.'

'You got a photo?' asked a lad at the back with his arm around a teenage girl.

Carter showed him the school photo she had tucked in her notebook.

'Yeah, that's Caitlin. Never seen her in prison clothes before.' The boy gave back the picture and looked at Carter. 'When did she take off?'

'She didn't go home on Thursday. Did you see her here?'

'I didn't. Any of you?'

The toast eaters shook their heads.

'Why do you think she's run away?' Carter kept her notebook open and got out a pencil.

The boy eyed the pad. 'I didn't say that. She's just a little kid, she hangs round here with her little friend, when we let her.'

Carter wrote something down. 'What's in it for you?'

The tall manager appeared at the table. 'Any luck?'

Carter noticed Nicola from the reception desk at the doorway.

'This gentleman was just about to tell me why he's friends with a girl from primary school.' Carter turned away from the teenagers. 'You got the tapes from Safecorps?'

'Safecorps?' The manager looked surprised. He indicated that Carter should step to one side with him. 'There's going to be a delay in accessing last Thursday's security footage.'

'Why is that?'

'I'm afraid I don't know the technicalities. Is there anything else I can help you with, officer?'

'If anyone recalls seeing Caitlin, or knows anyone else who might have been in contact with her, you can find me at Leabrook Station.'

One of the mothers stood up to address her as she walked to the exit, her voice lowered.

'Sergeant. Is there a predator in the area?'

'Right now, our concern is to find Caitlin. If we discover any wider public safety issues, we will of course let the community know.'

She took a last look around the room. The teenagers had returned to their bottle caps, and the parents were paying close attention to the children in the swimming pool.

Upstairs, Nicola had returned to her desk. Carter put down a card and asked her to call if she thought of anything. The young woman leant forward.

'The older kids let the younger ones hang around so they don't get thrown out,' she said. 'If they're keeping an eye on the little ones, Tony lets them stay.' She jerked her chin towards the hunched shoulders of the manager who stood staring at the main entrance as if willing Carter to leave.

'Peace on Earth' rang through the loudspeakers. 'Pa-rum pum pum pum,' sang Bing Crosby.

'Call the station when you have the footage.' Carter handed the manager her card. 'So we can rule out the leisure centre from our enquiries.'

The young man took the card, relieved at her imminent departure. 'There'll be a panic now. With the parents.'

'Then get me those tapes.' Carter walked back to her car, the December air icy after the humidity of the pool.

There was no reason for an over-promoted swimming pool manager to be concerned about a few parents. She looked back at the leisure centre as she got into the driver's seat. The bloke was still on the front step.

The radio screeched. Carter turned on the engine and boosted the heater before she answered it.

'Brecon's here and he wants you in for a meeting with DCI Atherton in thirty. Where are you?'

'On my way. Lafferty, I need the name of the security firm that handles the Mandela Leisure Centre. It's not Safecorps.'

Carter swung out of the car park. In her rear-view mirror she saw the manager rub his chin and go back inside. She abandoned her plan to visit the Thompsons and headed back to the station.

Brecon had summoned her earlier than Carter expected. There weren't many occasions Carter welcomed outside interference, especially Atherton's, but when it meant more resources, she coped. She checked in at the desk for a heads up and met the slight figure of DS Lafferty walking in the other direction.

'Atherton's already here.'

'You spoken to the desk?'

Lafferty nodded. 'Nothing coming up on family background checks. Photos are ready. No news on the number
plate yet. Security at the leisure centre was run by Holdings.
Said their contract was cancelled a few months ago.'

Carter turned and walked with Lafferty to the incident
room. 'So, no tapes?'

'Nothing. What's up?'

'I met your friend Tony at the leisure centre. Said he'd
track down the security coverage for Thursday. Only there's
not going to be any is there?' Carter opened the door.
'Because my bet is young Tony's been creaming the security
budget for himself.'

'Who the fuck is Tony?' Brecon stood in front of the
whiteboard with DCI Atherton, the office manager, WPC
Hill and other uniforms. Atherton had brought several
detectives with him, all men, all looking at Carter as though
she had walked into the wrong room.

Atherton was a formidable presence; short, stocky and
ex-military, he liked to attack new cases, especially if they
might be high profile. Carter guessed the budget allocated
to the disappearance of Caitlin Thompson had increased.

'The manager at Mandela Leisure Centre, sir. Both
Caitlin's parents and her best friend think she might have
gone there on Thursday.'

It was Atherton's room, but Brecon couldn't help himself. 'Lafferty went there yesterday and you weren't on
duty this morning so how the hell do we have this new
information?'

'I passed by there on the way in today, sir,' Carter said.
'Saw the CCTV cameras and asked if I could have a look at
the security tapes. But there are no tapes because Tony fired
the company three months ago.'

'Do you think this man is involved in Caitlin's disappearance?' Atherton took a step forward.

'I doubt it, sir, but it means we can't confirm whether she
went to the pool. No witnesses have come forward and there
is no CCTV along the route she takes.'

Atherton turned to Lafferty. 'Make sure there's no footage
of the girl at the leisure centre and report the manager to
his immediate bosses. So,' the super looked up as Dawson
and Marshall entered the room, 'could it be a pick-up from
the school?'

'If it was, someone should have seen them.' Carter pointed
at the timeline. 'She comes out of Leabrook South Primary
School with all the other kids, teachers see their classes out,
most parents are there to collect. Some of the Year Fives and
Sixes walk home independently.'

'So who would have noticed one child leave alone?'

'Her teacher could have, or another parent. So far, no
one has come forward. But the Thompsons have a routine.
Caitlin's friend Ruby Siltmore, she's waiting for her by
the gate.'

Brecon nodded at a photo of Leabrook South Primary that
Rebecca Hill had pulled from the files. 'It's chaos outside
that school.'

'Exactly,' Carter said, 'all potential witnesses. It only
takes one person to notice something out of the ordinary. If
Caitlin had walked out with an adult, Ruby certainly would
have seen.'

'Are we relying on the vigilance of a ten-year-old girl?'
Brecon asked.

Carter took a breath. 'And the hundreds of people who
would have been walking down the road from the school.'

Atherton nodded. 'What if she got into a car?'

'It would have been difficult to get Caitlin into a car against her will without drawing attention.'

Brecon looked smug. 'Unless she knew the driver.'

'The Thompsons don't drive.'

'Someone in that family must have a licence.'

'And even if she did get into a car with a person known to her, there should be at least one child or parent who saw her. Ruby Siltmore's class leaves before Caitlin's and Ruby says Caitlin didn't show.'

'Are there any other entrances to the school?' Atherton asked.

'I've found one that could have been used. But it would have been unusual, premeditated.'

Atherton looked at the timeline and the map. They were nearly at the 48-hour mark. 'As of now, all officers are recalled. I want a team with dogs starting at the Palmerston Estate door-to-door within the hour. DS Lafferty, you're in charge of that. Dawson and Marshall, stay with the parents. Carter, you visit Mr Moffatt at home, bring him in if you can. All uniforms on the street, WPC Hill, comb every nook and cranny near Leabrook South. All media outlets have been alerted. No statements, except from me or DI Brecon. Next briefing here at eighteen hundred hours.'

'I've got some questions for the headmaster,' Carter said.

'Can you talk to him later?'

'The school is closed.'

Brecon sighed. 'Carter, you searched the school yesterday and interviewed them all.' He turned to the rest of the room. 'Get the fuck out of here while it's still light.'

Carter stepped to one side as the room emptied. 'I did, sir. But I went back last night and I want to chase up a few things.'

'Find him and speak to him. But do not,' Brecon called to the back of Carter's head, 'spook him.'

At least Brecon knew a possible suspect when he heard of one. It would have made more sense for Carter to be in charge at the estate search, she knew the layout now and she was a familiar face for the Thompsons, but Carter wasn't going to argue with Atherton. This way she was free to follow her own instincts, chase up Fry. She would go to see Moffatt as directed, but at this point it was a fishing expedition; she had nothing on the guy.

In the hallway, she heard Rebecca Hill call her name.

'You put a trace on a plate this morning? I've just got it back.' Hill handed her the paperwork. 'Mean anything?'

'A Mr and Mrs Graham Lithgoe. Birmingham.' Carter shook her head. 'Need to check it against the list of staff names at Leabrook South.'

No obvious connection to Fry but at least she had a legitimate question to ask the headmaster. She looked at Hill.

'You're doing a search round the school? There's a side gate to the front yard, have it cordoned off. No one's to use it, might be fingerprints. I'm going to get the head on the phone. See if he'll open up the building.'

Hill nodded. 'See you back here at six.'

Carter caught Hill's eye.

'Yes,' she said, 'see you at six.'

7

Isobel woke early on Saturday morning, her lips raw from chewing them in her sleep. In her dream, Dan and her father were going on a train journey together. She wanted to stop them but was too late. By the time she reached the station they were disappearing into the distance and she knew they were never coming back.

She lay in the dark trying to separate the realities. She hardly knew Dan; until last night had only been into his flat once. Yet now he was invading her dreams. She had been suspicious when she saw him talking to the man outside the restaurant, but it wasn't Dan who frightened her.

She pushed back the covers and felt for her slippers under the bed. They weren't where they should be; nothing was in its right place since she had opened the letter from Agnes Spill the day before. The letter had brought the chaos she had shut away for fifteen years. It had conjured Jason Ryall from the cell that kept her safe. She looked around her room, at the things she had chosen, curtains and pictures, clothes and books. Talismans in their way, spells to keep out the past. She had made a new life, and he wasn't allowed back into it. None of them were.

The desire to undo what had happened the day before

overwhelmed her. She started with the letter, collecting it
from where it lay on the bathroom floor. There were things
in the letter she hadn't understood, but she couldn't read it
again. She replaced it in its envelope and folded it into her
handbag. Next, she put away the food from the uncooked
dinner, washed all the surfaces and swept the floor. With a
final inspection of the flat, Isobel put on her heavy coat and
went downstairs. She pulled her door shut and hesitated
in the hallway. Dan did not appear. She left before she was
forced to recognise the flutter of disappointment.

Her mother had given Miss Spill her home address. Clare
Williams lived a mile from Brighton station, in a large and
unkempt flat on the first floor of a Georgian terrace. From
there she ran workshops for prisoners' wives, and numerous
therapeutic courses, to which she was constantly adding. At
present, she was specialising in colour therapy. On Isobel's
last visit, at the end of September, every available surface in
the sitting room had been lined with glass vials of different
hues. A few had splintered on the parquet floor. Clare had
been uncharacteristically careful when cleaning them up.

'It's a natural process,' Clare had explained, picking an
unbroken lavender vial and pressing it into Isobel's hands. 'I
need to work with the messages that the colours are sending.
Oh, do take it Isobel,' Clare sighed, 'It's important to me.
And it should be to you.'

The fast train to Brighton would get her there by one
o'clock. She expected her mother to be at home. Isobel's
mother was always home. The last, and only, time Clare
had stayed with her daughter had been after the storms in
1987 when she turned up on Isobel's doorstep unannounced.
They were facing an apocalypse, her mother had said, Gaia
had abandoned them. She insisted that Isobel prepare for the

end. It seemed Clare had gone down to the seafront in her nightdress and attempted to calm the waves. A photograph was later published in the *Brighton Argus*. 'Clare Canute' said the headline and beneath it a picture of her mother swathed in voluminous white cotton, facing the roiling waters with arms raised in ecstasy. She attracted a certain type of troubled client to her therapy rooms in the following months. It was fortunate that her patients came to her flat in Brighton once Clare stopped leaving the house.

'It is better for me to do my work here,' she said the morning after the storm when Isobel returned her to Brighton, 'where my power is greatest.'

On the train, Isobel tried to prepare for her visit. She needed to persuade her mother of her independence and capability in order to prevent further letters and communication from people Clare thought 'helpful'.

Her mother answered the door the third time that Isobel pressed the buzzer. It was possible that Clare only ever answered after the third ring these days. It was equally possible that she had looked out of the window and, seeing Isobel, had waited to see if her daughter had changed her mind about not speaking and would shout up to her. Isobel did not look up. It had taken years for Clare to believe that her daughter's deafness was not a matter of choice and that if she would only start speaking properly again, she would soon remember how to hear.

'Isobel. How wonderful. Is everything all right? You look washed out.' Clare took a step back into the hall and put her arms out to her daughter. It was a gesture Isobel knew well, signifying warmth while firmly discouraging any actual physical contact.

I'm fine, Clare. Everything fine. Good to see you.

Isobel and her mother had invented the sign for *Clare* during Isobel's rehabilitation. Clare wanted an elaborate gesture involving beating hearts. Isobel compromised with clasped hands. It had been almost a joke on Isobel's part, given how rarely her mother touched her, but Clare had taken it as a symbol of good mothering. It did not occur to either of them to use the sign for 'mother'.

Clare started to walk upstairs, hands beckoning *Come in.*

The large entrance hall was dark and the stairs were littered with boxes and pieces of furniture. Isobel followed her mother up to the flat and saw through the door that the boxes continued into the sitting room. There were labelled tea chests and cardboard packing cases with 'Julian Williams' scrawled on the side. Some of the containers were open and piles of clothes and paper spilled onto the floor. Isobel looked at her mother.

'It's your father's stuff, from that ugly flat.' Clare spoke with an exaggerated expression and Isobel knew she was shouting. She waited. These days, her mother was a proficient signer and she liked an audience.

His sister got bored hoarding. Eight years gone. Clare swept her arm out in front of her.

Eight years. At Julian's funeral Aunt Sasha cornered Clare. Isobel had watched the sisters-in-law argue outside the crematorium, had read the furious whispers while they all waited for her father's ashes. The blame her aunt assigned to her 'negligent' mother, and Clare's insistence that it was only thanks to her that Julian had lived as long as he had. When the funeral director walked over with the urn, Clare and Sasha had turned to her. Your father, they seemed to say, your responsibility.

She sent to me. Taken valuables. Naturally.

Isobel did not believe her father had kept anything of value in the bed-sitting room where he ended his life, and she was surprised to see that his possessions filled so many boxes. The way she remembered it, he had taken nothing when he left Clare.

I will heat casserole. You are too thin, Isobel. Please eat.

It was not yet two o'clock. Isobel had arrived in time for lunch.

I have eaten, thanks. Isobel signed as casually as she could. It wasn't any easier to lie with your hands.

'Oh, don't do that awful smile, Isobel. I'm not going to force you to eat. You're hardly a child any more.' Clare turned her back to her daughter and went through to the kitchen. Isobel was sure her mother was still speaking. It was another of Clare's techniques, part of the plan to get Isobel to hear again. She followed her mother into the kitchen and put the kettle on. Eventually her mother continued signing.

Good timing. You will help me with your father's things.

Arrived when?

About one month ago.

One month? Isobel wondered if Clare had touched any of it since the initial ransacking.

I was busy. Clare shrugged. 'I have patients to see, Isobel.'

They sat at the kitchen table while Clare ate the reheated stew and Isobel sipped tea. The sea mist cast a diffused brightness about the flat, illuminating every surface. Through the doorway, Isobel could see the bay window in the sitting room, and the houses beyond leaning wearily down to the coast. Isobel didn't understand how anyone could live by the sea. The end of the world at the bottom of the street.

Someone called you, Clare? You gave my address to someone?

'No one can get in contact with you, Isobel. It's quite impossible. I don't know why you have that telephone.'

It was Clare who had insisted on Isobel buying the mini-com, 'In case you need to reach me.'

Did someone call you or write to you?

Clare flicked her gaze to the ceiling in the manner of someone trying to recall an insignificant detail. 'Oh, you mean your old teacher, the homeless one. Nice woman. Looked after you.'

She is not homeless.

'She was then. She wore that overcoat covered in stains. Terrible life. Violent husband and she'd had to leave with nothing. I asked your father to put her in touch with the right people at the council and I think he tried to talk to her but then he got side-tracked by that other one . . . well, you know what he was like.' Her mother checked to see if her daughter had read her. Isobel remembered all the arguments. She was glad when they separated and she could visit them on their own.

'Yes. I knew her quite well,' Clare continued. 'Of course I did, after what happened. She rang me last month about my workshops, or so she said. Then she started talking about you. She was going to write to you. Did she?'

She wants me to see her. Her house.

Clare smiled. 'You should go.'

Isobel stared at her mother. *Your idea?*

'It was not! But I expect she's lonely now. And I thought you should be in touch. We spoke a few times on the phone and she wrote me a wonderful letter. I've got it somewhere.' Clare glanced around the kitchen as though the letter might be caught in the lampshade or the curtain rail. 'It was a good school, you know. You should have left before you did but you were happy there.'

Isobel felt the danger pricking her fingertips. There were rules to their conversations, paths to follow. Clare could make offhand remarks about her father, her childhood, but they were never to go any further. Isobel would look away. If she had questions she wanted to ask, they were reserved for a day when she felt safe. When that day would come or how it would feel, she couldn't imagine. It wasn't today.

'Don't make that face, Isobel. I know it ended badly. That doesn't mean it didn't matter. Look how well you turned out.'

You think?

'Yes,' *I think*. Clare imitated Isobel's sarcastic sign.

This was a new tactic. If she was not careful she was going to be drawn into a discussion. She wanted to agree with her mother that the school was important, to tell her what it had meant and why it mattered. She closed her eyes so she could think. Her mother was lying. She did not believe her daughter had 'turned out well', for all the reasons Isobel didn't want to think about. Her accident, her father. Isobel knew the truth. She opened her eyes. Clare was smiling.

Please do not do that again. Please do not give my address.

Fine, Isobel. You have so many friends, you don't need any more.

Clare pushed her bowl away and went back to the sitting room. Isobel sat in the kitchen and stared at the mess. After a few minutes she filled the sink with dishes and left them to soak.

'I need to get rid of all this for my Christmas workshop. I've got a man coming to take it.' Clare stood in the middle of the room and waved at the boxes.

Isobel stared at what was left of her father's life. *Are there any letters?*

'I expect so. Take anything you want, Isobel. It's all going to be thrown away.' Clare peered at the nearest container. 'But careful what you wish for.'

Her mother was punishing her. If she hadn't come this weekend, would her father's things have remained where they were? Perhaps Clare had counted on her visiting once Agnes Spill had written. Isobel could see photograph albums and books lying among the debris. Would her mother really have junked them without telling her?

Sitting down by a brown plastic suitcase, she pulled out a sheaf of papers. There were letters and receipts from 1977. She thought how much she would like to see her father's handwriting again, the spidery eloquence of it. He had hated his own writing. 'Hideous,' he said, 'no style at all.' But Isobel loved it when he wrote something to her. She reached for another case.

Two hours later, Isobel had collected a small pile of photographs and books. All the containers had been brought into the flat and stacked against one wall. She managed to find a few letters her father had written to her, as well as some of his notepads. A few of the pages were covered with both their work, where Isobel had started a design for her fantasy house and her father had added suggestions. She put these to one side. He had always encouraged her architectural follies, but she remembered looking at him once, when she was in the middle of a particularly elaborate extension, and catching his unguarded expression as he stared down at her with what she thought of then as his sad face. She was not yet used to seeing the other side of her father, the world that seemed to exist behind his eyes. It was only after the accident that she grew accustomed to the way he watched her.

The accident. That was how she thought of it, even now.

'There are some other cases in my room,' Clare said when she saw Isobel was getting ready to leave, 'more of the same. It might take a while. Who knew your father was sentimental?'

Her mother never asked Isobel directly if she would stay the night.

Her bag was getting heavy but Clare had made it clear she would not keep any of the boxes left behind unless Isobel was prepared to bargain. Isobel felt she would rather take what she could carry and not call in the favour.

I have work.

Good. So do I.

The bags were on the floor of her mother's bedroom. She recognised one of them; a navy holdall with looping handles on top. Seeing it made her feel dizzy. She swung it onto the bed, guessing by the weight that it contained books. She hoped it might be the rest of his notebooks, maybe some of his architectural drawings. She opened the case and for a moment she didn't understand what she was looking at. There were bundles of letters in her handwriting and dozens of exercise books. At the bottom of the case was a hardback book with a cloth cover. She turned to see her mother watching her from the doorway.

Your old school things, Clare signed. *Your dad got the police to return them.*

Isobel turned back to the case. The chart books, the stories written in blue ink, the letters. She recognised the cloth-bound book now, the little silver padlock, long since broken, hanging from the side. Clare sat on the bed and tapped Isobel on the shoulder.

'Take it,' Clare said, 'I need the space for my patients. We can't all live in the past, Isobel.'

Thursday

There is a horse at school! He came in the Easter holidays and there is a shed for him that is his stable. It is part of Mr Sanders's plan to make the school better but we don't have the slide or the swimming pool yet. The horse's name is Turpin and he has straw on the ground and we can feed him and brush him whenever we want. He mustn't grow a tail or a mane because he is itchy. There is a special oil to rub into his coat to help him. We have to take turns cleaning his house. It's called mucking out. We can walk him round the yard but we can't ride him unless it is our day. Kathy doesn't like him, but I spent ages with Lucy cleaning up the shed and polishing the bridle. He doesn't have a saddle yet.

When it is my turn to ride him, I will take him to the park.

Tuesday

Tuesday is my favourite day because we go to the library. We can take out two books. It is quiet in the library and there are cushions that you can sit on and read any book you like. I got a book called *Thursday's Child* because it had a picture of a girl walking with a horse and the story was about a girl who does not go to school because she has to work on the canal and they use the horse to pull the boat along.

When we walked back from the library I sang the song from the television programme about white horses with Kathy.

> '. . . On white horses let me ride away /
> To my world of dreams so far away . . .'

If I had to run away I would take Turpin with me and maybe we could go to work at a canal but I don't think he would like to be tied up to a boat.

Wednesday

Kathy has told everyone that I went to a funfair in the sky. She is still my friend but I don't like her.

Monday

It was a horrible day. We started swimming lessons and we walked to the pool from school and queued outside by the shops. Kathy stood next to Steven the whole time we were waiting and Mark talked to Lucy. I don't think he minds that she can't hear him. I didn't have anyone to talk to so I read my book from the library.

I know how to swim and I used to really like the swimming pool because it smells nice and under the water it is a different world. One time I had a mask on and I could see all the legs like we were inside a television together.

I haven't been swimming with school before. When I changed into my swimming trunks, Kathy started laughing and she was pointing at me and everyone laughed. All the girls had swimming costumes or bikinis but Mum said I could just wear the bottoms because I'm not a woman yet.

Miss Spill said I didn't have to swim, so I went to the benches by the side of the pool and watched. I told Kathy I didn't care.

Steven came up to me after and said he was sorry he missed the show. I didn't walk back with them, I walked with Angie. She always wears a money belt with a fifty-pence piece inside it for emergencies. I made a plan with her that I would get some sweets from the newsagents and we could share them. Angie gave me the fifty pence but Miss Spill saw. She didn't say anything she just put her hand out and I gave back the money. She looked at me like I was stealing it.

Saturday

Dad took me to Wimpy for lunch as a treat. It is my favourite because they have ketchup in the shape of a tomato and you can have a Knickerbocker Glory for pudding. Mum doesn't like it so she didn't come.

After lunch Dad took me to his office and he asked me if I was happy at school. He said Miss Spill had called him for a chat.

I said Miss Spill was a nosy cow and he laughed. Then he put his arm around me and said, 'We all get into trouble sometimes. The important thing is how you behave when you get caught.'

I asked him when he ever got in trouble but he said, 'Better ask your mother.'

Thursday

I took Turpin to the park with Lucy. Angie wanted to come with us but Miss Spill said she couldn't because we were going without a teacher. Steven said I should take Angie with me. He said she would like to go on a horse ride.

Angie stared at us. She couldn't tell if Steven was serious. He pushes her around but sometimes he is kind to her. He's like that with everyone. I said she was not allowed. I wanted her to come and she had her money belt on but Miss Spill was looking at us from the window. I told her she couldn't come. Steven jumped on top of Mark and they galloped around the yard. Lucy and I left and Angie waved at us. I didn't feel bad because it's true that she doesn't know about horses.

It took ages to get to the park. It's only down the road but Turpin goes slowly. We didn't know whether to walk in the road or on the pavement. In the end, we went in the middle of the street until we got to the main crossing and then we waited at the lights as if we were in a car.

I let Lucy ride him first. She had to stand on one of the benches to get up because of not having a saddle. We only walked through the park, but Lucy was a bit scared. Then it was my turn. I thought I was going to slip, but I stayed on all the way round the lake. My legs were wobbly when I got off. When I have my own home, I'm going to have a field, and Turpin will have a mane and a tail and his own saddle.

8

Carter tried the number she had for Fry several times before
driving over to Moffatt's house. She asked Hill to keep trying
the headmaster.

Karl Moffatt lived with his mother in a modern semi
over a mile away from Leabrook South. Rows of identical
windows ablaze with Christmas decorations overlooked a
side street off the London Road. Carter stared at the house
from her car and wondered how Moffatt managed to spend
his days in the confinement of a two-up-two-down with his
mum. Carter couldn't do it, notwithstanding that she hadn't
had a mother for a long time. Possibly ever, she thought, if
you considered the act of mothering to be a prerequisite
for the title.

She frowned as she got out of the car, annoyed by the
memories that clouded her concentration. Unlike some of
her colleagues, she understood that emotional responses
could be helpful when problem-solving. Of course, Caitlin
Thompson's case was important to her, just as the missing
child from her early days on the job had been. Her insight
was an advantage but not if she had to haul her own childhood out of the way every time she saw a new piece of
evidence or interviewed a suspect.

She rang the doorbell and stood back while a yapping dog was shut in a room.

'Quiet, Lancey! Stay there. Good boy.' A woman's voice came from behind the door. 'Hello? Who's there?'

'Detective Sergeant Carter, Mrs Moffatt. I'm here to talk to you and your son.'

'I've already spoken to the police. And Karl came to the station himself.'

Carter wondered when everyone had decided they only needed to speak to the police once. Was it something they heard on television? 'I know, ma'am. I have some further questions. Do you think you could open the door?'

There was a pause before the deadbolt was unlocked and the safety chain slid into place. The door opened a few inches. A slim woman in her sixties with a peroxide beehive was visible in the gap.

Carter held up her badge.

'You can't talk to Karl without his solicitor present.'

'That's up to Karl.' Carter stepped forward as a man passed her on the pavement. 'We can certainly do this at the station if that's what he'd like.'

The chain slid away and the door swung open.

'Come in, come in.' Karl's mother leant forward to nod at the man who stood further down the road looking back at the Moffatt house. She shut the door and shouted up the stairs. 'Karl. Police.'

Carter followed her through to the living room where she was directed to a low sofa. The yapping dog threw itself against the other side of a pair of connecting doors. The mother perched on a chair opposite, her shiny hair reflecting the multi-coloured fairy lights that twinkled on the minia-ture Christmas tree. A plate of chocolate biscuits sat on the coffee table next to Jean Moffatt's cup of tea. Carter tried not to look at them. Breakfast seemed a long time ago.

'Mrs Moffatt . . .'

'Jean. Would you like a biscuit?'

'No, thank you. Jean.' Carter put a hand up to the plate being offered. 'If you could run through Thursday for me.' She opened her notebook.

'What did you say your name was?'

'Detective Sergeant Sally Carter.'

'Listen, Sally, since this is a friendly chat,' she glanced at the ceiling, 'I know my Karl has been in trouble before. Life's been difficult for him and that's hard for a mother to watch. I wasn't there for him when he was a little boy but now I take care of him and he looks after me and we have an understanding; no more funny business.'

In the next room, the dog had stopped its staccato barking and started a high-pitched howl.

'And on Thursday?'

Jean Moffatt shook her head. The beehive remained immobile. 'He's a sensitive man, Sally. It won't do any good all this talk of missing children.'

'I'm sorry. But Caitlin Thompson deserves a proper investigation. She may be lost, or had an accident, or she may have been taken. If Karl is involved it would be better for everybody if we find out now.'

From overhead, heavy footsteps shook the room. Mrs Moffatt leant towards Carter.

'Karl was here, in his room, all day on Thursday. The same as every day. He only goes out to help me with the shopping or to his work at night. Or Sundays, he likes to go with a friend to watch the birds at the nature reserve. Don't you, darling?'

The shambling figure of Karl Moffatt hovered at the doorway. He was still in his pyjamas.

Carter stood up. 'Hello again, Karl. I have a couple of questions for you and I hoped you'd answer them now rather than down at the station.'

'Sit down love.' Jean nodded at the sofa.

The large pale face looked from Carter to his mother. His appearance had deteriorated since the day before. Dark circles ringed his eyes and patches of stubble grazed his cheeks. The pyjama bottoms were tartan and they didn't meet the top.

'What do you want to know?' His voice was nasal, congested.

Carter looked at her notes as though reading the previous interview. 'You told us that you go to the nature reserve on Sundays.'

'Yeah.' Had he been crying?

'It's a bus ride from here and quite a walk the other end.'

'Yeah.'

Carter waited.

'Karl?' His mother prompted. 'Quiet, Lancey!'

After a moment the dog shut up.

'What?'

'Well, you don't go on the bus, do you darling?'

Moffatt looked at Carter. 'She told you?'

'It's a violation of your parole for you to consort with any known criminals.'

'He's not a criminal.'

'Who isn't? Billy? Oh no, Sally.' Jean Moffatt smiled at her son. 'Billy's just a bit slow, isn't he? Go on, do have a biscuit. I'll only have to put them away when Lancey comes in.'

'I'll need his name and address, Karl.' She took two milk

chocolate biscuits from the assortment and nodded at the Moffatts. 'We'll need to speak to Billy, too.'

Carter radioed the station as soon as she left the Moffatts and asked for verification on a William Rutherford. Hill picked up the call.

'He works with Karl Moffatt on the night shift at Briggs Biscuits. Any word on the headmaster?'

'No one answering that number. Shall I send a unit over?'

Carter was tempted to send some uniforms over, pick the guy up if he was there and sort it out when he was at the station but she knew better than to put that on Hill's shoulders.

'Negative. I'm on my way to Fry's now.'

Turning up unannounced at Fry's home address was bound to antagonise the man but they needed access to the school and if that rattled him, Carter might see a less professional side. Brecon was right, she didn't want to scare him away altogether, just force a mistake if there was one to be made.

It was after three o'clock and already near dark when she reached Fry's house in one of Leabrook's leafier neighbourhoods. Carter stood outside the large Victorian villa and looked up and down the street. No sign of the car Fry had driven from the school.

There were three doorbells. Fry's was Flat C. The lights on the third floor were off but Carter rang the bell, waited, and then held it down. After a minute the front door opened and a young woman in jeans and a jumper confronted her.

'We can hear that bell through the whole house. There's nobody in Flat C.'

The woman's hands and clothes were covered in a fine dust. She eyed Carter up and down and went to shut the door.

'Detective Sergeant Sally Carter, ma'am.' She held up her badge. 'I'm looking for your neighbour, Robert Fry.'

She peered at the badge.

'Really?'

'Yes. Has he been at home at all today?'

'I don't think so. What's it about?'

'It is quite urgent, ma'am.'

'Ma'am? Good god. Sorry. I'm making a Christmas cake, I wasn't expecting the Flying Squad . . . '

Carter's radio blared. She reached for it with a nod of apology.

'Carter.'

'It's Mrs Thompson. They're having some trouble with the search. She's asking for you.'

'I'll be there in twenty.' She turned back to the woman and took a deep breath.

'Do you know where Mr Fry might be?'

'He's away a lot. He has a girlfriend he stays with.'

Carter grabbed her notebook.

'I don't know her name, I'm afraid.' The woman tilted her head in concentration. 'Dark-haired. With a daughter. They used to come round here but I haven't seen them for a while.'

'Do you have any contact details for Mr Fry, for emergencies?'

'Oh, yes.' She smiled. 'Hang on.'

She left the door open and disappeared into the hallway. When she came back she held a pad of paper in the shape of a cauliflower.

'Leabrook South Primary School.'

'Yes?'

'That's where he works.'

'Right. Thank you, Miss . . . ?'

'Celia Whoolf.' She watched while Carter wrote it down. 'With an 'h', two 'o's and no 'e'. I could leave a message.'

'If you do see him,' Carter handed her a card.

The blue lights were visible long before Carter reached the main entrance for the Palmerston Estate. The uniforms on duty waved Carter through and she parked outside the stairwell leading to the Thompsons' flat. She could hear the dogs barking before she stepped out of the car. The noise echoed through the concrete walkways and tunnels. All the dogs on the estate could smell and hear the trained Alsatians.

At the top of the stairs PC Dawson stood with David Thompson watching the search below.

'She's asking for you,' David said. His eyes didn't meet Carter's. 'She's indoors.'

'Marshall's with her,' Dawson said. He lowered his head to Carter. 'Atherton's called in Underwater Search and Confined Spaces. Family services have been notified. Full station briefing nine am tomorrow.'

Atherton hadn't waited for the six o'clock meeting. Carter could only guess at the kind of attention the case was starting to gain.

Carter went through to the flat. The front door was on the latch and a dim light spilled onto the concourse. She could hear Susan Thompson crying and she paused before going in. It wasn't a sound you got used to, however many times you told a family that there'd been an accident, or an attack, or a suicide, or a murder. Caitlin had been missing for forty-eight hours, there was a good chance they would find her alive in the next twelve. But how much hope was kind to offer and how much hope was cruel?

December 1990

Sunday

9

The library was full of students on the last open Sunday before Christmas. Some of them must have been there all night. Isobel glanced around the room as she entered with her suitcase, trying to avoid eye contact with any of the visitors. Jenny did not work at the weekend and the returns trolleys were piled high. Melanie was on the telephone. She smiled at Isobel and made a gesture with her hand to indicate how busy she was. Isobel nodded but didn't take her coat off. She pushed the case under the desk counter, retrieved her flask and left for the canteen.

She walked to the opposite corner of the campus, taking the longer route via two sides of the square instead of going down the stairs and straight across. Her head was filled with thoughts of the weekend with her mother, but she felt less burdened, as though she had exchanged some of her anxiety for her father's belongings and the luggage was lighter.

It was late by the time she had collected everything she wanted from Clare's flat and she had been too tired to resist the ordered pizza and bottle of red wine. She sat on the bed with her mother and watched *Meet Me in St. Louis* on mute. When she was a child, Clare would have found a book for them to read together, taking a chapter in turns, and Isobel knew her mother missed that. Maybe she missed it too. She still felt her mother's voice when she read. Watching a film without the sound was Clare's attempt to recapture those evenings, and while her mother drank and asked what everyone in the film was saying, Isobel would make up whole conversations. She enjoyed the sense of the outside world receding.

They fell asleep on Clare's bed with their clothes on. Isobel woke up when it was light. Her mother slept turned towards her, on the same side she had always lain with Julian. Isobel didn't wake her. She called a cab on a number she had used before and got the early train to London.

As she approached the far side of the quad she tried to focus on the coffee she was going to have, the comfort of it, but when she stepped into the canteen, a tap on the shoulder brought her round to find Melanie Harris looking at her, concerned.

I am worried about you, Melanie signed. *On Friday you left. Everything OK?*

Melanie had watched over her in the early weeks of Isobel's internship at the library. It was Melanie who had taught the other staff some basic signs and she had refused to let go of her status as Isobel's mentor.

Fine. Isobel tried to breathe slowly. *I'm fine. Just tired.*

Melanie Harris nodded and waited while Isobel bought coffee. She reminded Isobel of Miss Peden, her old History teacher. Both women seemed to enjoy their responsibilities without ever actually smiling. But Melanie would never wear patent blue shoes with a gold buckle; she was a cords and sandals woman. Isobel wasn't sure where you bought clothes like that. Greenham Common chic.

They walked back to the library together.

Good half-weekend? It was Melanie's line that neither of

them had much of a life outside the library. If Isobel let her, she would talk about her cats. Melanie was of the opinion that Isobel should get a pet even though she had made it clear that she didn't like animals. It wasn't true, but Isobel had no intention of acquiring a pet. She knew how that ended.

Melanie waited for an answer. Head to one side.

Isobel looked at her and thought of Dan standing in the hallway waiting for a kiss. Monday was her day off. There was still time to see him 'over the weekend'.

Clare, she finger-spelled her mother's name.

I see. Melanie raised an eyebrow as though Clare was a cross they both had to bear.

Isobel turned back to the quad as they approached the library and took a sip from her flask. She had the sense that the ground was shifting beneath her but she was not sure, now, if she minded.

Winter. Too dark. Melanie held the door open.

'Thank you,' Isobel forced the words out. It was the only way she could fight against the Melanies; push them away from her world. Isobel's mother might be in denial, but at least she didn't feel sorry for her daughter or feign understanding.

Melanie looked uncomfortable. *See you later*, she signed, and went back to her desk. Isobel watched her retreating form with something like triumph.

The library had emptied a little. A young trainee from the university pushed a book trolley around the shelves. The Sunday papers were scattered across the chairs in Periodicals and Isobel went over to pick them up. One of the headlines caught her eye, 'Please Find Caitlin'. A photo of a schoolgirl was printed below, taking up most of the front page. The corner image was a photograph of a man and woman, huddled in the back of a car. 'Thompson Family Misery'; the other papers carried the same photos. Isobel sat down.

The child's fine hair was held in a ponytail, blonde wisps framing a small face with pale eyes. She wore a look of indifference, staring out from the paper as if determined not to be impressed by her own disappearance. In smaller print at the bottom of the page Isobel read, 'Mother's plea for missing 10-year-old. Can you help?' Isobel recognised the girl immediately. The picture was not recent but she was quite sure. On Friday, the child had been sitting just across from where Isobel sat now.

Fifteen years flashed through her mind, past the job, the flat, the institute and beyond, to the hospital, her hospital, the one she came to think of as home. Sitting in the family room staring at the papers, the photos of Angie Mason plastered across the front of the tabloids. 'Down's Syndrome Child Missing'. Isobel had seen the headlines. She had turned each paper over and gone back to the ward.

Something brushed her leg and she looked up to see Melanie in front of her.

'I need you on the *desk*, *Isobel*. Isobel?' Melanie's expression changed from impatience to alarm. Isobel looked down at the newspaper and stayed very still. She wanted to read the rest of the story but the print was blurring. She closed her eyes and waited for everything to go away. When she opened them again, Melanie was sitting on the seat in front of her.

What is wrong? Isobel? What happened?

Isobel pushed the newspaper over to Melanie and pointed at the photograph of the missing child.

That girl, you remember? She was here last week. Sitting with a friend. They were reading. Remember?

Melanie glanced at the picture then back at Isobel, her forehead corrugated with concern.

Isobel, this missing child. She was taken.

She was here Friday.

Melanie shook her head. She opened the paper and found the rest of the story. She handed it back to Isobel.

Caitlin Thompson was missing Thursday after school. In Leabrook. Melanie rubbed her face with both hands.

Isobel scanned the report for more details.

She was here with another girl. Sitting here.

Melanie didn't reply. She was looking into the middle distance, her mouth pursed. After a minute, she put her hands on one of the empty chairs and heaved herself upright.

You saw this girl on Friday, after she was missing, in the library reading?

A few students stood nearby, watching the silent drama. Isobel nodded.

OK. We will call police. Melanie didn't pause for Isobel to object. *Go to staff room and wait. I will phone.*

She turned her back to Isobel and headed towards the office. One of the students reached into her pocket and handed Isobel a tissue. She took it and walked away from the reading area, leaving the students peering at the photograph of Caitlin Thompson. It was only when she was climbing the stairs to the upper floor that she realised her face was wet.

May 1975

Wednesday

I asked Kathy if Steven is her boyfriend. She doesn't think Steven is old enough for her but she says he will do for now. He is thirteen. Kathy says she likes older men because they know what to do.

Thursday

I did Maths with Miss Spill today. Her face was right up close to me and I could see all the scabs on her skin and her hands had bits of blood on them. When she signed my chart book she said she wanted to talk to me about Angie. She said Angie looked up to me and I had a responsibility to be her friend and to take care of her. She looked at me as though she could see all the way through my head. I was taking care of Angie. I was buying sweets. Now Miss Spill says I have to go to the after-school club on Fridays and be with Angie every Friday. Steven and Kathy said, 'Wow, thank you so much, Miss Spill. That will really be so nice for Izzy.' They always pretend to be nice to her because I think they are a bit scared of her.

No one goes to Friday club except the kids who are not allowed on the bus.

Friday

Kathy gave me a card in lunch break on the way to Luigi's. It had a picture of a cat on the front and inside she had written a list. It was called 'How to have an orgasm'. She said I should keep it to read at home. I only saw the beginning of the list. It said, 'First wash your hands'. I put the card in my blazer pocket. I don't want to read the rest of it.

I went to Friday club with Angie and we cleaned bells with Brasso which smells really nice but is hard to get off the brass. I don't mind being with her because it's us and a couple of kids in wheelchairs and the two girls who are sisters but don't speak at all. They are called Jolie and Belle, and Kathy says they were going to die because they were born so small but they are OK now apart from not talking.

When Angie's mother came to pick her up, she gave me a lift home.

Saturday

I had a big row with Mum. She found Kathy's card in my blazer and she was really angry. She took all the magazines out of my room and said I was wasting my time and what was I learning at school? She wanted to know why I had the card. I said I didn't know; someone gave it to me. I said I hadn't even read it and she could keep the stupid card. She calmed down after that but she said she's going to speak to Mr Sanders. That must not happen.

She said it was Dad's idea for me to go to the Schoolhouse but I don't think that is true. I have been there for six years and she always says how much she loves it. 'You've got to grow up a bit, Isobel,' she said, 'I can't be worrying about you as well as everyone else.'

Sunday

Dad took me to the park because the sun was shining and he bought me a Vimto Jubbly ice-lolly and I sucked all the syrup out of it until it was just a triangle of ice. He asked me how everything was and I said fine. He said, 'Things can be complicated, Izzy.' I said what things, and he looked at me funny. He asked me what I liked most about school and I told him about Turpin, how he was such a good horse even though he did not have a mane or a tail, and Dad laughed.

Monday

When I woke up this morning the sun was shining so I wore my summer uniform dress and I got the early bus to school. It's a smaller bus and it has special seats with seat belts. None of the rest of our gang at school get the early bus any more but Patrick was there and I was scared because he sat next to me but he didn't talk. It was so cold and not summer at all. I was shivering and Patrick gave me his blazer.

When school started I told Kathy that maybe Patrick is OK. He doesn't smell of gravy any more. Kathy said that Steven smells of Old Spice, which is a scent for men.

Tuesday

Mark is going out with Lucy and it is just me that doesn't have a boyfriend. Kathy and Steven said they would find someone for me but then Steven said I could go out with Patrick. I said I didn't love Patrick and they laughed.

Dad came to pick me up. He was there for ages before I finished school so he had to wait for me outside and talk to Miss Coburn who was already in the yard.

Friday

Kathy asked me to go to her house tomorrow to talk about everything.

I went to the after-school club and I took Angie around the yard on Turpin. I said 'Hug horse' and she held on. Turpin was on a lead but when Mrs Mason came to collect Angie she was worried. I told her I thought it was safe. Angie was hugging Turpin, and her mum looked like she was going to cry and she told Mr Dickens that Angie couldn't go on the horse without a teacher there again. If I was Angie's mum I would want her to go on the horse all the time because it makes her happy.

The Masons took me back to their house for tea. They have a big house and it is all new inside. I had chicken in breadcrumbs and chips that cook in the oven which Mum says are bad for you. It was lovely. I said I would come back next Friday.

Saturday

I went to Kathy's house and she told me so many things about Steven. His dad hits him and his big brother is in trouble with the police. She let me put on some of her make-up and we read all her *Jackie* magazines and she let me keep some of the old ones. We listened to the radio in her room and they played 'Seasons in the Sun'. Kathy said it was a romantic song and that it was a shame I didn't have a boyfriend. She said, 'Lucky you got my card, Izzy.'

Monday

We went to Joe's café for lunch and Mr Dickens sat with us. I didn't want to eat anything and Mr Dickens said I was too skinny and then he squeezed the meat pie he was eating through his teeth and onto his beard and said I could eat that. I had that feeling like I was going to be sick when spit comes into your mouth and Kathy got hysterical she was laughing so much, and when we got back to school he made us write out 'I think Mr Dickens is funny' one hundred times.

When I saw Steven I said I was sorry about his dad and he said what did I know about it, and I said, 'Nothing.'

Tuesday

I spent the whole day with Turpin, showing Angie how to take care of him, what he likes to eat and how he likes to have his coat brushed and where he goes for a walk. His itch is much better, maybe because I always rub oil into him. He has a saddle now. Miss Spill got one from a lady who goes to her church. It is small on him because he is quite big in the middle, but if you tie some string underneath it stays on. I still like to ride him without a saddle.

Steven and Mark came outside and hung around Turpin's shed. Angie tried to leave when she saw them but the boys wouldn't let her out. I told them to move and Steven kicked me in the legs. It hurt but I didn't cry.

Wednesday

Mum wanted to know how I got the big bruise on my leg. I said I fell over. If she talks to Mr Sanders he will tell everyone I am a weed again and he might not let me go on the trip to the seaside next month. What if she tells him about the sex card? I said everything was fine, and my leg was fine and I can go back to school tomorrow.

10

Rebecca Hill had some coffee standing by for Carter when she walked in for the morning briefing.

'You stood me up. Ma'am.' She handed Carter the cup with a smile.

Carter stared at her for a moment. She appreciated that the regulation gear was no match for Hill's personality. She always looked as if she had been brushed backward, like velvet. Carter smiled. They had their own easy relationship at work. Outside of the station, it was more complicated. They didn't usually confuse the two. As far as she was concerned no one at work knew about her private life and she wanted it to stay that way. 'Oh. Yeah, sorry. Got held up at the Palmerston Estate. How did the school search go?'

'Busy. Dogs picked up a trace where you said, round the back of the shed and down the alley. Then it went cold. We searched the houses, the locals helped, but possibly she was picked up by car from there. We bagged up all the rubbish from round the side gate.'

They headed to the incident room.

'But there was definitely trace in the alley?'

'Search and Rescue were positive.'

'You got into the school?'

'Front yard only. Atherton's orders.'

Carter wondered if the school governing board were involved in the decision. She took a swig of coffee and pushed at the door.

The room was full. Carter looked around for Dawson and Marshall, they had worked late into the night at the Thompsons'. Odds were the two of them were back at the estate and Carter silently thanked them for it.

A collage of suspects' photos dominated the board: the Thompsons, Karl and Jean Moffatt, Billy Rutherford. Tony Crouch from the leisure centre. The collator had found three more paedophiles living in the area. All the photos were cross-marked 'Alibi' except for the Moffats'. Robert Fry's picture was not on the board.

Atherton and Brecon waited for the room to settle. Neither man appeared to have got much sleep. The DCI nodded to his second-in-command.

'Billy Rutherford,' Brecon pointed to the board, 'has no criminal record and is registered disabled. He has an alibi for Thursday, firstly at the residential home where he lives and then at his place of work, which is where he and Karl were for the night shift. Before then, Karl's only alibi is his mother, Jean. Karl Moffatt has a history of public nuisance and has done time for exposing himself to minors. One of his previous victims was from Leabrook South Primary School. Both Karl and Jean are coming to the station in two hours' time.' Brecon looked at Carter. She had phoned in a report the night before, after she'd left the Palmerston Estate. Billy Rutherford and Karl Moffatt were low priority as far as Carter was concerned, and as for the mother, Carter doubted she ever went further than the end of the road to walk her tiny dog.

'Tony Crouch has been relieved of his duties at the leisure centre and will be charged with embezzlement, but he was at work on Thursday until late. As of now he is removed from this case.'

Lafferty took down the photo as Brecon continued. 'DS Carter. Could you go over what you've found?'

Carter ran through the findings from the Palmerston Estate and the school. 'If she was collected by prior arrangement with another adult, from a different exit point, that would explain why nobody saw her after school on Thursday.'

'We should get the parents back in here,' Lafferty said.

'For now, we are treating the Thompsons as victims,' Atherton said. 'Many of the papers have led with the story today. There will be a press conference this afternoon where the family will have a chance to make an appeal. With any luck, we'll get some witnesses coming forward.'

'What's the status with the search teams, sir?'' Carter asked.

'USCS are combing the local parks and smaller waterways until dark but we are not expanding a body search at this stage. It's important we all understand we are still hoping for Caitlin Thompson to be found alive and well.'

Carter looked at Brecon. They both knew the DCI had his own career in mind as much as anything. The politics of the Met reached beyond the Borough of Waltham Forest and flowed along the sewers to Westminster without any help from USCS. Carter didn't think Brecon cared much for the politicians, but he had a pension to protect and that came with more responsibility to those in power than those without.

The room broke up and Carter approached her DI. 'Sir? The headmaster, Robert Fry.' Brecon stared at the meagre collection of suspects and evidence. 'He was in the school building all day and at a staff meeting most of the evening.'

'But he might not have been acting alone.'

'A planned abduction, from his own school? The press are on this now, Carter. If we bring him in for questioning and we haven't got anything solid, and I mean air-fucking-tight, we'll be up to our necks in it, from the school governors, not just Fry.'

An operator put her head round the door of the incident room. 'We've had a call from Whittington Park Library regarding a possible sighting of Caitlin Thompson on Friday afternoon.'

Carter turned round. 'Student?'

'No,' the operator looked at her notes. 'A member of staff.'

Brecon looked at Carter. 'You should have a uniform take a statement.'

A phone-in from a member of the public. It was outside the local area and Moffatt was due back at the station for interrogation. Still – Carter returned Brecon's look – this was the first witness to come forward that had made it past the switchboard.

'Go on then,' the DI sighed. 'What the fuck are you waiting for?'

11

They arrived within an hour. Isobel watched them through the glass porthole in the staff room door as they followed Melanie to an office. An overweight woman in a dark suit and a woman about Isobel's age with a scarf draped over her coat. What was Isobel supposed to say to them? Melanie and Jenny should have noticed the girls, or any of the dozens of other people on the campus, but she was the one who was to be questioned by the police. She thought of their pocket books with curling pages. Isobel knew those notepads, filled with words no one read, children no one saw.

After a few minutes, Melanie came in and went to the coffee machine.

I will interpret. She pushed one corduroyed hip against the worktop. The percolator dripped coffee from a funnel.

Thank you.

'Yeah, well . . .'

Isobel could see the tension in Melanie's face. She wondered what the police had said.

Isobel, the university has got involved. I don't know what you think you saw, but the girl is still missing. They're going to want a statement and they might need you to go to the station.

The water finished draining through the coffee grounds in a cloud of steam.

You want this? Official?

Official. That was how you turned a messy human event into paperwork. The police were part of the clean-up but they could only manage the words, the way things looked, they couldn't change the feelings. Isobel thought of Lucy, the words she had were signs and she made a world from them. Lucy Monero had built a successful business that taught other companies how to include sign language and subtitles in their staff training. If only she could have stayed with Lucy fifteen years ago, learned how to sculpt her soul in the air. Isobel stifled a sob at the thought of what she had done instead. The memory of Angie crying at the top of the stairs rushed at her. Angie reaching out, swollen mouth opening and closing, snot and tears pooling at the edges of her lips.

I must tell them what I saw.

The woman in the navy suit stood by the window, watching students in the square below. The younger woman sat at the desk with a cigarette in one hand, tipping a saucer full of paper clips onto the desk with the other. When Isobel came in, she stopped to look up at her. The woman at the window turned round. For a moment, all three studied each other. Then Melanie heaved past with a tray and the watchful faces resumed their ordinary civility.

Once she had set the tray down, Melanie began the introductions.

Her name Valerie Jenkins. Whittington Park Liaison Officer. Melanie waited while Isobel and the woman in the scarf shook hands. The liaison officer maintained eye contact with Isobel throughout the introduction, blowing the cigarette smoke carefully from the side of her mouth. Isobel continued to stare at her as they drew apart. She saw angular features, the contours converging in a slash of claret lipstick.

'I'm here as a point of contact between the university and the police. To facilitate relations.' Isobel understood much of what Valerie was saying, she knew the PR wheels were already in motion, but she turned expectantly to Melanie and nodded while she translated.

Detective Sergeant Carter.

The woman in the suit took Isobel's hand and Melanie explained that she could lip-read. The policewoman looked straight at Isobel, eyebrows raised. Isobel saw how she took her in as something more than just a witness. She remembered wanting to join the police once. The people who were supposed to protect you. What would it be like, Isobel thought, to remember the faces of all the damaged children you found?

She took a step back and tried to concentrate on Melanie's signing.

'I am not,' Valerie Jenkins glanced at Detective Sergeant Carter, 'part of the police force. I am just here to help. We all appreciate your coming forward, Isobel. It can't have been easy.'

Isobel noted the assumption that there was more to her story. *It can't have been easy.* She hadn't told them what she'd seen yet. They only had Melanie's second-hand version and unless she wrote it down herself, that's all they'd ever get.

Melanie carried two more chairs over from the edge of the room and indicated that they should sit down.

'DS Carter, if you can talk directly to Isobel, I will sign when needed.' Melanie spoke and signed simultaneously.

'Miss Williams, could you identify yourself formally.'

Notebook pages flipped back and forth. Carter took a folded piece of A4 paper from the back of the book and searched for her pen. Isobel watched as Valerie Jenkins offered her a pen and the policewoman held up a hand, reached into her jacket pocket and took out a set of keys, a crumpled packet of gold Marlboro Lights and a Bic biro. The keys were held together on a keyring with a plastic hamburger in a bun. Isobel could see a green plastic pickle. She winced as she imagined carrying the keyring in her pocket all day. Dirt, and crumbs and food, the idea of food, all mixed together.

Carter kept the biro and replaced the cigarettes and keys in her jacket. She wrote on the paper and turned the page and the notebook to Isobel.

'Is this your correct name and address?'

Isobel read the small account of her life in the pocket book. Name, address, date of birth. They had already seen her employment file.

Yes.

Carter recorded her assent and looked back at Isobel.

'Right. Your colleague tells us that you read about Caitlin Thompson in the newspaper this morning and recognised her from the photograph?'

Yes.

'Do you know her?'

Isobel read the question. She turned to Melanie and signed.

No. I saw her here, at the library, Friday.

'What time was this?'

About four o'clock.

'Did you speak to her?'

No.

'And she was with another girl?'

Yes. About the same age.

Valerie Jenkins looked at Melanie.

'You must get a lot of children in the library?'

'No, not really. Sometimes they might come in with a parent.' The faculty allowed interested visitors, in principle. 'This isn't a public library, Sergeant, it's for academic research, not much in here for children.'

Carter looked up from the pages in front of her.

'So, if two girls came in, they'd have had to be with someone else? Someone who was a member?'

'You're supposed to show your library card when you come in. But if I'm not at my desk, then people could just walk in. It's not locked or anything.'

Melanie made a show of interpreting the conversation but she paused before she began speaking again and her hands fell to her sides. 'Jenny and I were both on duty on Friday afternoon, neither of us saw these children.'

Everyone turned to Isobel.

'Miss Williams, you were at your desk on Friday afternoon and you saw Caitlin Thompson, with another girl, enter the library?' The policewoman held up her notebook, but she wasn't reading from it. She didn't take her eyes off Isobel as she started signing.

I did not see the girls come in. No. I was at my desk—

Melanie interrupted again.

'Jenny shares the desk with Isobel.'

I was at the desk, alone. Jenny was on coffee break. She got back, I went for a walk. I got back. The girls were gone.

Carter wrote for a minute before looking at Isobel.

'So you didn't see them come in and you didn't see them leave?'

I don't watch doors, I work. I looked up. The girls were in the

magazine section. Reading. Homework, maybe. Something not right.
Isobel added the sign for *'scary'* and *'little'*.

Melanie said, 'She says the children were behaving strangely.'

'Strangely? How?'

'They gave her the creeps.'

Not what I said.

I help.

Again tell them.

Melanie frowned.

They were scared. Isobel signed. *The girls.*

Isobel saw the policewoman's head tilt with interest as she waited for Melanie to translate.

'She says they seemed a little scared.'

Detective Sergeant Carter turned back to her notes. 'Thank you for your time. We are trying to investigate every sighting of Caitlin. This one doesn't appear to fit the profile.'

The policewoman rocked the chair with the back of her knees as she stood up. She was in a hurry.

She offered Isobel the covering statement for her signature. Valerie Jenkins put out a hand to read the statement first. She smiled but the emotion didn't reach her eyes. Isobel sensed her relief. The university appeared to be off the hook.

Miss Jenkins handed Isobel the statement to sign and stood to shake the Detective Sergeant's hand.

She wants description friend?

Carter glanced down at Isobel. 'Is there anything else you'd like to tell me?'

Melanie interpreted but Carter frowned at the difference between Melanie's careful tone and Isobel's more urgent actions. Isobel could see the indecision in the policewoman's face, the conflict between a practical world of deadlines and hard facts, and whatever Isobel was offering. Isobel hadn't imagined seeing the girls. Was her testimony less reliable because it was unspoken?

After a moment Carter sat down. 'Write a description. I'll take it with me.' She opened her notepad and waited for Isobel to add to her statement.

Isobel looked at the black book for a moment. She thought about those other police notepads; what might be recorded in them, things she had said, the absence of things she should have said. At the hospital, the police had given her pens and drawing paper, asked her to try and remember every detail of the night. The paper had remained blank.

She took a library pen from the desk and looked over the loose page. Added to the information was a summary of the conversation between Melanie, Carter and herself. Isobel turned the page. She wrote: **The two girls looked about ten. They were thin and pale with straight, fair hair. They were wearing jeans and they had different colour polo neck jumpers, one was dark red and the other one was blue.**

She paused. Was she supposed to describe their behaviour, or just what they looked like? She added, **'They had a secret.'** Carter read the page over Isobel's shoulder. She reached out for the pad and nodded when Isobel signed and handed it back to her.

'That's fine.' She stood up again. 'Miss Williams, we'll be in touch if there is anything else we need.'

Isobel rose to shake the hand Carter offered and met her gaze. The policewoman's head tilted again as though she knew Isobel had more to say. She blanched. She had told them all she knew about Caitlin Thompson, and she had hidden all the words for the other missing girl, years

ago. Sewn them up with the scar tissue, deep in the back
of her mind.

Valerie followed Detective Sergeant Carter to the door.
'If you want to speak to Isobel again, we'll need a qualified
interpreter.'

The DS closed her notepad and placed it back in her
pocket. 'It's good of you to be here today.'

'Of course.'

The DS paused. 'Well, Miss Williams may have been mis-
taken, but we'll have the statement on file.' Holding up her
hand in a gesture that was a combination of surrender and
departure, she nodded at Isobel and left.

Melanie started to clear away the coffee cups and Isobel
watched as Valerie sat down and lit another cigarette. Her
face had slackened, as though she had stopped holding
it in place.

Nearly lunch. Melanie picked up the tray and headed
to the door.

Isobel glanced at Valerie, cigarette in one hand, the other
pressed to her temples. She held the door open for Melanie
and slipped out behind her.

She picked up her case from under the desk but decided
against going to the staff room for her coat. She did not want
to see Melanie again, or find Valerie Jenkins waiting in the
corridor when she left. She headed to the street and flagged
down the first taxi that passed. Speaking slowly, she made
sure the driver understood where she wanted to go and the
pointlessness of pursuing a conversation.

When the taxi pulled into Bowman Road, she leaned
forward to tap on the glass partition as they approached her
flat. She could see several people standing by the low wall

outside the house. A police car was parked opposite. The cab driver slowed down. They drew parallel to the house. A uniformed officer stood inside her hallway talking to a man with a drill. The front door was lying on the pavement, the hinges still attached.

The policeman looked up as the taxi stopped. Isobel heaved her case out and thrust the exact change through the driver's window, turning her head away before she could make sense of whatever he had to say. She met the policeman at the gate.

'Miss Williams? PC Garvey.' He was younger than DS Carter but he had the same air of forced neutrality about him. Isobel nodded and put her index and middle fingers against her ear. Most police officers knew some rudimentary signs.

'You're deaf?'

Isobel nodded again.

'But you can lip-read?' PC Garvey collected himself. 'It's your neighbour, Mr Nash. He's been assaulted. They forced their way in.' He glanced over at the guy with the drill and shrugged. 'Mr Nash sent someone to fix the door.'

Isobel tried to process the information.

'He's ok, but he'll be in hospital for a day or two.'

Dan had been attacked at home. He was in hospital.

'We don't know when the incident took place. Have you seen him recently?'

She thought back over the past two days and shook her head.

'We'll get his full statement this afternoon,' the policeman prompted Isobel.

'You've been away?' He indicated the suitcase.

She wanted to help Dan. 'Friday,' she said. And, 'Brighton.'

She looked at the unfamiliar faces hovering in the street and steeled herself to keep speaking. 'Mother.'

PC Garvey recovered his notebook from his jacket pocket and started writing.

June 1975

Wednesday

We had the police quiz again today. I was on the team with Lucy and Mark and Christopher. We went to the police station that is near my house and we won the quiz. I could be a policewoman.

Thursday

Steven's big brother started at school today. He is fifteen and his name is Jason Ryall. He was expelled from his other school and Mr Sanders said it would be good for him at the Schoolhouse.

To make him feel welcome we all sat in the main hall in a circle and we had to say what we wanted to do when we grow up. I said I wanted to be a cook but Mr Sanders said I couldn't because I would sneeze all my germs into the food. When it got to Jason's turn he said he wanted to spread germs too and he winked at me. Mr Sanders told Jason he was being silly and the Schoolhouse was not for silly people.

Jason made me feel better. He looks like Steven, they have got kind of red hair and some freckles. They are even the same height but Jason is more muscly than Steven and he understands more.

Friday

The whole day was hot and we were allowed to stay outside and do what we wanted. I cleaned out Turpin's house
and tried to keep him cool by sponging him with cold
water. Kathy wouldn't help but Lucy stayed. She likes
to hold him.

After lunch, Jason got the hosepipe and sprayed everyone
in the playground because we were so hot. Even Christopher
wanted to be sprayed in his wheelchair. But Patrick got angry
when some of the water splashed him and he tried to get
the hose from Jason. Jason gave him the hose and said, 'Go
crazy.' Patrick did go crazy and when Mr Dickens came out,
Patrick sprayed him too.

There was supposed to be a parents' meeting about next
week's seaside trip but our clothes were dripping water
on the floor. So when the parents came we had to have the
meeting outside.

Patrick is banned from the school trip.

Sunday

We are staying the night at the seaside so I had to pack a bag
with things I might need. There was a list from school but
Mum said it was ridiculous so we put in a nightdress and
underwear and a proper swimming costume for girls and a
toothbrush. We have to wear school uniform so I don't need
any extra clothes and there was room left over in the blue
suitcase so I put in my books and Dad gave me a packet of
hard sweets for the coach journey and my own fifty pence
to put in my money belt.

Dad told me to have a lovely time and not get into too

much trouble and Mum said Lorraine wasn't going so that would help, and Dad said, 'For God's sake, Clare.'

I don't know Lorraine.

Monday

There are twelve of us on the trip. If we had one more teacher then maybe Angie could have come but Angie's mum said the teachers will have enough on their hands. So there is Kathy, Lucy, Steven, Jason, Mark, Christopher, Drew, Jolie and Belle, and me and Mr Dickens and Miss Peden.

Mr Sanders made a speech before we left about the reputation of the Schoolhouse and wearing our uniform with pride. Jason is lucky because he doesn't have a uniform yet.

The journey took three hours because we had to stop for people to be sick. I didn't feel sick and I had my books with me, and mostly I talked with Kathy because Jolie and Belle don't talk, and the boys were all mucking about together. Jason calls Mark 'Bishop' because that is his second name. So now we all call him Bishop and sometimes Jason just shouts out 'Bish!' and it makes him laugh. There is so much to talk about now that Jason is at the school. Kathy says he is dishy but she already has a boyfriend and he is Jason's brother so she can't swap.

The place we are staying is called a youth hostel and there are bunk beds with sleeping bags. We are supposed to have sleeping bag liners but that is one of the things Mum said was ridiculous so Kathy said I have to sleep in all my clothes or I will catch something. The boys are in one room and the girls are in another.

We played on the beach but it was rainy and Mr Dickens took us to an amusement arcade, which was brilliant. There was a machine to drop two-pence pieces into and money spilled down. That was Jolie and Belle's favourite. And there was a table where you could play bingo, and there was a shooting game. I tried to shoot at a target but I missed and Jason came up behind me and held my arm and I missed again because I felt funny with Jason's hands on me. His fingers pressed on my skin and left a mark.

Kathy said my face was red and I think she is jealous.

Now we are waiting to go for chicken and chips.

*

Lucy has gone to hospital and Kathy is not in her bed.

We had supper and went back to the arcade for a bit but Jason didn't come with us. Steven said he'd gone to get something for later.

When we got back to the hostel, we all went to the games room and Jason was there. Mr Dickens and Miss Peden were outside smoking. We played ping-pong and we had the radio on and we danced to 'Kung Fu Fighting' and the Bay City Rollers and Jason got a big bottle of cider from his bag and we all drank some. It tasted really nice. And Jason had got real darts from a pub.

We chalked a darts board on the wall. Drew said it was a stupid game but Jason said he would help him and that you didn't need to see the board to throw a dart.

We made up a game where you had to run around the room and then throw a dart. Christopher only did the darts bit because the room was too small to keep moving his chair round. We went round and round. Jason stood behind Drew and held his arm to throw the dart, but then Lucy ran in front of the board and the dart hit her. It was lucky she had her arms up or it would have hit her in the face but it went really far into her hand. Even with Jason holding his arm, Drew is not a good darts player.

Mr Dickens took Lucy to hospital in a taxi and we had to go to bed. After Miss Peden left the girls' room, Kathy went to see the boys, and that was an hour ago and she hasn't come back. So I am on my own with Jolie and Belle and I don't know if they are awake.

Wednesday

Lucy came back from hospital in the night. She has a bandage around her hand and stitches in her skin. At breakfast Mr Dickens told me he wanted to know how Lucy hurt her arm, like it was my fault, but then they saw Kathy wasn't there. They did a search of the building and they found her in a bedroom on her own and she had been sick.

We weren't allowed to go back to the arcade and we all had to go for a walk, with Mr Dickens pushing Christopher, and Lucy and Kathy and Drew stayed with Miss Peden at the hostel. Jason was in a funny mood and Bishop wasn't talking to anyone so I walked with Steven. He said he hated his brother and I said Jason was really nice but he shouldn't have thrown the dart at Lucy, and he said, 'What do you know about it, you stupid bitch?'

I wanted to cry but I didn't because then Steven would think I care and I don't.

We had to leave after lunch. Miss Peden took me out of the queue when we were getting on the bus. She put her nose really close to my face.

She said she wanted me to tell the truth and she asked if anyone had tried to get me to be a naughty girl.

Her face was angry. I said no.

I don't know what she was talking about. She looked like when Mum found that card from Kathy. She made me feel guilty even though I hadn't done anything.

I asked why and she said, 'Nothing, Isobel. Oh, God.' And told me to get on the bus.

Mr Dickens stared at me when I got back in the queue. If I was naughty I would not tell Miss Peden. I would not tell anybody.

12

Returning to her office from the library on Sunday, Carter picked up a sandwich and drove past the entrance to the Palmerston Estate. She parked on the street close enough to see the several journalists and photographers on the overhead walkway leading to the Thompsons' front door. The figures of two uniformed constables were visible directly outside the flat. Carter recognised one of them as a friend of Hill's. They'd been to the pub together a few times, on a girls' night. Evenings that were never acknowledged at work. Only Hill seemed unaware of the rules.

'You'll get us . . . noticed,' Carter said to her once, on a rare lunch together.

'If you think they haven't noticed, you should turn your badge in,' Hill had laughed. 'It's pretty obvious, Sally. Anyway,' she held Carter's hand up to her face and kissed the soft knuckles, 'things are changing. We don't have to pretend any more.'

Pretend, Carter thought, as she looked around the estate, sandwich in hand. Is that what she did? She'd seen senior women leave the force, without explanation. She wanted to believe in Hill's vision but there was little evidence to support her optimism. Life didn't magically improve. You had to work for it.

'Letting people know who you are, Sally. That's work too.'

It was hard enough to find out for yourself. She grabbed a Fanta from the glove compartment, pulled open a bag of crisps and stuck a few into the sandwich. Maybe she did pretend. As much as anyone, she supposed. No one could know what you really thought. Who you really were. It was impossible. You let people see you a little bit at a time, if you trusted them. Hill might be an exception, but most people seemed to hide behind something, to try being someone else.

She thought about the witness from the library. Isobel Williams. She hadn't spoken but she was present in the room in a particular way. You had to slow down to see her clearly. Carter wondered if that was because of the silence.

Above her, Carter heard a photographer shout out for Susan Thompson. She swallowed the rest of the sandwich and headed back to the station before the uniforms noticed her.

In the incident room, she stared at the operations board with Caitlin's timeline and map.

'I've got a bloody press conference in an hour.' DI Brecon stood behind Carter and looked at the unpromising information in front of them. 'How's that witness?'

'She thinks she saw Caitlin on Friday, with another girl.'

'The Siltmore girl?'

'Ruby? No, she was at school on Friday. And the description of Caitlin doesn't really match. The clothes are different, it's the wrong area.'

'She could have changed clothes, Carter. She could have

dyed her hair black and be living in Timbuktu by now.'
Brecon waved an arm in the direction of the street. As far
as he was concerned, anywhere outside the jurisdiction of
the Met was a lost cause.

'Susan Thompson says no clothes were missing, no
money, no bags.'

'But the witness is good?'

'She's a librarian. She's deaf. Very observant. She came
forward when she saw the papers today.'

'And?'

'She was upset.'

'Why?'

Carter looked directly at her DI. Ninety per cent of
everything the man said was unhelpful. Ten percent was
good enough.

'I'll put in a request for a background check.' She headed
towards the office.

Brecon called after her.

'And pick up the Thompsons for the press call. You're the
only one the mother will deal with.'

For a moment, Carter saw the Thompsons as the public
would. Grey faces and unwashed hair, filtered through a
journalist's lens. People tended to err on the side of suspicion
when presented with a choice.

Hill came into the office as Carter was getting
ready to leave.

'Scenes of Crime Officers made Caitlin's prints from the
ones in her bedroom. They have a positive match on her at the
side gate. And this.' Hill handed Carter a photograph. Her
fingers were spattered with ink from the whiteboard marker.
'It's the rubbish from round the back of the bike shed.'

Carter sat down and looked at the photograph, all the

stuff she had seen on Friday night in the torchlight. Crisp packets, Coke cans. Caitlin could have been at the gate at any time, but having a positive ID at least meant she might have used the gate to get out of the yard without being seen. At the bottom corner of the picture, something red caught Carter's eye.

'What do you think that is?'

Hill peered at the photo. 'Elastic, rubber? Some kind of band.'

'A hairband?'

'Could be.' She smiled at Carter. Sally probably hadn't worn a hairband since school. 'More like the bands you get around envelopes, office stuff.'

'She left her classroom to get a hairband for her gym class.'

Hill's notes were open in front of her. 'Did she come back?'

'Her form teacher says she was in class at the end of the day. She may have got that wrong, but no one's come forward with a different story.'

Carter held on to the photograph of crisp packets and kids' rubbish and thought about the cocky teenager in the pool café. He had recognised Caitlin straight away. He'd said the girl might have run off. Carter wondered who he thought she was running from.

'Right. I've got to get the parents for the TV appeal. Follow up that number plate. Give the owners a call and see if they know our Mr Fry.'

'How was your witness from the university?'

Carter sighed. Brecon had called her on it and now she had to ask herself why she hadn't listened to the librarian.

'What is it?' Hill took a file from the desk and waited.

'I . . . ' Carter stopped. 'I'd written her off as a dead end.' She took a deep breath.

'Waste of time?'

'It wasn't that. The description didn't quite fit. I don't know . . . '

Hill frowned. 'Sally?'

It wasn't the description. The description matched well enough to follow up. It was the witness. She had seen something in Isobel Williams but it didn't belong to this case.

'We need to do a background check on her. Follow up her statement.'

'Will do,' Hill held Carter's eye. 'You ok?'

'I'm fine. I just . . . ' Carter glanced at the open door.

Hill nodded. 'Fuck 'em. You know what you're doing.' She put an inky hand on the table next to Carter's.

Carter took a breath. Hill would be a DS in the next year or so, but she wasn't yet. She looked at their hands, Hill's more slender. She had seen their fingers intertwined, felt Hill's palm pressed against hers. Now she could only clear her throat and offer her girlfriend a raised eyebrow. She wasn't a coward, she didn't really care what people thought. She just couldn't imagine how it would all work out.

Hill took her hand back. 'I'll get on with it then, Sarge.'

'Thank you.' Carter heaved herself out of the plastic chair and went back to the incident room, taking another look at the map on the wall. Prison clothes. The boy had mentioned prison clothes. He'd laughed at the picture of Caitlin because kids don't like being seen out in school uniform, it embarrasses them.

On the map, Hill had put a pin into the university on Holloway Road. During a regular day, Caitlin changed clothes before she went out after school. Carter followed a route across the map to Leabrook South Primary. Two main roads, almost a straight line.

Her mum had said no clothes were missing and if she was right, Caitlin hadn't gone home to change. Carter looked again at the photo of the school gate, the red band. If it was the same band Caitlin got from the office for gym class, she could have ditched it at the gate before leaving the school premises. Just as she would have wanted to get rid of her uniform. Carter nodded. The girl didn't have to go home. She had been given a change of clothes by someone she knew. They were waiting for her on the other side of the gate.

From the open door, she heard Hill calling after her.

'Carter, I've got Fortis Green nick on the line. A PC Garvey. Says he wants to talk to you about an Isobel Williams?'

Hill was standing in the office holding up the telephone receiver.

'Who's that?' Hill covered the mouthpiece when she saw Carter's reaction.

She reached for the phone, closing her hand for a moment over Hill's.

'That,' she said, 'is my dead end.'

13

The crowd on Bowman Road had dispersed by the time PC Garvey left. Both the main door and Dan's front door were back in place and the new keys lay in plastic envelopes on the hall table. Isobel was grateful that the locks were changed but she had no intention of staying in her flat. She closed the door behind the policeman and ran up the stairs two at a time.

Needles of panic flicked at her fingertips. A world in which children were abducted and neighbours assaulted was closing around her. Isobel told herself there was no connection between the two events and immediately realised this was no longer true. She was now the link.

For the second time that day she had given a statement to the police. She had tried to be as detailed as possible, passed the notebook back to the policeman and watched while he told her that she should keep an eye out for anything suspicious, get in contact if she thought of anything that seemed relevant. She was already listed as a witness in the disappearance of Caitlin Thompson. PC Garvey said Isobel had been the last person to see Dan and the first person to arrive back at the scene. He made sure she'd understood that. She showed Garvey out of the flat and didn't mention the man at the restaurant.

Isobel recalled the man smoking in the lane that night, the pat on Dan's back as they parted. The same man who pushed her on the High Street. Jason Ryall was out of prison but the smoker wasn't one of the Ryall brothers. She hadn't recognised him outside the newsagents, the craggy face and balding scalp of a middle-aged man. But he'd recognised her. Jason Ryall had his old sidekick on the case. Bish bash bosh. Mark Bishop.

She needed to leave. The police weren't going to help her. Isobel went into her bedroom and placed her father's suitcase onto the bed. She removed the books and letters and started to pack.

She tried to think who she could stay with. She refused to go to Melanie Harris or her mother; the two people who had been officially charged with her care in the past, and the last people she would ask for help. She placed her clothes in the suitcase and imagined the pleasure both women would feel at seeing Isobel on their doorstep. It was not a gift she wanted to give.

She went through to the kitchen and binned the fresh food. There was a number for her social worker on the fridge but social services were not sentimental when it came to life in the real world. As far as they were concerned, Isobel had plenty of support. Anything more serious might reawaken her involvement in past crimes, the spectre of the care system, or worse.

She didn't want to leave her father's letters and drawings behind. She went through the pile and placed a selection of the most precious items back in the case. She added the legal letters and the bundle tied with ribbon, pushed another jumper in and sat on top of it while she forced the clasps together.

The remaining books and papers were laid out on the floor below her. Evidence of her father's life, and her own. She had always been told she looked like him, the same fair colouring and broad cheekbones. But she didn't want to be like her father. She had been the one to find him, on a day out from the shared accommodation where she lived during the week. She had let herself in with her own keys and seen him straight away. He was lying back in his chair, face white, eyes closed, but he wasn't asleep. She was eighteen.

People stopped remarking on the likeness after that. Her mother, their old friends. Maybe they, too, imagined his dead, marbled face when they thought of him. They didn't have to see it every time they looked in the mirror, though. The faces of the girls in the library floated into her thoughts, staring back at her, willing her to help. She shuddered. It hadn't been like that. She wasn't the person you asked for help.

She looked at the smallest pile of books that lay on the pillow next to her. Her favourite Puffin stories. Water-stained covers and coarse pages. Clare said her dad had kept them. A hardback volume on top, with a cartoon picture of a girl in a pinafore dress and a huge cloth cap, read '1975'. The diary Lucy Monero had given her for her eleventh birthday. The last year she had gone to school.

She had not forgotten. She reached over to pick it up, tucked it into her lap, and started to read.

Tuesday

Everything is different since we came back from the seaside. Mr Sanders told my parents that I was copying the older boys and girls and I needed to stand up for myself. I don't know what he was talking about. It was Kathy who was in trouble, not me. Mum has banned me from seeing my friends after school and she told Dad it was time to look for new schools for me next term.

I don't want to go to another school. They would make me do lessons and I couldn't have Turpin.

Wednesday

Lucy had her stitches out and she had to stay in hospital for the night because they were infected. She came back to school in the middle of Mr Sanders' speech about a new future for the Schoolhouse. We are not going to have a sports day this term because of what happened on the school trip.

Lucy's hand is still sore from the dart.

Kathy has been off school all week but Steven said she will be back soon.

Thursday

Jason came into the stable when I was mucking out Turpin. He wanted to know why I was bothering to clean up a horse at school. I said I wanted Turpin to have a nice home. Jason said Turpin was a stupid name because Dick Turpin was a famous robber and Turpin was just a horse. Then he grabbed the broom and climbed the outside of the building and banged on the iron roof.

'Stand and deliver!' he shouted over and over. He was really loud and it was lucky Turpin was outside. Mr Dickens came and told Jason to get down but Jason didn't stop for ages. In the end, we went into school together and Jason put his arm around me and everyone saw.

Friday

Patrick punched me in the stomach. We were playing truth or dare at break time and I had to go and tell Patrick that I didn't love him. He punched me straight away. It was a weird feeling and I couldn't breathe. But it didn't hurt like a pain when you have a headache or scab your knee on the ground.

Jason came over and stood next to Patrick. He asked if I was OK and kneeled down by my head and whispered in my ear. I could feel his breath on my neck, 'I'll sort out the little fucker.'

He stood up and threw his head against Patrick's chin and Patrick fell over.

Patrick and Jason had to go to Mr Sanders' office and Patrick lost a tooth.

Monday

When I got on the bus this morning Steven had a tape recorder and he played 'I'm Not in Love' and everyone on the bus sang along. They thought it was so funny. Patrick was on the bus and I felt bad even though he was the one who punched me.

At break time, Steven told Jason that he'd seen me without my pants on. That was from when we played kiss chase on Valentine's day. I said that wasn't my fault but Jason said he would give me money if I took my pants off again.

Wednesday

Kathy is back at school but she didn't want to come to the park with Turpin, and Lucy is not allowed out of school with any of us because of what happened at the seaside. So I went on my own. When I got to the park there was a lady with a pram who wanted to know what I was doing there. She said it was dangerous and she said she was going to report me to the school.

Turpin knew I was in trouble. He is like a person inside a horse body and he isn't very good at being a horse. He only likes to walk and his mane had to be cut off again. But when you speak to him he looks at you like he understands what you are saying.

Thursday

Kathy says she thinks Jason could be my boyfriend. She said she was jealous because she always liked him and he is older so he knows more about sex. I didn't tell her what Jason said about taking off my pants.

Friday

In break time Jason gave me forty pence and I pulled down my pants and let him look. We were round the side of Turpin's shed. I spent some of the money on biscuits. I wanted to buy Caramel Wafers but they cost too much so I got a packet of Happy Faces from the shop at the end of the road. I took the top off each one and licked the jam first and then the icing. It was like a meal.

14

Carter waited as Susan Thompson stared at the mass of photographers and reporters in confusion, the mother's misery glowing in every flash. Neither parent wept, but they provided a good enough show for the press to decide in their favour and grant a sympathetic portrait for the viewers and readers. The story would sell better as a traditional tragedy, particularly in December.

The Thompsons had read from a prepared statement. Mr Thompson described Caitlin as a 'ray of sunshine' and talked about her love for her dog, Spencer.

'Spencer's missing you, love. He's got a new collar but we're waiting for you to come home and put it on him.'

Carter took hold of Susan's arm and concentrated on escorting the couple back to the car.

'Christmas is a time for children,' the BBC journalist announced gravely outside Leabrook town hall. 'The Thompson family is waiting for news of their own child. Waiting to give her the best Christmas. Hoping they get the chance to celebrate it together.'

As she drove away, several photographers tried to get a last shot, a glimpse into the family that the official conference pictures hadn't captured. Carter knew an unguarded photograph was valuable publicity, but she couldn't help the jolt of contempt that pushed her foot down on the accelerator, forcing the men to drop the cameras from their faces and jump away from the lurching vehicle.

Mr and Mrs Thompson slumped silently in the rear seat. Carter studied them in the mirror as she drove back to the estate. They were both staring into the distance, faces immobile. If they were faking, it was the best performance she'd ever seen. The traces of guilt she looked for behind the eyes or in the set of the jaw were missing. The couple looked empty, like a mouth without teeth.

When she had handed them over to Dawson and Marshall on duty outside their flat, she turned the car round and headed south. Isobel Williams lived a couple of miles from the library where she worked. No one had been able to reach her on the adapted phone she was supposed to have, and Carter wanted to talk to her. Last thing on a Sunday night was not a good time to find an interpreter but she was confident they could communicate with each other. She thought about Williams' determination to provide a witness statement earlier that day. Carter recognised the impulse, the desire to right a wrong. It stemmed from all the wrongs done to you along the way. And sometimes, from the wrongs you had done to others.

The officer from Fortis Green station who had reported Williams' break-in was young, a Constable Garvey, but he'd been thorough and had called her employers.

'Why did you call the library?' Carter asked over the phone.

Garvey had hesitated. 'I wasn't sure I'd got the whole story.'

'And you spoke to Melanie Harris?'

'Yes, but she didn't want to discuss Isobel Williams without more information. She put me in touch with a Valerie Jenkins who said she was worried about Williams and gave me your name.'

Carter took the details of the attack on Williams' downstairs neighbour, Dan Nash. He was in the Whittington hospital and his preliminary statement said the men who assaulted him were after Isobel. Garvey had been unable to contact Williams since taking the statement. Carter assured the PC that she would go to the house.

'He didn't tell them much,' Garvey said, 'Mr Nash. Probably why he got lamped. But they know where she lives.'

Carter pulled into Fortis Green High Street and drove for a few hundred yards. In the A–Z, Bowman Road was further down to the left. She found it after a minute and radioed the station.

'Anything further on our witness?'

'No, Sarge. We've got a lot of calls coming in from the TV appeal. A couple from Wood Green. Walthamstow. And lots around Archway.'

Near the library.

'Log everything round Archway as a priority. I'm at Williams' address.'

'Also, one of our suspects, Karl Moffatt, has gone AWOL. Not turned up for work. Not at home.'

Sunday night. Moffatt's shift started at eight. Carter checked her watch, half-past ten. The manager at the company he worked for, Briggs, had called it in promptly, which meant Moffatt was on notice and everyone at the factory probably knew why. No wonder he didn't want to show up at work.

Midway down the terrace, she pulled up a few doors past

number 47 and looked back at the house. The curtains in the upstairs windows were closed, but it looked like all the house lights were off. She grabbed her jacket from the car and walked to the front door, noticing the new lock.

The doorbells were numbered but unnamed. According to PC Garvey, the assailants got hold of Dan Nash because he answered the door, but they couldn't reach Williams. Her doorbell had a flashing light. Carter wondered if it was easy to ignore.

She pressed both bells, waited for a few minutes and tapped on the downstairs window in case a friend or relative of the victim was staying at his place. When there was no reply, she headed back to the car.

If Caitlin Thompson was at the library on Friday with another child, in a change of clothes and reading, she would have have been with someone she knew. That would fit with her leaving school by the side gate for a pre-arranged meeting; she thought she was seeing a friend.

On the pavement opposite a woman studied the number on one of the front doors and crossed the road. Carter turned on the engine and radioed the station as the car warmed up. Through the windscreen she watched the woman walk down the street.

'No response at Isobel Williams' flat. Call Fortis Green and see if they have any other contact numbers for our witness.'

Williams was the only link she had so far between the library and Caitlin, but there was nothing she knew of to connect her to any of the Thompsons. Now it seemed she was involved with another crime.

Hill came to the radio. 'We've got Moffatt's mother here and every hack in London's camped out front.'

'On my way.'

The woman ahead walked under the streetlight and Carter saw her face. The liaison officer from Whittington Park. Hair swept into a scarf, dark lipstick. She stopped outside number 47. After a moment she pressed a bell, stood back and lit a cigarette. Carter got out of the car and went to meet her.

'Miss Jenkins?'

The woman started. 'I . . . yes . . . Oh.'

'Detective Sergeant Sally Carter. We met this morning.'

'I remember. I was just . . . ' She waved the cigarette at the darkened house. 'Hoping to catch Isobel. Make sure she was all right.'

'There's no answer. I've already tried. Do you have any idea where she might have gone?'

Valerie Jenkins sighed, shadowed eyes belying her young face. 'Our office is closed on a Sunday night. I just have her home address from the library.'

'It's good of you to come by.' Carter glanced up at the window.

'She's not the easiest person to get hold of by phone.'

'No.' Carter's call sign blared from her personal radio. She put her hand up to apologise.

'Go ahead.'

Jenkins turned to leave and Carter waited to answer the radio.

'If you could call me at Leabrook Station when you get into work tomorrow?'

'Of course.' Valerie Jenkins took another drag on her cigarette and walked back in the direction she had come from.

'Yes?' Carter returned to the radio as she reached the car.

'Jean Moffatt says she hasn't seen Karl since this morning.'

Where was he? Carter was sure she hadn't been wrong

about him. In her experience, the men who had done for her when she was in care, the men who had done for her friends, were on the inside, the authority figures. Or those who had connections. She knew this was her particular prejudice, but it was also an advantage. She'd seen how these men operate, up close. She knew the combination of power and impotence that motivated them. Of course there were other kinds of men who hurt children, everywhere, every kind. But she hadn't thought Moffatt was one of them and now he had fled. She sat down heavily in the car seat and leant back against the headrest.

15

Isobel woke with her head pressed against the suitcase on her bed. It was dark. The floor was covered with fallen books and clothes. Hours, she had slept for hours and now it was late. She couldn't risk leaving the flat at night, not without help.

She reached down the side of the bed for her handbag. The lavender vial from Brighton rolled onto the floor and she shoved it back into the bag before she had to think about her mother. She had three pounds in her purse. The rest of her cash had gone on the black cab she'd taken home. She didn't have enough for another taxi but the minicab company would accept her signature on account. With a car waiting outside, she would feel safe enough to leave. She wanted to see Dan. Beyond that, she had nowhere to go.

She plugged the minicom in, pressed the pre-set button for the cab company and waited for the confirmation of her request.

She went back to the bedroom, took the sheets off the bed and put them in the laundry basket. She emptied all the bins, turned the boiler off and pushed a few more clothes into her bag. She thought of Dan in the hospital. She had let him get close to her. The familiar guilt burned in her throat and she swallowed hard.

She wondered if the policewoman from the library could help. Isobel worked hard to stop people seeing her clearly. To prevent them looking beyond her careful clothes and neat hair. DS Carter had seen her, though. It wasn't that Carter had been kind, she hadn't, merely professional, or that she believed Caitlin Thompson had been in the library; Isobel wasn't sure she did. It was the way she had focused on Isobel without judgement or pity.

She picked up the diary she had been holding when she fell asleep. The pages were creased where she had lain on them. 'So I will write this diary and then they will see.' Sally Carter wasn't going to save her. The residue of her childhood was powdered glass underfoot. Crunch, crunch, crunch. She could never escape.

The light on the minicom was flashing. Isobel shoved the diary into her suitcase and looked around. Already she felt far away, as though the things in her home belonged to someone else. She put the diary in her handbag, locked the flat, carried her bags and the rubbish downstairs and stood at the front door to make sure she could see the taxi. She left the black bin liner in the wheelie bin and walked over to the car. The driver got out and opened the boot when he saw she had luggage.

'Airport? Station?' He was careful to say the words clearly.

'Hospital,' Isobel said.

The driver pushed his lips together in an expression of sympathy. He had a small beard that bobbed about when he moved his mouth.

'Which one?' he asked.

PC Garvey had told her where Dan had been taken.

'The Whittington,' she said.

He nodded and they both got in the car.

She looked out of the rear window as they drove away. No one was following them. They were near, though, she was sure of it. The hospital was public and staffed, even in the middle of the night. She could check on Dan and wait there while she decided on her next move.

Watching the closed shops and restaurants flashing past, Isobel realised she had no idea of the time. She peered over the driver's shoulder at the dashboard. Two o'clock. Were visitors even allowed at two o'clock in the morning? The memory of her own hospital bed loomed and she sat back in the seat and focused on Dan. There was an emergency department; people must arrive all through the night. But he had been admitted hours ago; he wasn't in casualty any more.

The driver pulled up at the A & E drop off and held out the invoice for her to sign. She gave him a pound coin when he put her suitcase on the pavement. The driver placed his hand on Isobel's shoulder and frowned.

'Good luck,' he said. The small beard bobbed.

Isobel ducked into the nearest doorway to get out of the cold, wishing her heavy coat was not still in the library staff room. The doors swished open and the hot breath of an overhead heater blasted down as she stepped into the A & E admittance hall. She hesitated for a moment at the smell that enveloped her when she got past the doors. It was the same smell, imprinted on her sinuses, as unmistakeable as the lump at the back of her head that she now instinctively stroked with the palm of her hand. Nothing had changed.

The nurse at the reception desk didn't look up when she approached. Isobel took her exercise book and a pen out of her shoulder bag and wrote down Dan's name. The nurse didn't move and Isobel added a question mark, stabbing the bottom of the punctuation mark with some force to get her attention.

'Yes?' The nurse was younger than Isobel. She had purple smudges around her eyes and mouth. 'What's the matter?'

Isobel made the sign for deafness and held out the page with Dan's name on. The nurse looked at the paper and back at Isobel.

'Daniel Nash? Is he a patient?'

Isobel nodded.

'Hang on a minute.' The nurse held up a hand to Isobel. With deliberate slowness, she picked up the telephone and dialled a three-digit number.

'Nick?' Isobel could make out some of the words. 'You got a Daniel Nash back there? No? I have a woman in reception.' She looked at Isobel. 'She's asking for him.'

There was a pause.

'Thanks, yeah, I know. What can you do?' The nurse replaced the phone.

'He came in about lunchtime. He's been admitted. You a relative?'

Isobel pointed to herself and smiled. It seemed to work. The nurse picked up the pen and wrote 'Forrester Ward third floor'. She pointed in the direction of the main building as she spoke. 'You can visit tomorrow . . .'

Isobel gathered her things back into her bag, turned away and walked towards the hallway marked 'Main Reception'.

In the large entrance hall, two cleaners pushed mops around the locked front doors. The reception desk was closed. Isobel walked over to the lifts and tried to look purposeful. The suitcase made her more conspicuous but also provided a plausible alibi; she was dropping clothes off for Dan.

On the third floor there was a pair of double doors to either side of the hallway. Above each was a sign with the name of the ward and its function. She stood in front of Forrester and peered through the glass panel into a room with six beds arranged in opposite pairs. The curtains around the nearest beds were drawn, blocking her view of those beyond.

She should have come to the hospital as soon as the police had told her. Isobel knew what happened when your world began unravelling. She should have been here for Dan.

A face framed with neat braids appeared on the other side of the glass and the door was unlocked. Isobel stepped back.

'What can I do for you?' The nurse tilted her head, but Isobel could read what she said. 'They're all sleeping right now.'

Isobel did not think it was possible to really sleep in hospital. She remembered nights of staring at the ceiling, watching the shadows of the nurses glide past the ward. She pressed two fingers to her ear and waited while the nurse registered the information.

'D-A-N N-A-S-H.' Isobel signed the letters and mouthed his full name. She wanted the nurse to be on her side. She needed to see Dan. She could not leave until she knew what had happened to him.

'Mister Nash?' The nurse leaned towards Isobel, eager to understand her.

Isobel nodded. 'Dan Nash.'

'He is here. But you can't see him now. He's asleep.'

'Please.' Isobel took care not to speak too clearly. 'Please.'

The nurse looked down.

'You can't bring that in.' She pointed at the suitcase.

Isobel smiled. *Thank you.*

She slid the case to the wall and stepped onto the ward. The smell was worse inside. Less human but more desperate. As though the drips and tubes were syphoning out blood and replacing it with bleach. Four of the six beds were occupied. She waited for the nurse to indicate Dan but the woman walked straight ahead and went to speak to a porter standing by a door at the far end of the ward.

She wanted to find Dan before the nurse turned around and wondered just how well she knew him. She stepped up to a bed with a curtain drawn around it and pulled the thin fabric aside. Dan was lying with his eyes closed. His shoulder was bandaged and there were cuts on his face. She moved towards him and looked up at the nurse. The woman was talking to the porter, pointing at the door. Isobel turned to see two men with thinning red hair staring directly at her from behind the glass-panelled entrance. Steven and Jason Ryall.

Before the nurse reached the locked door, Isobel was at the back of the room. The porter moved forward to talk to her as she pushed at the exit bar. Isobel didn't try to read what he was saying. She gave the door another shove and stepped into the corridor, turning round long enough to see that the nurse, the porter and the Ryalls were all watching her. The brothers had not been admitted to the ward.

'Stop them,' Isobel said. *Stop them.* She shut the door and ran.

The corridor at this end of the ward led to a service elevator and a staircase. Isobel took the stairs down to the ground floor and followed the green signs to the emergency exit. She calculated she was heading in the opposite direction to the main reception. There were several doors leading off the hallway and Isobel willed herself to slow down in case she met anyone. She relaxed her grip on her handbag and started to think about where she would go next.

A door in front of her opened and a woman with a lab coat came out. She nodded at Isobel as she passed her. For a second Isobel imagined a world where she was entitled to walk confidently among her peers at work, unafraid, knowing she belonged. At the library, she had been close to achieving that. How quickly everything had been stripped away.

Isobel reached the exit and walked out into the car park. She inhaled the night air, thankful to be outside. Streetlights stretched ahead up towards Highgate and in the distance she saw the roof of the 271 bus lurching down the hill. She had two pounds in her purse. She started to run.

She reached the stop just in time to flag the bus down and took a seat near the back, turning round for one last look at the hospital. Several people stood at the main entrance but there was no sign of the brothers. The bus circled Archway and the Whittington was obscured. She opened her bag to get out her purse. It was only then she remembered that her suitcase was still sitting by the wall outside Forrester Ward.

August 1975

Thursday

Mrs Mason wants me to go over and play with Angie next week and keep her company. She is going to pay me. It is my first proper job. I said I would start work on Monday but I didn't say 'work' because I don't want her to think that I am just doing it for the money.

There are loads of toys at Angie's house but she doesn't play with them. She has her own record player. It is blue and it has a lid, and you can balance the records in the middle and then they drop down. Angie talks a lot and she likes to dress up and pretend. She wears a princess costume. I don't mind pretend games with her because she is good at doing what I say.

Dad was at home today. He was drawing in the kitchen and he let me sit with him and draw too. He makes people's houses bigger and nicer, and I helped him. I did a picture of my dream house with a big playroom on the side for all the children.

Monday

Mrs Mason took us to the cinema on Holloway Road to see *Escape to Witch Mountain*. Even the music was scary. And there

was a trailer for a film about a shark that made Angie laugh
but I didn't like it. We had popcorn and I had to share it
with Angie. When we got back to her house, Angie wanted
to pretend we were the children in the film. We made an
obstacle course in Angie's bedroom and played at running
away and Angie put on her angel costume from school. We
screamed when her mum opened the door. Angie can scream
so high it hurts your ears. I laughed, so she screamed again.

There was a message from Kathy when I got home, but all
Mum said was, 'That girl Kathy called', and I had to call her
back to find out if she wanted to see me.

Tuesday

Mrs Mason said I can't take Angie to see Turpin but we
are allowed to walk to the shops together. When we went
out I told Angie I wanted to get on the tube. You can ride
around all day on the tube for ten pence if you don't get off.
Sometimes I go to Trafalgar Square and feed the pigeons.
Even if you don't have any food for them they fly at you and
they have poorly feet even though they look fat.

I know most of the tube map now but I can't take Angie in
case she tells her mum. She was cross with me because she
says she can keep a secret. We got some sweets instead and
went back to her house and I read her some stories.

Tomorrow I am going out with Kathy and Lucy. Mum
said I can go as long as it is just the girls. I will wear my new
shoes. They are platform wedges and they are made out of
denim with a daisy sewn on top and ties that go round my
ankles and I can walk in them even though they are high.

Wednesday

I met Kathy and Lucy at Victoria Park and we sunbathed on the grass. Kathy had brought a tub of coconut oil to help us get brown. Lucy still has a scar from the dart and Kathy said a suntan would help it not to show, but it was so hot in the park that the coconut oil melted and we were all greasy. So we went back to Kathy's house and dried off. Kathy wanted to see the boys. I told them my mum said I couldn't, but Kathy said did I do everything my parents told me, and I said no, but then her mum came in and went mental about us using all the towels and Kathy told her to fuck off and we left.

We got the bus to the Sobell Centre because it is lovely and cold with the ice rink, and when we got there Jason and Steven were outside waiting for us so Kathy must have rung them anyway. It was weird seeing Jason outside school. Like when we went to the seaside, only this time there were no teachers. I said I couldn't stay long and Jason said that was a shame because he had plans for me.

We went skating but Lucy was on her own without Bishop there, so Jason said he would keep her company when they did the dancing competition. She is a better skater than me. Even though she can't hear the music she can feel it in her body. They came second and Jason said it was stupid, but I would have been so happy to come second in an ice-skating competition.

My skin was sore from the sun and the towel rubbing. I felt sick. I tried to go home but when I took my skates off Steven and Jason got them and ran away so I couldn't get my shoes back. When I went to find Kathy and Lucy they were in the changing rooms and my shoes were in the loo. Actually in the water. Lucy said she was sorry but Kathy said the boys did it. The water in the loo was maybe clean but I washed the shoes anyway.

When we left, Kathy and Lucy said the boys had gone home and they were going to get some chips, so I went home on my own on the bus and I had to wear my wet shoes.

Thursday

I was supposed to go to Angie's but Mum said I had to stay in because she says I have sunstroke. She is cross about my shoes but it wasn't my fault. Mum says they are ruined. I don't really want to wear them again anyway because they were in the loo.

Friday

Today was my last day working and Mrs Mason gave me £10. Now I can go to the bookshop and buy any book I like. And Mrs Mason took us to the Schoolhouse to see Turpin. We all went to the park and I rode him and then Angie got on with me. I was worried we would be too heavy for Turpin but he is a strong horse. I thought Angie's mum would be pleased to see Angie be happy but she looked like Dad when I was drawing houses with him.

After tea I said goodbye to Angie and she gave me a fifty-pence piece, and she put her finger over her mouth and said 'Shhh'. Angie is my real friend. And not just because of the money.

16

The librarian stood up as soon as Carter walked into the reception at Leabrook police station.

'Miss Harris. Thanks for coming in at this hour. And on a Sunday,' Carter shook her head. 'This way, please.'

Melanie Harris looked over her shoulder as she approached Carter. Half a dozen photographers and journalists waited in the street outside the police station.

Carter met her eye. 'Caitlin Thompson.'

'You've got someone?'

'We might have.'

She showed Harris into one of the interview rooms and indicated where she should sit.

'Miss Harris?'

'I'm worried about Isobel.'

Carter nodded. 'Have you been in touch with her?'

'Not since we saw you. She left work and then another policeman called to ask about her, but he didn't say what it was. I spoke to Valerie Jenkins and she said there had been an attack at Isobel's house, a neighbour was injured? And no one can get hold of her.'

'Do you have any reason to be concerned for her welfare?'

The woman frowned. 'There was a break-in, at her house.'

Carter waited.

'And you saw her this morning; she was worried.'

'What do you think she was worried about?'

'I don't know. She was in a state about the missing girl and then I heard about her neighbour. I'm her main contact, but she wouldn't call me.'

'You're not close?'

Harris paused and before she could answer, there was a knock on the door and PC Dawson put his head round.

'Meeting in ten, Sarge.'

'Thanks. Coffee.' Carter looked at her guest. 'You?'

'No, thank you.'

Dawson left and the librarian put her hand to her bag as if to leave.

'Miss Harris, is there anything you'd like to tell me about Isobel Williams? Do you know where she might be?'

The woman's hand stayed on her bag. 'She doesn't have any family in London. Her mum is in Brighton. I feel . . . responsible for her. We were both worried, me and Valerie. Valerie wasn't even supposed to be working today, she came in specially when she heard.'

'But you didn't go to her house. You came here. There's something particular you know that might be relevant?'

Harris took a deep breath.

'Isobel wasn't born deaf. She was hurt, pushed down the stairs, when she was a child.'

'Right.' Carter wondered how many stairs you had to fall down to hit your head that hard.

'She was in hospital for months. Lots of operations. Afterwards her social worker said she had a breakdown.'

'Social worker?'

'The police were involved. She refused to speak. Isobel ended up in some sort of care home for a while. When I saw her in the library this morning she had the newspaper in her hand and she was crying. I tried to stop her from calling you, thought she might be imagining things . . .'

That's what Carter had seen, what she recognised. Isobel Williams was a child of the system.

'Do you have any contact numbers? For her mother? Her social worker?' Carter grabbed her notebook.

'I have her social worker's number but Isobel wouldn't want you to talk to her.'

'We need to think about her safety. And Caitlin Thompson.'

Melanie Harris raised her eyebrows. 'You think Isobel actually saw her?'

Dawson knocked and walked in, cup in hand. 'They're ready.'

'Take Miss Harris's details and call Isobel Williams' social worker.'

'It's the middle of the night.'

Carter took the coffee from the PC. 'There must be an emergency number. Get it.' She turned to Melanie Harris at the door. 'Thank you for coming in. We'll be in touch.'

Carter saw the regret in her eyes. Harris hadn't believed Williams before and now she was reporting her to the police. Isobel Williams had a case file. It had not come up in a basic search because she had been a child when the incident had occurred, but the social worker would know where the file was kept. Carter took a gulp of the coffee as she walked to the incident room. Brecon stood by the board with Atherton. Everyone else was perched on tables and chairs.

WPC Hill stopped Carter by the door. 'I've had the head-master on the phone He's been away for the weekend.'

'Where is he now?'

'He's at his place. Said he would be happy to meet you in the morning.'

'And the number plate? Any luck with the owners?'

'Local shop sent a uniform round.'

'The . . . Lithgoes?' Carter checked her notes.

'Yes. Newbury way. They sold the car a couple of weeks ago. A woman picked it up but the paperwork's in transit apparently.'

'Did they know Fry?'

'They'd never heard of him.'

Carter stared at Hill. 'So the woman who bought the car is the connection. She might be Fry's girlfriend.'

'We're tracking the paperwork now.'

'Carter?' Brecon called across the room. 'You joining us?'

A staff photo of Isobel Williams had been enlarged and pinned up along with two other eyewitnesses, and a new map had been added; a blown-up detail covering a mile of the river Lea. A member of the USCS team was marking several points along the riverbank.

'The nature reserve?' Carter looked at Brecon. 'Where's Moffatt's friend, Billy Rutherford?'

'He's at his residential home. Been there all day. Moffatt called him this morning and cancelled their trip. The mother says Moffatt left for the river as usual. Then he didn't turn up for his shift later. We've had a team on it but it's too dark to see much. Right,' he addressed the room, 'we're looking for Karl Moffatt. I'm going to check out the factory. Lafferty, go over to Rutherford's care home, bring him in if necessary. And find him an appropriate adult for the interview. Also, there's been some trouble at Moffatt's house, local vigilantes, so Jean Moffatt will not be going back there. Carter, Hill tells me you're at the school first thing.' Brecon paused. 'DCI Atherton?'

Atherton looked round the room. 'Everything points to someone local, someone Caitlin Thompson knew. Witness reports stop two days ago and we have had no contact from her abductor. As soon as the full search and rescue begins, the press will know that we have changed the direction of the investigation.' The DCI straightened his back. 'She's on the front page of the tabloids. Her parents are on TV. If Moffatt has her, he might panic. Let's find her before that happens.'

The uniforms in the room dispersed. Brecon stood by the door to talk to each officer as they left. Atherton turned to Carter.

'I want you here for the briefing and the press call tomorrow.'

'Yes, sir.' Carter glanced over at Brecon. 'I'm following up some information from the school.'

Carter hadn't stepped entirely out of her remit yet, but she was getting close. Someone was going to be charged with Caitlin's abduction soon, whether the girl turned up or not.

'The parents are still high on the list, but we're also looking for the convicted paedophile, he has targeted the school before, he is local and his only alibi is his mother.'

'Moffatt was done for indecent exposure, sir.'

'To children, and he was deemed a risk.' Atherton shook his head. 'Try to keep your attention on the case in hand, DS Carter, and not let your personal life confuse things.'

It wasn't the first time that Atherton had referenced Carter's past. He would stand well back if Carter's adolescent troubles made it into the papers. It didn't matter that she had won then, being wrong now would leave her open to all the old accusations. She hadn't missed the double threat either. Her 'personal life' could be used against her in more than historical terms.

On the other hand, if the DCI was lining her up as a scapegoat, she might as well keep following her instincts. She wouldn't get any credit if she was right, but she was used to that.

'Sir, Karl Moffatt flashed a boy in a playground who happened to go to Leabrook South, he has no connection with the school or Caitlin Thompson and I don't believe he's capable of an organised abduction.'

Atherton stared directly at Carter, his mouth a thin line of disapproval.

'This is not your own case, Carter, but your name is on the file.'

The DCI walked over to Brecon and Carter turned back to the board. She had accepted Atherton, and all the others like him, since she joined the force. They were part of the job. Occasionally, she had been luckier, as she was with Brecon. The DI had the same belligerent manner and unshakeable confidence in his own rules as the rest of them, but he was one of the few to treat her as her job, nothing more nor less.

Isobel Williams and Caitlin Thompson stared out at her. Two girls, Williams had said, two children in the library. Who was the other girl?

'Sarge?'

Carter turned to see PC Dawson, paper in hand.

'I've spoken to the social worker in Islington. She supervised Williams' transfer from residential care five years ago. She'll send the case file over in the morning.'

Carter stared at the paper. 'There was no mention of a criminal record on the PNC.'

'No charges against her.' Dawson handed Carter the information sheet.

'We've got five hours until sunrise, Dawson. Get home.'

Dawson checked the board behind them. 'I'll just run past the Palmerston Estate. Marshall's there and Hill's on her way.'

Carter nodded and left the incident room. She swapped out her radio battery, got back to the car and headed south. She needed more information on Isobel Williams.

This was Caitlin Thompson's fourth night away. No one was going to get any sleep.

17

The bus reached the bottom of the hill and rattled along the Holloway Road. The deepest hours of the night, and only delivery vans and lorries were on the streets. In a little while she would be in Hackney, towards the park and all the roads that reminded her of school. Isobel stared at her own reflection, yellowed and damp in the bus window. Like a fish tank, she thought, and shrank away from the glass. She remembered seeing a trailer for *Jaws* when she was a child. The swimmer from the shark's point of view, bare limbs glowing in the sea. Here she was again. Lit up like a prize. Jason Ryall hardly had to search at all.

They found her the night Agnes Spill's letter arrived, outside the newsagents. She had stayed so close to her past life. Maybe she wanted to keep watch, but after everything, she was still the one in the water.

Now they had her suitcase. Apart from clothes, there were books, her prescription packets, her father's papers, the few letters he had written to her, some of his drawings, and his cancelled passport from 1968. She gripped the seat and tried to block the image of Jason's hands going through her life.

The bus swung round Highbury Corner and Isobel rang the bell to get off. She didn't want to get any closer to the old haunts but immediately she regretted leaving the warmth and light of the bus. She huddled into the bus shelter and waited for a moment before checking her bag. The diary was there, her purse and keys, the glass vial from her mother and, at the bottom, the letter from Agnes Spill.

She stared at the teacher's address. Walthamstow. She didn't know the area but it wasn't far. A direct link from Highbury and Islington. She looked over the roundabout to the tube station. The gates were closed. She needed some money and for the first time she could remember since she was a child, she was hungry.

At a hole in the wall, she collected the maximum she was allowed, thirty pounds, in ten-pound notes. The receipt from the cashpoint said it was 04.37. The tubes would be running in an hour. She needed somewhere to keep warm.

Every shop and restaurant she walked past was shuttered behind iron grilles, but by the side of the station the lights of a small caff reflected off the parked black taxis.

The place was full of cabbies getting breakfast at the end of their shift. There was a toilet at the back, and she ducked in. She thought of all the strange little caffs she had found on her trips round London as a child, tube ticket in her pocket. Back before dark and no questions asked.

Maybe when she reached Walthamstow she should call the police. She would have a context then, a story of some description; the authorities placed a value on that, however rickety the structure. They didn't look beyond the basics unless forced. Mother, child, home. Tick. She knew there was a file on her somewhere, a collection of questions without answers. There would be a file on Jason. And Angie. Isobel turned on the hot tap and tried to soak in some of the warmth.

At the counter she ordered a tea, added four sachets of sugar and took it to a table where a man with a lively face started talking to her. She looked over at him and put her fingers to her ear, shrugging.

'Yeah,' he said, 'you can't hear yourself think in here.'

She drank her tea in long gulps.

A waitress with a notepad asked if she wanted anything to eat. Isobel glanced over at the glass display cabinet. There were sandwiches and pies on plates. Containers of cheese, and tuna fish. Eggs were frying next to a stack of sliced bread. She was still hungry but she couldn't imagine eating anything on offer. She reached up for the paper and pencil. The waitress raised her eyebrows and handed them over.

'More tea and some biscuits?' The woman frowned as she peered down at the page.

The man next to her laughed.

'It's not much of a breakfast, love.'

At the table beside them, two men were reading the tabloid sports sections, shouting about football scores. Isobel saw the front page. 'Haunted' ran the headline. In the photo a man and a woman slumped in the back of a car, looking straight through the camera. Caitlin Thompson's parents.

Isobel's blood thumped through her temples. She told herself she had reported what she had seen. There was nothing more she could have done. But she didn't believe that. There was always more.

The tea arrived and the waitress handed her a packet of biscuits. Isobel recognised the blue foil wrapping of her childhood favourites.

'Help yourself, love.'

She couldn't eat the biscuits with the man watching her. They would stick in her throat. Her appetite had gone, in any

case. Isobel drank more tea, gathered her things, and paid at
the counter. She took her change but the waitress held up a
hand as if to stop her. Isobel waited.

'Never mind, love.' The waitress winked at her.

It wasn't until she was walking over to buy her ticket at the
station that she realised she had left the caff with the whole
packet of biscuits in her bag.

She got her ticket and stood in the entrance hall.
Everything seemed brighter than she remembered. Banks of
stainless steel replaced the blue machines of her childhood
and white paint covered the tobacco-stained walls.

Gathered around a tinselled Christmas tree, Salvation
Army singers shook collection boxes at the workers in heavy
boots returning from night shifts. Isobel watched the singers
and thought of carols at the meat market. Butchers' draped
in pig carcasses. Angel costumes with a blood-soaked hem.

She turned away and went through the ticket barrier,
looking back one more time before descending the escalator
in the flush of hot air from the tunnels below.

Monday

Dad drove me to school. He said it was because of the bombs last week but they were miles away. He came in to talk to the teachers about me. He went to the Maths room first, so I think he wanted to see Miss Spill, but she wasn't teaching today and I couldn't find him after assembly.

Jason came into the shed when Angie and I were brushing Turpin. He said he wants me to kiss him every day. I said I thought he liked Lucy more than me but he laughed and said I was being stupid and he gave me more money, so I kissed him. Angie told him to go away but Jason just laughed.

I don't think Dad was worried about bombs after school because he didn't pick me up. I went to the shops and spent some of my money. I bought some mint-flavoured lip gloss from the chemist and from the bookshop I got *Dinky Hocker Shoots Smack* about a girl with a mother who is a counsellor too. I showed it to my mum when I got home and she was shocked because it is about taking drugs. It is a good book though.

Tuesday

I did all my work at school in the morning so I could be with Turpin in the afternoon. I need to keep his shed clean because Mr Sanders said there is going to be an inspection soon. Jason came in and kissed me and he told me to pull down my pants again but I said no and he said I would do it later.

I went to the park with Kathy. She is still going out with Steven and Lucy is with Mark and she says Jason is my boyfriend but I don't think he is. I don't even know if I like him. He shouts at Turpin and frightens him. Kathy still thinks he's sexy but I only kiss him when he gives me money. I didn't tell her that.

When I got home Mum had taken my new book out of my room and all my magazines. She said they were a load of rubbish and my mind was going to rot. She said I should be reading Simone de Beauvoir and what was I doing at school all day. I told her dad had come to the school to talk to the teachers about me and she said of course he had. She said it like she didn't believe me but she said it wasn't me she didn't believe.

Friday

Miss Spill waited at Friday club with Angie and me. She doesn't look so bad these days. But Jason won't do Maths with her. He won't even pretend to be nice to her like the others do. He does Maths with Miss Coburn. Lots of people like Miss Coburn, but she smiles all the time even when nothing good has happened.

When Mrs Mason came to pick up Angie she had a talk with Miss Spill about the help I did in the summer. Miss Spill gave me a funny look but they said I could take Angie home on the bus and wait at her house every Friday until her mum finishes work. It will be a babysitting job like in the holidays.

Saturday

Mum and Dad had an argument about whether I could babysit Angie. Mum said it would be good for me and Dad said he thinks it is too much responsibility. Mum said that just because he never grew up it doesn't mean his daughter can't.

They said I could go as long as Mrs Mason was in the house with us when we got home from school. I said she would be but it doesn't make a difference because we just play in Angie's room anyway. Dad went out for the rest of the day and Mum read me the first chapter of *Jane Eyre*. She was going to listen when I read the second chapter but she had to make a phone call so I read it by myself.

I wanted to make everyone in the book say sorry to Jane.

Friday

There weren't many kids at the club today and Angie took care of Turpin with me. She is gentle with him.

It was my first day taking Angie home by myself. We got the school bus back to her house. We weren't on our own because Mrs Mason has a cleaning lady who stayed late so I wasn't lying to Mum. I made Angie some dinner. We had Heinz tomato soup and chips that I cooked in the oven.

We took the food up to her room and put a blanket on the floor like a picnic. The soup was in cups and we dipped the chips in it. If restaurants had food like that I would be happy. The last time Mum and Dad took me to a proper restaurant was on holiday and they ordered lamb and when it came it had a big bone in the middle because it was a leg.

Angie wanted to play 'Escape to Witch Mountain'. We dressed up and acted out the story. We turned it into a dance and showed it to Angie's mum when she got back from work. She gave me one pound so maybe I can stop kissing Jason now.

18

It was nearly 3 a.m. but Carter was buzzed into the front reception of Islington police station and shown through to the Sergeant on duty.

'You been demoted already?' WPS Elizabeth Woodford shook Carter's hand. She was older than Carter but they'd worked together for a couple of years before Woodford was made Sergeant. She was glad to see she had stuck it out.

'It's only a matter of time.'

Woodford nodded. 'So, why are you working the graveyard shift?'

Carter followed her through to the small staff room.

'I'm on the Caitlin Thompson case and something came up that I wanted to check. A burglary. Thought you might still have the file.'

'How long ago are we talking?'

'Fourteen years. Finch worked the case. Any chance I could look at the old file?'

'1976? Finch retired last year.'

Carter nodded. She hadn't gone to his leaving drinks, but she was still grateful to the man. He'd helped her when she started on patrol and he hadn't stood in the way of her

Detective badge, which was more than could be said for most of them.

'Right. Well, the new stuff gets taken away but they haven't got round to the old cases. You know where to look?'

'I remember.'

'Tea?'

'I remember that, too.'

Woodford smiled and left her to it. Carter didn't ask why she was working nights. It was hard enough for a WPC to become a Sergeant. If she wanted to make Inspector, Carter knew she'd have to do the work no one else wanted.

She made some tea and took it down to the filing room. Rows of steel cabinets lined the walls but she knew where to look, the same place that held all the files the year that she started. The paperwork had been easier then, just a few forms in duplicate. As the years went by the files had grown fatter and now they were being taken away and loaded onto computers. Carter wondered who in government had shares in the data systems company and what happened to the original paperwork once it was digitised.

The contents of the cabinets for 1976 were divided by surname. There was no file on Williams. That might mean there was no paperwork for her, or it might mean that it was sealed as a juvenile record. The notes Dawson had given her named the address of a Patricia Mason. She found the files for M, and the name Mason. She took the paperwork to the desk at the back of the room. Inside, the folder was arranged with the most recent document first.

MISSING PERSONS REPORT
ISLINGTON POLICE STATION

23 March 1976

Name Angela Margaret Mason

Gender Female

Date of Birth 18 April 1961

Address 37, Perseus Road. London N1

Reported Missing 18:30 23/03/1976

Next of Kin Patricia Diane Mason

Address Same as above

Relationship Mother

Information Child was reported missing
by mother after she failed to return
from school. Officers searched the
family residence. The school, known as
the Schoolhouse, has been notified and
interviews pending. The missing child has
Down's syndrome and requires supervision.

Statement Signed Detective Sergeant
Leonard Finch

There was no mention of Isobel Williams, but Carter recognised the case. The child abduction she had worked on when she first started at Islington. Included in the file was a photograph of Angela Mason, with her arm around a horse, and a group school photo from the Schoolhouse. There were witness statements from the mother and a schoolteacher, Agnes Spill, who was directly responsible for the girl on the day she disappeared. Carter remembered Finch had gone in quickly because although she was fourteen, Angela Mason was considered especially vulnerable and unlikely to have run away.

Carter read the short statement again. The Schoolhouse. She remembered it had been one of the schools that took part in the Met police quiz. Primary school children from the borough came to the station. The Schoolhouse team had been different. She remembered a little boy in a wheelchair, a girl who had taught her some sign language, and there were older kids too. The school had moved out of the area midway through the year, but they'd been allowed to finish the contest in Islington. When Angela Mason was abducted, Carter had gone to check out the new grounds.

She stirred her tea and tried to recall the details of her visit. A Victorian school built like a warehouse to store children, two tall stories of grimy red brick. It must have been a weekend and there were no pupils, but there was no indication of the building's use either, no kids' art in the high windows and no playground, just a bleak gravel yard with a couple of sheds and some barbed wire. A knotted rope hung from the only tree. She thought of the boy in the wheelchair and the others. A mixed school, they'd called it. A charity school. Carter had had her own encounters with charity when she was a child. That had been mixed too.

She turned over the next file.

SUMMARY OF CASE

Angela Mason was found alive at 11.28 on
27.03.76 at 202, Albermarle Place, London
E2. She had been held against her will
and suffered minor physical injuries. She
was admitted to Homerton Hospital in
distress. Jason Ryall, a former pupil
at the same school as the victim was
arrested and charged with abduction.

Signed Detective Sergeant Leonard Finch

There were two cross-references for the case file, one listed under the name Jason Ryall and another under Patricia Mason, December 1975.

Carter returned to the cabinet and found Ryall's folder.

CHARGE SHEET ISLINGTON POLICE STATION

29 March 1976

Name Jason John Ryall

Gender Male

Date of Birth 18 February 1960

Address Flat 18, 149 St Edward
Avenue. London E2

Charge Kidnap and false imprisonment of
a minor, Angela Margaret Mason

There was no statement from Ryall but his photograph and record were included. He had several juvenile arrests for theft and assault and had served time in a juvenile detention centre and in community service. The sentence for abduction had been three years' detainment at Reading Young Offender Institution. The last case in his file was for Pentonville. Ryall had been sentenced to sixteen years for grievous bodily harm of a detention officer while in Reading. There was no record of a release date, if he had one.

Jason Ryall had been fifteen at the time of his arrest. Carter didn't recognise the face. She hadn't seen Ryall then, and he'd been a minor, his name kept out of the papers, his identity protected. If he was still inside, he would have a record as an adult. This one should already have been sealed. There was unlikely to be a court transcription from his trial.

There was one further report. A faded photocopy with 'Ryall' handwritten at the top.

CRIME REPORT ISLINGTON POLICE STATION

22 December 1975

Incident Attempted burglary

Location 37, Perseus Road. London N1

Victim Patricia Diane Mason

Information At approximately 9 p.m. two men gained entry and attempted to steal property from the ground floor. Eleven-year-old Isobel Williams who was in sole charge disturbed their efforts. Miss Williams was employed by the owner to take care of her daughter for the evening. When Miss Williams disturbed the burglars they attempted to intimidate her. Miss Williams became upset and, in the ensuing argument, she has stated that she missed her footing and fell down the stairs. The men escaped. Miss Williams is currently unable to provide a full description or statement due to the nature of her injuries.

The night of the burglary, Isobel Williams was babysitting Angela Mason.

Carter sat down with all the reports and read them again. An unsolved burglary at the Masons', three months later the abduction of Angela Mason, and then the trial and conviction of Jason Ryall. She drank the lukewarm tea. Melanie Harris had told her Williams' injuries had occurred when she was a child. She picked up the school photo from Angela Mason's file. A black-and-white photo taken in the school yard, as bleak as Carter remembered. Underneath, all the children's names in small but elaborate italics. Carter peered at the faces and traced the names. The boy in the wheelchair, and another boy she recognised. Christopher Nicolson, Mark Bishop. She scanned the others. There was a Steven Ryall, but no Jason. The girls from the police quiz team – Kathy Binks, the deaf girl was Lucy Monero, and Angela Mason, smiling in her neat school uniform. Sitting between them, her hair loose and long around her small, white face, was Isobel Williams.

19

The last time she had seen Jason was in the weeks after the accident. He was a few feet from her hospital bed. She had screamed until a nurse came running. The nurse thought Isobel was imagining things, that it was a bad dream. Isobel couldn't understand exactly what was said to reassure her but she knew what it meant: it was no use telling people that Jason had found her, no one could stop him.

He had visited her before, when she was in intensive care. That wasn't a dream either but when she told her father that a kid from school was hanging around he said it was impossible. She wasn't allowed visitors apart from family. She had wanted to believe her father and not think about Jason, so she accepted she had imagined him looming between the tubes and monitors while she drifted in and out of consciousness.

Her parents had stopped all visitors when they found the police trying to question her as she came round from surgery. With the help of a consultant her father succeeded in preventing any further unauthorised interviews, but the ban meant Isobel lay on her back and stared at the ceiling all day. Her father spent every evening with her. Clare would arrive in the morning with books and Lucozade, upset the nurses and leave when it became clear that Isobel was still not speaking. The rest of the time, Isobel depended on the company of the porters and cleaners who stopped by her bed to try and make her smile.

It was better once she moved out of intensive care. At least Jason didn't come into the new ward. There were four other children: a baby in a cot, a young girl with dark hair who slept all the time and two boys nearer her age who ignored Isobel when they realised she couldn't hear them. The ban on visitors remained while the Williamses sought legal advice.

Without the shunt that drained fluid from the top of her skull, Isobel was at least mobile. She could sit up unaided and read her books but she wasn't allowed to leave the ward alone. She refused to use the potty that the nurses said she could slip under the bedcovers and 'no one will notice'. So every time she needed the toilet, she had to wait for a member of staff to walk with her to the cubicle at the end of the corridor. There was no bell or buzzer for emergencies; the ward sister said the children didn't need them with a nurse's station in the room.

Sometimes at night, a nurse sat at the desk reading a book or a magazine, but the station was unstaffed for long hours during the day. The boys would jump from bed to bed trying to get around the room without touching the floor, or wheel each other about in the spare cot. Isobel couldn't tell what was wrong with them, they seemed perfectly healthy, then one of them was discharged and the other boy stopped jumping and after a while he was moved to another ward. No one told Isobel anything about the new children she lay next to every day; they left as mysteriously as they arrived. Isobel didn't ask; she wanted to keep away from questions of any kind.

They had cut a hole into her head. The doctor drew a

picture of it, a tiny door through to her brain. Before the operation her head was swollen and she was dizzy. There was blood coming out of her ears. She remembered the ambulance ride from Angie's house; she'd been awake the whole time. Her father was waiting for her outside the hospital, running alongside the trolley as they wheeled her in. That was when she realised there was something wrong with her head, she couldn't hear what he was saying. Her ears felt full and sticky and when she poked inside to clear them her fingers were wet and she saw they were red. She didn't start to panic until she tried to tell him. She couldn't hear her own voice.

The best thing about screaming was how it felt. In her chest, in her throat. She hadn't screamed when she fell down the stairs because it hadn't hurt. It was more surprising than painful, one minute on the first floor landing outside Mrs Mason's bedroom with Angie and Jason and Steven, everybody shouting, and the next minute, the world turning upside down. Little flashes of the house as she fell, the ceiling, the banisters, enough time to wonder at each frozen image. What is happening? Where am I? When she stopped falling, she looked back up the stairs and the brothers were gone. Angie was crying and shaking her head the way she did when she didn't want to do something, the way she had when Isobel found her sitting on the double bed.

They were both still there when Mrs Mason came home. Angie at the top of the stairs, Isobel at the bottom. Isobel didn't know how much time had passed. It felt as though it was no time at all. And it felt as though they had always been there, Angie staring down at broken Isobel, Isobel looking up at the child she should have protected.

Apart from the screaming, she didn't make any sounds.

Clare, the doctors and nurses, the social worker and the police, all assumed it must be terrifying to be suddenly deaf. 'Not so bad as blind,' one of the nurses mimed to her sitting by the bed in the early days on the children's ward, 'you're a lucky little girl.' The nurse ran out of ideas to express 'lucky' and was reduced to writing in the pad of large-rule paper on top of the cabinet. This nurse, who spent the most time at her bedside that week, was the first one to lose patience with her. Isobel just wouldn't appreciate how fortunate she was.

Only her father seemed to know that Isobel's screams and silence were not about her deafness. He didn't ask her what was wrong. He stood by the bed at the beginning and end of each visit and looked down at her with the same expression she had seen at the kitchen table, the day she glanced over from her drawing. The melancholy seemed focused now, directed entirely at Isobel. She tried to imagine that he was sorry for her but when she closed her eyes at night she would shift and wriggle to escape the truth. The reason her father was sad was not because of what had been done to her, but because of what she'd done.

October 1975

Monday

I told Jason that I didn't want to kiss him any more. He laughed. I let him cut some of the knots out of my hair to make up for it. He likes cutting things.

Angie wanted to come out with Turpin again. I said she was not allowed to and she tried to hug me. She is not my friend at school but I can't tell her that. I let her stroke Turpin.

Tuesday

Next week is half term. Steven wanted to make a guy and take it to the market at the weekend so we can get some money for fireworks. Jason said it would be better to have a Halloween party. I said we should go to a haunted house. Kathy told us we could stay in the basement at school and have a séance.

I wish I hadn't said about the haunted house. I saw it in a film that Dad showed for his birthday party last year. They put it on the wall in the sitting room and their friends watched it with them. I only saw the beginning and I couldn't sleep after.

Wednesday

The school sent a report to my house. Mum and Dad wanted us to have supper together so I knew something was wrong. They said they were worried I was not learning anything. Mum said all I know about is boys and horses. I don't even like the boys any more and what is wrong with liking horses?

Dad said again that he wants me to go a different school and Mum said it was a shame that people couldn't do better. I didn't know if she meant me or the school, and Dad said, 'Jesus, Clare.'

Thursday

Jason got a detention today because he put a bag on Drew's head and made him walk around. Jason said Drew was blind so it wouldn't make any difference but Drew couldn't breathe. Instead of the detention Jason walked outside and climbed up on Turpin's shed and banged on the roof again. I could hear Turpin but I wasn't allowed in the playground. Mr Sanders said we had to ignore Jason because he wanted attention. He was still on the roof when I went home.

Friday

As soon as I got to school I went to see Turpin. He was tied up to a tree and there were men putting barbed wire on the roof of his shed. He looked lonely. Miss Peden shouted at me from the window to leave the horse and get inside. She called Turpin a 'filthy animal'.

Jason came and put his arms around me when he saw I was crying. He said we would put a spell on her when we do the séance.

We had to bring Angie to the Halloween party because I was her babysitter. I told Jason that they could have the party without me but Jason said I could bring Angie if she was quiet so I told Angie she was invited to a party.

She clapped her hands when we walked round the back of the school because she was expecting a birthday party with cake. I told her it wasn't that kind of party. We had to climb through the fence and go down the steps to the basement without Miss Spill seeing us.

There is a space under the big stairs that Mr Sanders wants to make into a changing room for when they have the swimming pool. Kathy and Lucy and Steven and Mark Bishop and Jason were waiting there. Steven had stuck some candles in the milk bottles from kindergarten. Angie stopped clapping when she saw the room. The floor is dusty in the basement so we sat on our coats and Kathy told us to draw letters out to make a Ouija board. We heard the teachers upstairs locking the school for the weekend and the boys stood guard at the bottom of the stairs in case they came down.

I was glad Angie was quiet because the others didn't want her there and Kathy was in a bad mood already. Lucy sat in the corner with Bishop but she did not smile at me.

When the boys got back we finished the letters in a circle on the ground. Angie didn't want to play but Jason laughed and said it would be fun. I held Angie's other hand and she squeezed it really hard.

Jason asked for the first question and looked at us.

One of the candles blew out and Kathy squealed and I jumped.

Angie said she wanted to go home but Jason told her to shut up.

We put our fingers on the stone and Bishop and Steven giggled but Jason wasn't laughing any more.

It was hard to see everyone's face but I think Kathy was scared. She pushed against Steven.

My arm was shaking but when I looked down the stone was moving. We all looked at each other to see who was pushing it. The stone stopped on the letter B.

We still had our fingers on the stone and it started moving again. It stopped on the E.

Angie was making a noise almost like singing but it echoed in the room under the stairs.

Jason said the ghost wanted to talk to us.

We watched our hands and the stone moved around the letter O. I held my breath. Angie kept whining and I was scared Jason would shout at her but I didn't take my hand off the stone when it stopped again.

Jason jumped up and shouted BOO and we all screamed.

Jason laughed so hard. He kept saying 'Bish!' pointing at us and laughing.

I could feel my heart.

I grabbed Angie and tried to pull her up. She had her hands over her ears and she was rocking.

Bishop had his arm round Lucy and they were staring at me. Lucy's eyes were so big and she was trying not to cry. Jason leaned over the board and moved his mouth at her. I couldn't tell if they were real words.

I had a pain like a stitch and it was hard to breathe.

I pulled Angie's hands away from her ears. She looked at me but she didn't move.

She got up.

We tried to get past Jason but he didn't move out of the way. He said we should take the party to Angie's house but I said her mum would be there.

Steven and Bishop were making ghost noises and Kathy was giggling but I know she was scared too. I wanted Lucy to come with us but she didn't move.

I said to Jason we would have the party another time and he winked at me.

As soon as Angie and I got out of the basement we ran. We didn't even stop to see Turpin.

At the bus stop Angie said, 'We have to get out of here. We have to escape from Witch Mountain.' She remembered the words from the film.

We got home before Mrs Mason, and Angie promised not to say anything. I told her that Jason would find out if she did.

December 1990

Monday

20

The divers had been in the water for over an hour when Carter drove into the temporary car park. A low haze lay over the marshes. The team had moved upriver from the sports field. She cursed the white tent USCS had put up beside the towpath. The press hadn't been told about the search and the tent could be seen for miles.

Lafferty was leaning against his car, peeling an orange.

'Come for the show?' he held out a segment of fruit. 'You look like shit.'

Carter shook her head and turned to the riverbank. She had been home to wash and change her clothes and had slept for an hour after she'd eaten. She wasn't tired but she'd need more than an orange to get her through the day. Half a cold pizza and a takeaway coffee waited in the car.

There were half a dozen officers standing on each side of the river. That meant at least three in the water.

'What is this? I thought we were going in with a small team.'

'Got a tip this morning. Moffatt comes out here for his R and R. Bird watching, his mum says. Finds it relaxing.' Lafferty made a tossing motion with his hand. It still had some orange in it. 'Fuck.'

'We were going to keep it small and mobile. And he's got an alibi.'

Lafferty wiped at the juice on his trousers. 'Yeah, well he might have an alibi but now he's taken off. We've got his pal Billy Rutherford at the station. Can't interview him until he gets an AA. But he did say Moffatt never came out here on his own.'

'What does Jean Moffatt say?'

'She said he's gone.'

'Gone?'

'No forwarding address, Carter, and I don't think you'll be getting a postcard.'

There was a shout from the riverbank.

Carter took her time walking over to the man in charge. The activity in the water had increased. She had seen a few water recoveries before, but not on her own case, and never a child. If Moffatt had killed Caitlin Thompson, he must have done it in the first twenty-four hours she had gone missing. He couldn't have hidden her. Unless he had an accomplice. Carter had looked in the wrong places. She hadn't made any difference at all.

'Morning, Carter.'

Carter recognised the Sergeant, MacInley, an experienced diver. Brecon had really gone to town.

'Morning, Mac. Something?'

The older man nodded, his mouth tight.

'Don't know what. It's stuck well in there.'

It. Carter looked away. *She.* A girl. Not floating yet, so maybe tied down. Or worse, only just gone. There were no good possibilities, no comforts. Only this: a dead child at the bottom of a filthy river.

The divers were surfacing, necklace formation. They held

on to the line as they moved back to the bank, signalling to the officers on land. One of the officers spoke to Sergeant MacInley who waved to his colleagues on the other side.

'Suit up,' he shouted to one of them.

Carter looked at him.

'We need another diver. The body's weighted.' MacInley didn't meet Carter's eye. 'Adult male.'

The sky had darkened again and the mist thickened to rain. Carter sat in the car with the engine running and finished her breakfast. There were other places Carter should be but she gave herself a moment to be grateful that it wasn't Caitlin Thompson in the water. Karl Moffatt shouldn't have been there either, but she doubted there would even be an inquiry. Carter thought of Jean Moffatt and her dog.

She wanted to visit Isobel Williams but there was still no reply at her flat and the library didn't open until 10 a.m. She'd radioed the station first thing for a check on the man mentioned in the paperwork, Jason Ryall, and just caught Hill back from another night shift at Palmerston Estate. She'd told her what she'd found in Islington. Hill promised to chase it up when she came back on duty.

Her priority, though, was Caitlin's school. She could drive there in time for morning registration and grab the list of vehicles from Fry, see whether he had claimed a car for himself. If the headmaster was involved this was an opportunity to interview him before he learned the official suspect was dead. Carter turned out of the field and headed towards Leabrook South.

On Friday, the DI had left her alone with Moffatt and his solicitor on several occasions during the interview. Carter had gone over some of the statement with them but the solicitor had been guarded. If the interview were scrutinised, Carter was on the outside, the one who had pressed Moffatt, and Atherton wouldn't hesitate to put her in the spotlight and protect Brecon. That was why Carter kept so few notes. Take all the statements you can, but never record your own thoughts. DS Finch had encouraged her imagination, just not on paper. It was harder to get you for what you hadn't written.

She thought back to the Angela Mason case and the sparse files held at Islington. If she'd kept more notes she might have placed Isobel Williams and the Mason girl sooner. But Finch was right, she'd learned early how her own words could be used against her. Even a letter to a friend at school. Once the authorities took an interest in your private thoughts, they were open to interpretation, and rarely in your favour.

Take Robert Fry. Carter had copied the car number plate and radioed it in as soon as the office opened. She had not, however, written anything about the bicycle clips. That was the sort of detail that could get you in trouble if there was a later investigation or a lawsuit. Accusations of paranoia or bias. Carter frowned as she pulled into the street next to Leabrook South Primary. The focus would be on Moffat this morning and she guessed the news media would be camped out at the riverbank by lunchtime. She had another chance. Caitlin Thompson might still be alive and Carter was free to continue her own line of questioning while Brecon was looking the other way.

The rain had slowed. She stood by the gate in the alleyway behind the bicycle shed and pulled hard on the wet iron handle. The gate didn't move. Someone had secured the padlock. There was a shuffling on the other side.

'Hello?' She tried out her friendly voice. A squeal behind

the gate ended with a flurry of retreating footsteps. So much
for friendly.

In the reception area Mr Fry was directing damp children
to their classrooms and smiling at parents as they passed by.

'Oh, yes, they all seem to keep a trained spider to write
their homework at that age, Mrs Ogupunde. I don't expect it
to make any sense until Year Six. Mr De Souza knows what
he's doing.' The headmaster continued to placate the mother
as he acknowledged Carter behind her.

'Plenty of time for Simon, don't worry at all. You again.'
Fry indicated his office further down the corridor, 'Shall we?'

They moved slowly through the sea of children, many of
whom appeared to be going in the wrong direction. Carter
wondered again how it was possible for anyone to keep track
of who came and went.

'DS Carter.' Fry closed the door on the tide of tiny ruck-
sacks. 'We're a small school. And, as I told you, no one can
come into a classroom and collect a child without the teacher
being informed. After school, the form teachers take them
out to meet their parents in the front playground. By Years
Five and Six, most of them are allowed to walk home by
themselves. Like Caitlin.'

'Like Caitlin was supposed to.' Carter flipped open
her notebook.

'Indeed. We can't keep an eye on them outside the school
gates. More's the pity.'

Carter looked around the room while Fry retrieved the
paperwork from his desk and added a few more number
plates to the list he had prepared for the Detective. Carter
had only been in the office once, briefly, on the Friday at
her first visit. The other interviews had been conducted in
the staffroom. Every wall was filled with shelves and all the

shelves were stacked with box files. There was no décor to speak of, not even a photo frame. On the desk, the red rubber bands spilling out of an ashtray triggered a memory. The red bands on the ground outside the bike shed. The receptionist said Caitlin had borrowed one from her on Thursday.

'I've managed to put together a list of most of the vehicles owned by school staff. The dinner ladies won't come in for another hour or so and I have absolutely no idea what the cleaning staff drive. Some sort of van, but they usually arrive after I've left. Yes, fine,' Fry held out the handwritten list and offered it to Carter with a look of distaste, 'I will get in touch with the cleaning company. But really, I would prefer it if you could call Miss Traynor in future, and not make any further unscheduled visits during school hours. The children, and their parents, are upset enough. They are holding some sort of vigil for Caitlin this evening. And the staff are under a lot of pressure. They feel . . . scrutinised.'

Carter allowed the headmaster's speech to settle. The unprompted declarations of suspects often gave away more than her own notes ever could.

'What about the caretaker? Did you speak to him about the gate?'

'Yes, he's secured it properly. Doesn't know what happened to the padlock. He's in the yard now if you'd like a chat.'

Carter wondered if Robert Fry had ever had to face serious consequences or if he had sailed through his life so far enjoying 'chats' with everyone he met. She glanced at the paper Fry had given her. She didn't think the number of the car the headmaster had driven had been included.

'And the attendance records? The school building plans?'

'No luck with the plans, I'm afraid that might take a while.

Miss Traynor has copies of last week's registration for you. The actual registers are with the teachers right now for morning attendance.'

An incomplete list of cars, no school plans, records in different places, more staff that Fry hadn't questioned. He couldn't have made the visit more complicated. She looked at the headmaster. If he had something to do with Caitlin's disappearance he was only drawing attention by being deliberately unhelpful. On the other hand, if he was not involved, he had no reason to be obstructive. Carter felt like shaking the complacency from his well-cut suit.

'DS Carter, I'm sure you understand that we still have to run the school as best we can in the middle of this . . . event. It's the last few days of term, we're supposed to be rehearsing the Nativity play but the children cannot concentrate. We've had newspapers and television cameras, and of course your good selves. You have your job to do, and we all hope that you will find Caitlin safe and sound . . . '

He tailed off and for a moment the alternative fates of Caitlin Thompson filled the room like so many ghost children lined up against the shelving.

Carter closed her notebook and looked directly at the headmaster.

'Of course. Let me speak with Miss Traynor, and I would like another word with Caitlin's form teacher, then I'll be out of your way, Mr Fry. I should advise you, however, that one thing we don't have in this case is time and I would like you to get the rest of the requested information to me as soon as possible.'

Fry held himself perfectly still, his priestly hands clasped before him. She had pressed a button.

'Advise me, DS Carter?'

'Informally.'

'I see. Well, thank you. I believe you know where to find Miss Traynor.'

The headmaster returned to his desk and gathered a pile of papers.

Catherine Traynor was stationed behind the glass partition at the main entrance to the school. Carter was glad to see her as she left Fry's office; she was a known quantity. The feeling didn't last.

'They haven't found her then?' The receptionist pushed open the window.

Carter shook her head.

'I've got Thursday's registration for you. I thought you already had all the kid's names?'

'We do, but not a record of who was in the school that day.'

'The school? I've only got a copy of Caitlin's class.' Her voice rose slightly.

Carter recognised the defensiveness from Friday.

'I told Mr Fry I needed the registration record of every child in the building on the day that Caitlin went missing.'

She looked back to see if Fry was still in his office. The door was closed.

Traynor paused as she thought through the task. 'I have to get the books from the teachers and then type them up. There are six years, two classes in each year and about thirty children in each class. That's three hundred and sixty registrations, minus the thirty I've already got.' Carter was going to have to leave the school without any of the information she had asked for. Tightening her grip on the reception desk, she tried to remember that it was not the receptionist's fault.

'Can't I just take the books with me? Or you could use your photocopier.'

'Look,' she pulled out a pad of Post-it Notes, 'tell me exactly what it is you want and I'll get it ready as soon as I can.'

Carter heard a door click shut and turned around. The corridor was empty. Catherine Traynor was waiting for her instructions, pen poised above the pad. Carter wondered if she should order the removal of all the registers. She noticed the pen in the receptionist's hand, a transparent biro with red stripes at the top and bottom.

'Can I see that? The pen?'

The receptionist passed it to her.

'Sure. Why?'

Carter turned the pen repeatedly in her hand. The wording was printed in black capitals around the clear plastic tube. Whittington Park University.

'One of our young mums gets them for us,' the receptionist smiled, realising she could offer a bit of gossip. 'She was on the list, she comes in to drop off leaflets and arrange meetings for the PTA. Does loads for the school, Val.'

One of the parents Lafferty had interviewed.

Carter spoke as calmly as she could. 'Val? Valerie what?'

'Sorry?'

'Her second name. What is her second name?'

'Oh. Valerie Jenkins, Rowena's mum. Nice girl. Year below Caitlin. She's not been well, off school for a few days now.'

Carter made for Fry's office. The door was locked.

'Mr Fry's gone to a meeting,' Miss Traynor called behind her.

Carter turned. 'Where?'

'In the staff room. You can't go in there. DS Carter?'

Carter headed towards the back of the building, radio in hand. The teenage lothario from the swimming pool had mentioned Caitlin's 'little friend'. Not Ruby Siltmore. She was Caitlin's 'little' friend but that wasn't what the boy had meant. He had dismissed the girls because of their age, not their size. Caitlin's friend was Rowena Jenkins. The two girls in the library.

'We need to find a Valerie Jenkins, she works at Whittington Park University. And send a car to Isobel Williams, same campus, or at her home address, Bowman Road. She's a witness. Bring her in.'

21

It was only five stops to Walthamstow but the heat of the
tunnels and the strong vibration through the seats made
Isobel drowsy. She thought of Lucy dancing at school when
no one else could hear any music. Isobel didn't dance, but
she liked to feel the rumbling of the sound.

'Compensatory plasticity' was the term the doctors used
in the hospital. They wanted to run tests on Isobel to gauge
if her other senses improved after such profound and sudden
deafness. She refused. Months of invasive treatments had left
her without any desire for further explorations. In any case,
there was no system that could measure how the world had
changed for her. The doctors and nurses, even her parents,
saw an absence where her hearing had been but the silence
in her head was not empty. She was full of sensations; she
just couldn't easily distinguish between them.

They told her what had happened to Angie. The police
started questioning her and she stopped speaking. Soon she
noticed how the nurses looked at a point beyond her head.
Pity relied on the pitied accepting their position but she had
learned from the best. At the Schoolhouse you didn't feel
sorry for anyone.

It took almost an hour to find the house. She got lost

several times and had to stop for directions. Finally, some-
body recognised the address on the letter and pointed
her to 'the old railway track'. She walked slowly down
a street with a gate at the far end, looking at every front
door, wondering about the lives inside. The thoughts came
in signs, not words. *Christmas tree. Family. Home.* She felt
so tired and distant from the people getting up, going to
work or school. Back at the library, they would be busy
with the last rush before the holiday. She wondered if she
would ever see them again. She longed to be in her warm
flat with all the doors shut and the heavy curtains drawn.
It started to rain.

She reached the gate. On the other side was a cattle grid
and a path that lead into wild, deep-green fields with a strip
of stormy grey above the horizon. She had never seen a
cattle grid in London. Isobel found a metal walkway beside
the gate, and crossed over. She looked around. No farm.
No cows. The path curved ahead. She could see a brick wall
high between the trees. A bridge. She walked on for a few
minutes and at the next bend she saw a row of three cottages
knocked together.

She looked around. The street was out of view but the
bridge was clearer now, and the path ran on and narrowed
in the distance. She couldn't see the railway, but there was
a cluster of overgrown fencing.

On the doorstep, she stared at a single milk bottle, the
silver foil lid stretched tight above the frozen cream top.
She thought of all the little bottles of milk that sat in crates
outside the Schoolhouse, curdling in the sun.

'Isobel?'

She was older, of course, but that only showed in her hair,
which had been greying and thin then, and was now a few

white wisps wound into a bun, and in the fat of her cheeks, which had drooped.

'Miss Spill.' Isobel felt the words escaping before she could stop them.

The woman nodded. 'Agnes.' She didn't move from the doorway.

'Agnes,' Isobel repeated.

They stood, each regarding the other. Agnes bent down to pick up the milk bottle and the smaller figure of a teenage girl was revealed in the hallway, hair tied back and brow furrowed. She stared straight at her. Isobel caught her breath.

The girl walked to the door.

'Who's this?'

Isobel could just make out the girl's mouth.

'It's Isobel Williams,' said Agnes. 'You remember who that is, don't you?'

Isobel took a step back into the rain. All the effort of the night, the lack of food and sleep. All that way, the years of running, years and years of running. She clutched at the air as she fell.

Monday

Mum and Dad think I have gone to sleep but I have not. I must write down everything.

Today was the first day back to school after half term. We had a special assembly and Mr Sanders gave a speech about personal responsibility and telling the truth. He said some of us don't understand how lucky we are and the Schoolhouse might be our last chance to do something with our lives. Jason shouted, 'Speak for yourself, mate,' and Mr Sanders sent him out of the room.

Mr Sanders said inspectors were going to come to the school and they wanted to talk to everyone to make sure we were all safe. Some of the kids started to boo but Kathy was sitting next to me and she looked scared. I was going to ask her what was wrong but then the banging started.

We followed Mr Sanders outside and there was Jason on the roof of the school. He must have climbed up the fire escape. It was high up. Mr Sanders got his megaphone from sports day and shouted for him to come down. Bishop and Steven were cheering and clapping.

Mr Sanders said he was calling the police. Jason grabbed a tile off the roof and threw it into the playground. Turpin was at the back fence and his rope was loose. Jason was smashing more tiles and Mr Sanders was shouting and the kids were going mad. The teachers tried to push them inside.

I went to get Turpin. I could hear Mr Sanders shouting through the megaphone about the police. I could hear Jason banging on the roof with his stick.

Turpin was frightened. He was kicking out, trying to get the rope off and I thought I could stop him and I would hold him and everything would be all right.

I opened my arms but he pushed past me and I couldn't catch the rope. He got to his shed and was kicking and bucking and the barbed wire was outside and it got caught up in his legs and it hurt him. He tried to run and he dragged the wire with him. Then I saw Christopher. He was sitting in his chair watching Jason. I called out but Turpin kicked the wheelchair and Christopher fell into the mud and Turpin kept kicking at the rope and the wire and the wheelchair.

I couldn't stop him. Miss Spill and Miss Coburn grabbed at the rope and Mr Dickens shouted 'Lorraine' and I saw Miss Coburn on the ground as well. Then the police came and then an ambulance came for Miss Coburn who needed stitches on her face, and for Christopher who has broken bones, and no one could tell me what happened to Turpin.

Tuesday

When I got to school they said that Christopher was going to be in hospital for a long time. Miss Coburn is not coming back to the school ever. Turpin's shed was empty. I couldn't find him. I went to Mr Sanders and he said the vet had to come and it was the kindest thing because he was a very old horse.

After school Mum and Dad were waiting to talk to me and

they said they knew what had happened. I didn't tell them before because they don't even like Turpin, and what if they say it was his fault that everyone got hurt. I cried even though I didn't want to and Mum said it was just as well Lorraine had called and Dad said he thought Mum had done enough for one day and she laughed and said it was Lorraine's choice and she'd chosen to leave and not to get fired.

They had a big argument and I went to bed. Lorraine is Miss Coburn because I heard Mr Dickens say it.

Thursday

I am going to leave this school after Christmas. I don't ever want to go back but Dad told me I have to go to school because it is the law.

Mum put a photograph of Angie, me and Turpin in a frame by my bed. Mrs Mason must have given her the photograph because I have never seen Mum take a picture of anything. I put it under my pillow because I want to keep it near but I don't want to look at it.

The Schoolhouse should not be the law. Is it the law to kill your horse because he is frightened?

22

Television crews were huddled on the steps of Leabrook station, trying to chase up a link between the dead man and Caitlin Thompson. Atherton was making an impromptu statement. Robert Fry ducked down in the back seat as Carter drove past.

Carter checked him in the rear-view mirror. 'We won't go in the front way, sir.'

Fry didn't answer. He had hardly spoken since Carter asked him to accompany her to the station, except to ask for Atherton. He hadn't asked for a lawyer, and Carter hadn't suggested he needed one. She was going by PACE rules, but she had insisted that he needed to answer questions.

As they entered the station, Lafferty appeared.

'What's going on? Atherton's fighting off the News of the Screws. Is this him?' Lafferty nodded in Fry's direction.

Not for the first time, Carter wondered if Lafferty ever thought before he spoke. She glared at her colleague as she introduced the headmaster.

'This is Robert Fry, Mr Fry, this is Detective Sergeant Lafferty. Mr Fry is the head at Leabrook South. He's helping us with our enquiries now that we have information about one of the mothers at the school.'

Lafferty nodded. 'Brecon's waiting for you.'

'DS Lafferty, could you find an interview room for Mr Fry while I chase up a few things? Thank you,' Carter added before Lafferty could answer. 'I'll be right with you, Mr Fry.'

Carter turned her back on the two men who looked equally displeased with each other's company. On her way to the office she passed Dawson and Marshall, temporarily relieved from duty at the Thompsons'. They moved towards Carter when they saw her, keeping step with her.

'We've got two cars out looking for Jenkins, one at the address she gave her work,' said Dawson.

'There's no answer at the door there,' said Marshall.

'Or the phone.'

'But we've found an address for the car you reported. There's a Panda on its way now. Finsbury Park. Dartington Street.'

Carter looked at the paperwork in Marshall's hand. 'Tell them not to approach.'

As soon as they reached the office she exchanged her radio handset for a fresh one, made sure it was turned off, and started to gather the paperwork she was going to need for the interview.

They needed to know what they were dealing with at Jenkins's place. Find out as much as they could from Fry first. She had seen the headmaster driving the car from the school. If it was Jenkins' car, that was confirmation of a relationship. It was possible the two of them had the girls at his place. She needed Fry to give permission for a search. There was still a chance he might cooperate.

The people Carter usually faced on the other side of the interview desk were misfits, like Moffatt, the ones who never stood a chance. They were wrong but they were

suffering. Not Fry. He seemed confused and irritated, neither innocent nor guilty.

'Think out loud, Carter.'

She turned to see Brecon. His face was blotched red and
white from standing in the cold watching Atherton bluffing.

'This is not your personal case. The press is outside stok-
ing some story about kidnapped girls. Atherton told them
we have a suspect. We've got the guy here, right?'

'The headmaster is here, sir. I'm just about to start the
interview.' Carter gripped the files.

'You think he's got the girls?'

'It looks like he's involved with the woman who might
have them, Valerie Jenkins. We need access to his address.'

'He's not going to volunteer it if the girls are there, is he?
Marshall, get someone over to his house now. Dawson, tell
Lafferty to start a warrant. I take it you haven't charged him?'

Carter watched Dawson and Marshall leave. With Moffatt
dead and nothing on the parents, Atherton must have let it be
known he was willing to flush out the headmaster and local
damage be damned.

'If he'd been at his premises, it would have been worth
arresting him. But he was at the school. He hasn't asked for
a solicitor, he might still talk.'

'What else?'

Carter thought about their conversation on Friday. Either
Brecon had forgotten that she was the one who had pushed
for the case or he had filed it under 'proper procedure'. She
wondered if power made it impossible to do the right thing.
Or if Brecon knew something she didn't. Either way, he was
changing the rules with the benefit of hindsight.

'If Caitlin is at Valerie Jenkins' place,' Carter said, 'we
might be looking at two girls.'

Through the doorway, Carter could see Lafferty heading towards them.

'Is that on?' Lafferty looked at the mute radio in Carter's hand. 'Hill radioed in. She's left some files for you on Isobel Williams. Fortis Green are looking for her too. There's an incident report from the Whittington Hospital last night.'

Brecon turned to Carter.

'What's she got to do with this?'

'It's thanks to her we're looking at the headmaster and Valerie Jenkins. She gave us the connection.'

Carter didn't share her own connection to Williams.

'Christ alive.' Brecon held Carter's look. 'What have you got involved with? Atherton's called a meeting in twenty minutes, he'll want to take the lead on Valerie Jenkins . . . '

Carter cut in. 'That would be a mistake, sir.'

'Well, you can tell him why. We need to talk to Fry, find the girl, or girls. Carter, you're with me. Lafferty, you're supposed to be on the warrant.'

Brecon put out his hand for the files.

'I'll be right there.' Carter said.

'Let's get on with it. I don't want to wait for his lawyer any more than you do.' Brecon nodded at Carter and headed to the interview room.

Carter cradled the radio. She wanted to talk to Hill. She had got her in trouble, chasing after Isobel Williams. Doing double shifts. They could have left it all with Fortis Green to sort out. But they were both involved now, and Hill had some new information.

On her way to the interview room she stopped Marshall.

'Where did you say on the address for Jenkins' car? Dartington Street?' She scanned the map. Since the press conference the flags had multiplied with possible sightings.

Only the red ones indicated confirmed movements of Caitlin Thompson on Thursday morning and they hadn't changed. Dartington Street was located a couple of miles west of Leabrook. She'd almost passed it on her way back from the library at Whittington Park.

She looked at Marshall. 'Who's on it?'

'Two of our uniforms and two more from Finsbury Park. There's no sign of Jenkins' car.'

'Who ordered the others?'

Marshall glanced over Carter's shoulder. The SIO was still outside. 'DCI Atherton.'

'Tell them to wait and don't approach the property. She's already been spooked. No lights, no sirens. Just observe for now.' Carter turned to go. Her radio was still switched off for the interview with Fry. She wanted to turn it on, apologise to Rebecca, make contact. She picked up the files her girlfriend had left for her. They were marked 'Angela Mason'. 'Oh, and Marshall, radio Hill would you? Tell her to keep her head down when she gets in.'

Homerton Hospital Antenatal Record

02/04/1976

Name Angela Margaret Mason

DOB 18/04/1960

Blood Group O Positive

Height of Fundus by exam. 16

Weight 10st.

Height 5ft 4in

BP 160/105

Oedema Periorbital.

Further exam. needed

Urine Trace protein

Remarks History of cardiac disease. Refer.

Autopsy Report St Pancras Coroner's Court

14/07/76

Patient Angela Margaret Mason

Address 37, Perseus Road N1

Date of Birth 18 April 1960

Date of Death 9 July 1976

Report Patient died in childbirth. Myocardial infarction caused by congenital heart disease. Infant survived delivery by Caesarean section. Mother and baby both positive for Down's syndrome, Trisomy 21. Infant: Term minus 9 weeks.

23

When Isobel came to she was lying on a linoleum kitchen floor, her feet resting on a folded blanket. Her eyes were sore and tight in their sockets and when she moved them a sharp pain shot through to the back of her head. She turned on her side. The floor was warm and smelled of oranges.

A hand clasped her shoulder and pulled her up a little, the other hand offering a glass of water. Isobel took a few sips and sat up. The pain settled round her right temple and stayed there like a bruise.

Agnes was standing over her, stooping as Isobel handed the glass back.

'You took a fall,' she said, 'take it easy now.'

Isobel stared at her.

'You're all right,' the teacher said. 'Mary caught you.'

Isobel continued to look up at Agnes. She didn't want to see the girl crouched beside her, the ghost with a hand on her shoulder.

'Isobel,' Agnes said, 'this is Mary Mason, Angela's girl.'

Isobel knew the name; she had read Miss Spill's letter enough times. 'The house belongs to Mary but she can't stay here alone.'

She allowed herself to look a little to the teacher's left.

Wavy brown hair, tracksuit, small hands fluttering at her sides. Her face, leaner than Angie's, the lines stronger. She saw her fully now. Angela's girl. Maybe she had always known.

'Would you like some bread?' Mary was talking, her words easy to read. 'Would you like a cup of tea?'

Isobel nodded.

'Feel like getting off the floor?' Agnes offered Isobel a hand. 'Let's make you comfortable.'

Isobel sat at the kitchen table. She felt her appetite again and remembered the biscuits in her bag. She reached down for the handbag which was on the floor by the folded blanket, took out the packet and offered them to Agnes. The plastic wrapping was crumpled.

'Ah, yes. Sorry your bag took a spill as well.' Agnes tipped the biscuits onto a plate. A few remained intact. Isobel watched as Mary bit off the top half and gnawed at the cream and jam. Like a meal, she remembered, and took one herself.

Mary chattered away. Isobel followed part of the conversation, drinking the tea and feeling the blood return to her hands and face. Nobody asked her any questions. Outside, it had stopped raining. Sitting in the kitchen with flashes of sunlight glancing through the window, they let her collect herself.

Beyond the garden, tall, windswept grass was visible. Isobel tried to not think about the world outside the room but each time she looked up to see Mary's animated features her mind switched track. Angie's daughter. Isobel could cry to think of her being here all these years. She pressed at the sore place in her temple. She was so tired.

Mary wanted to take their guest on a tour of the house. Isobel watched Miss Spill calm her, the teacher's expression so familiar. An incline of her head, the folds at the corner of her pursed lips as she listened. She remembered why she had never wanted to see her teacher again. Agnes had always understood too much. The dread of being known by her was undiminished.

She couldn't recollect when the story of the teacher's homelessness had started to circulate. It explained so much about the woman in a stained macintosh who took such trouble with their work. Of course Miss Spill was happy at the Schoolhouse, she had nowhere else to go, Steven said so and Kathy agreed. They made it into a game to be sarcastic to her and pretend she didn't notice. If Isobel ever objected, they turned their attention to her. It was never the sort of attention you wanted.

She hadn't said she liked Miss Spill, and even if she had been brave enough it would not have been quite accurate; but she did like the Maths room, where it was quiet, and there were tables to sit at, not just mats on the floor like in the main room. And she had a sort of fascination with the teacher, when you got over the strangeness. Looking at her neat appearance now, it was hard to believe how odd she had seemed at school. Isobel retained an image of her arriving at the gates each day as though she had just walked away from a car accident. She hadn't known then about the husband. Walked away with nothing, her mother had said. Isobel wondered about her own appearance on Agnes's doorstep. She had also walked away with nothing. She didn't imagine she looked any more presentable than her teacher had done.

Isobel was still staring when Agnes Spill turned to her.

'Have I changed so much?'

Isobel flushed and shook her head.

More clean? Miss Spill signed.

Some of the teachers signed at the Schoolhouse. Lucy wasn't the only deaf pupil. When Miss Spill had visited Isobel in hospital after the accident she encouraged her to sign. They had sat in the children's ward for over an hour while Isobel wondered if the teacher could hear her heart pounding. That night she had reminded her father of the ban on non-family visitors.

'She was worried about you,' her dad had written in her hospital notebook, 'and she promised not to talk about the burglary.'

Agnes poured some more tea. 'Your father was kind to me.'

Isobel started. The teacher could still read her mind. Her father and Miss Spill. She had a sudden memory of him in the Maths room.

'He used to come and talk to me, he wanted to help get me rehomed, part of his work with the council. That's how he met Lorraine. Miss Coburn.' Agnes checked Isobel was following what she said.

Clare had told her. 'I asked him to help her but he got side-tracked.'

Mary had moved her chair closer to Isobel.

You sign? The small hands formed the question as soon as Isobel looked at her.

Isobel nodded.

Mary nodded with her. From the pocket of her tracksuit bottoms she took a lump of flesh-coloured plastic and put it on the table.

You want?

All three of them studied Mary's hearing aid.

'She doesn't need it, Mary,' Agnes said after a moment.

Mary smiled and put the lump back in her pocket. The smile faded as she looked up at Isobel. *You ok?*

'She has a lot to take in,' Agnes patted Mary's hand. 'I'm not sure what your mother told you, Isobel.'

She thought back to the night she'd got the letter.

Nothing.

Agnes frowned. 'To be fair to her, I didn't tell her that much. Just that I wanted to get in touch with you. And a little about Mary. I didn't say why I was writing. It was between us.'

There it was.

Her secret. Laid bare on the table with the bread and jam.

'That boy, the man, I didn't know if the police would contact you. They told us, of course.'

Of course.

The man? Mary looked at the two women. *The prison man?*

'Yes,' Agnes said. 'The prison man.'

The teacher was as calm and steady as she had been at school. Isobel had thought of her as an immoveable object when she was a child. Always there, even when you didn't want her to be.

'I thought you should meet Mary. It's what her grand-mother wanted as well. I wasn't expecting you to come so soon though.'

She could tell her now. Tell the teacher that the brothers had found her.

You knew my granny?

Isobel's head was heavy. She couldn't meet the child's eye. She pressed her palms to her face, her elbows braced against the table in an effort to keep upright.

Agnes stood to collect the tea things without taking her eyes off Isobel. 'I think you could do with a rest. Why don't you take her to your room, Mary? Have a sleep, Isobel, and we'll go for a walk later, if the storm blows over.'

Mary was thrilled to give a tour on her own. She pulled Isobel to her feet and tipped from side to side as she ran ahead.

Hallway. Cupboard. Loo. Sitting room.

They were back at the front door, Mary skipping to the staircase Isobel had seen from the doorstep.

She could leave now; walk out of the house and on to somewhere else. It had ceased to matter where.

My sign name . . . Mary put three fingers on her palm for the letter M and then twisted her hands at the wrists in a little burst. The sign for applause.

Isobel blinked hard.

Agnes named me. Because I like singing and making shows. Mary paused. *Your sign name what?*

Isobel shrugged.

Will give you sign name. She walked away, beckoning Isobel to follow her.

From the other end of the hall, Isobel saw Miss Spill coming out of the kitchen, wiping her hands on a tea towel. Isobel felt a flash of hatred. She didn't want to be here, scared in the hallway and ready to run. She had rebuilt her life and these people were not supposed to be part of it. Her teacher from the Schoolhouse, Angie's daughter . . . Jason's daughter.

She felt the old hurt rising in her chest. So I will write this diary and then they will see.

The hardest part of the life she had made was not keeping other people out. People fell away easily, put off by her silence, satisfied with their attempt at simple communication. No. The hardest part of her life was knowing herself. She could shut herself up in her small, solid flat for as long as she wanted but she couldn't escape the truth. She looked back at Agnes, framed by the kitchen doorway, and she wanted to rail against the understanding in her eyes.

Mary stood on the bottom stair, hands clasped round the banister, her body swaying. Isobel realised she was singing. Eyes closed, heart-shaped face dipping in time to the music in her head.

Isobel moved away from the front door.

'I'm going to call your mother,' Agnes said. 'Let her know you're here. I saw you brought one of the vials.' Agnes tilted her head at Isobel's handbag. 'Such a lovely memory to have. She was always clever like that, your mother.'

What song? Isobel signed when Mary opened her eyes.

'Abracadabra' by the Steve Miller Band. I have a dance. Do you want to see?

Tuesday

Jason has been expelled even though they don't call it that. Mr Sanders said Jason was old enough and didn't need to be at school. I can't tell the others I'm glad because they like him and Steven is sulking. I would tell Lucy but she is leaving as well. She is going to another school. Ever since the Ouija board she just comes in the mornings now and she doesn't hang out with us any more. I tried to talk to her in break time but she wouldn't look at my face and I don't know enough signs to make her understand.

Wednesday

We went singing in Smithfield meat market to get money for the school. Every year we dress up as angels with white dresses and tinsel in our hair for halos and wings on our back which I like. But we have to put our ballet shoes inside our socks so they don't show and it was very cold today. I couldn't feel my toes or my fingers.

The men who carry the meat put money in our buckets when we sing hymns and they are nice, but they have whole pigs and bits of cow on their shoulders and the blood drips

down their backs. My socks were pink when I got home and
Mum made me throw them away.

Thursday

The police were at the school today. They went into the Art
room and stayed all day. Mr Sanders made an announcement
over the Tannoy system. If we had anything to say to the
police we were supposed to go to the Art room and talk to
them. I don't know what we were supposed to talk about.

Kathy didn't come to Joe's for lunch and when I got back
to school she had gone home.

Friday

Kathy said I could meet her at the park after school and she
would tell me everything. I didn't really want to see Kathy
after school. She makes me feel like I have done something
bad. I had to wait until Friday club was finished. I took Angie.

All the way to the park Angie asked where Turpin had
gone. I didn't know what to say. It was horrible going to the
park without him. I said he was dead but I don't think she
understands what that means.

When we got to the park Steven and Kathy were sitting
on the bench kissing. I should have known Kathy was going
to meet the boys. It was freezing but Bishop said I had to stay
because we were going to have a funeral for Turpin. Then
Jason arrived.

I didn't want to have a funeral but Jason told us we must
show respect. He said we could have a cremation. He said
a cremation is where you burn the body but even without
the body we could still have a fire. We all walked to the

flower garden and no one was there. Jason made a fire out of newspapers and bits of stick and told us to stand around it and hold hands.

Jason said we were praying for a horse called Turpin, to make sure he was in heaven. But Bishop said he was a mean horse. I was still holding Angie's hand. We tried to leave and Jason started shouting. He ran up and pushed his face close to me and told me I was being rude. I had a feeling in my legs like they had electricity in them, like they might fall down or like I might fly into the clouds.

He told me to say something. I squeezed Angie's hand so I wouldn't cry. I said thank you and Jason let us go.

Angie was upset with the boys but not in a sad way. She was angry and I had to make her promise not to say anything about the fire. She said it was dangerous and the boys were rude and I said she was right.

It is Jason's fault that Turpin was killed.

Tuesday

Jason was outside school today at break. He was with Bishop and Steven but I stayed in the playground. Kathy asked me if we could talk. She said she was in trouble and she wasn't allowed to hang out with the boys.

I asked her if it was something to do with Jason and she said he made her do things when we were all at the seaside. She was crying and she told me not to tell anyone. Especially Steven. She said he would go mental if he finds out. She said she had to go with her mum to the police station and make a statement.

I didn't know what she meant but I didn't ask any more questions because Steven came back. He said he is coming to the party. I didn't know what party and he said we were going to have a party at Angie's house and it was going to be a Christmas party and he was going to do it in a proper bed with Kathy.

He squeezed Kathy and she looked at me over his shoulder to check I wouldn't tell about Jason.

Wednesday

There are only two more days of school before the Christmas holidays and then I do not have to go back. Mum and Dad are sending me to the comprehensive and I will sit in a classroom like my cousins do and have lessons at a desk.

I am going to tell Kathy and Mark and Steven that I am leaving. I will tell them tomorrow and then we won't have to have the party.

Thursday

I told Kathy first. Kathy said she hated me and she will tell the boys and they will hate me too.

So that is it. I will leave school and never see them again.

Friday

I said goodbye to everyone and especially to Lucy because I miss her. Patrick shook my hand really hard and told me to be careful. Christopher is not coming back to the Schoolhouse. He is not in hospital any more but he is going to another school. We made a card for him and Miss Spill took it to his house.

I'm seeing Angie in the holidays, which is my job.

Lucy wrote her telephone number on a piece of paper even though I can't call her because her new hearing aids don't work on the telephone. I was happy that she gave me her number.

Mr Sanders was not at school this week but I said goodbye to Mr Dickens and Miss Bannister. Miss Spill just nodded at me like I was only going away for the night.

Angie's mother came to pick her up after Friday club and asked me if I would play with Angie on Monday next week. I will get some money to buy presents, so I said yes.

Kathy said she wanted to talk to me. She said she was sorry she was angry and she would miss me. I said it was ok even though it is not.

She asked me about the party like that was all she wanted to talk about in the first place.

I told her we couldn't have the party. I said it is not my house and Mrs Mason would not like it. I said she wasn't supposed to see the boys anyway. She said it was none of my business and I better not be a tell-tale and she would talk to Jason about the party.

I shouldn't have told her I was leaving.

24

Robert Fry sat on the plastic chair in the small interview room, an untouched cup of tea on the table between him and DI Brecon. Carter stood by the door as Brecon acknowledged the change of personnel on tape.

'10.38 a.m. Robert Fry and DI Brecon have been joined by DS Carter. I believe you've spoken with Detective Sergeant Carter a few times already, Mr Fry?'

The headmaster looked at Carter as she sat down. 'Maybe I should have legal representation.'

Carter nodded and waited for Brecon to reply. Fry was clearly capable of understanding police hierarchy and manipulating it to his own advantage if necessary, but Brecon was asking the questions.

'You haven't been charged with any crime, Mr Fry. We simply want to know about Valerie Jenkins, and we appreciate your cooperation.'

The DI could hold the line for longer than Carter had thought possible and still stay on the right side of the rules. She had sat in on other interviews to find out how he got away with it so often, imagining there was a special talent that she had yet to learn as a newly qualified DS. Now she saw the trick for what it was, law on one side, authority on the other, a quick sleight of hand, and the two were one. She supposed you could still call it a skill.

'Of course, should you require one we would be happy to provide a solicitor, if you don't have one of your own. But I would remind you that we urgently need to find Caitlin.'

'I know that.'

'Before you came in, DS Carter, Mr Fry was telling me Valerie Jenkins is a parent at Leabrook South Primary. Is that right, Mr Fry?'

'She is. As I told DS Carter. A new parent.'

'And what counts as "new"?'

Fry sighed. 'I think Rowena arrived halfway through the last school year.'

'Rowena?'

'The daughter.'

Carter considered how the confines of an interview room made everything a little clearer than in the outside world. At school, Fry had seemed unshakeable. Two feet across from them in the station, Carter noted his agitation. Brecon had picked up on it too.

'Rowena.' Her DI said the name slowly. 'She's in Caitlin Thompson's class. And DS Carter has found a connection between the mother and a sighting of Caitlin.'

'That's why I agreed to come and talk to you. When I spoke to DCI Atherton, he assured me that the school would be protected. We break up for the Christmas holidays in two days. The children can't have any more disruption.'

'Valerie Jenkins.' Brecon looked up from the file. 'She's a volunteer at the school?'

'She does some reading with the children. She's on the PTA. Our receptionist, Miss Traynor, can help you with that.'

'And do you know where she is?' Brecon didn't change his tone, but Carter knew he was pushing whatever limits were left.

'I'm sorry?'

'Do you know where Valerie Jenkins, the mother of your pupil Rowena Jenkins, might be?'

Fry sniffed hard, his lips against his teeth. 'I have no idea. At home, I assume. I've been told Rowena has been off school for a few days.'

'We checked "at home", and she's not there.'

Carter noted Fry's breath deepen. Relief.

'I can only tell you what I know from school.'

The statement from Fry's neighbour Celia Whoolf was in the file. A girlfriend. With a daughter.

Brecon looked up again. 'Would you mind if, just to eliminate you from our inquiries, we searched your address?'

Carter saw the hesitation.

'My home? Why on earth would you want to do that? What is this?'

'We are looking at every possibility, Mr Fry. We need to find Caitlin, and we don't have many leads. We are asking anyone who has been in regular contact with Caitlin or her family to cooperate.'

'I've been more than helpful, DI Brecon. I shall be talking to DCI Atherton about the way you and DS Carter have led this investigation.'

Carter stood up as Fry did. She needed as much information as she could get before she confronted Valerie Jenkins. 'It's an informal search, Mr Fry. If you give us permission then it makes everything much quicker, and it will be better for you. That you helped us.'

Hey presto, law on one side, authority on the other.

'What are you talking about? Are you detaining me? I want to see DCI Atherton.'

'Do sit down, Mr Fry.' Brecon let his impatience surface. 'Are you helping us or not?'

'You said you wanted me to answer some questions. You did not say I was a suspect. If you don't let me leave immediately then I want my lawyer.'

Carter remained standing opposite Fry. 'We are going door-to-door again, and visiting all those who we know had contact with Caitlin Thompson on the day she went missing. That includes her teachers, yourself, and Miss Jenkins.'

The headmaster stared at her. 'When you have located everyone, let me know. I can meet you, with my lawyer present, at my house. At an agreed time. Otherwise, you will have to get a warrant.'

His confidence was telling. He didn't have Caitlin at his place, and Carter didn't think the child had ever been there. He was lying, but it wasn't about that.

'Sit down, Mr Fry.' It was hardly a request, and they would have to caution him if he was no longer a voluntary witness. 'DS Carter, please bring Valerie Jenkins into the station.'

'Yes, guv.'

Fry sat down, his eyes flickering.

'You know where Valerie is?'

Valerie. Brecon nodded as Carter stood back and addressed Fry.

'Yes, Mr Fry, we do. I saw you drive her car away from the school. The car that is registered at her actual address.'

She waited for the information to land.

A hissing sound escaped from Fry's rigid mouth. Carter thought of Caitlin Thompson's friend Ruby and her wail of distress. A child's sense of guilt for what she hadn't done. Maybe we never grow out of that shame. She wondered what Fry believed he hadn't done.

'They're together. Valerie and the girls.'

Carter didn't move.

Fry's voice rose. 'She's crazy. She followed me here from my last school. She's trying to destroy me.'

Carter looked at Brecon. They would have to arrest him now and hope that he would keep talking while they waited for the lawyer. Carter suspected Fry was giving as much of a performance now as he did in the school hall.

'When did you last see them, Mr Fry?'

'I . . . Not since Thursday. Caitlin came into the office, Valerie was there . . .'

'Caitlin came into your office?'

Fry hesitated and Carter immediately regretted interrupting him.

'She came into your office and Valerie Jenkins was there?'

Carter made sure not to change Fry's wording. The interview was balanced on the edge of an interrogation and Fry was on his own.

He nodded.

'Mr Fry,' she pushed, 'What is your relationship with Valerie Jenkins?'

The headmaster fell back in his chair, his voice almost a sob. 'I told you. She's crazy. This has nothing to do with me. I want my lawyer. This isn't right. This is not right . . .'

Brecon cleared his throat. 'Robert Fry, you do not have to say anything. But it may harm your defence if you do not mention when questioned something which you later rely on in court. Anything you do say may be given in evidence.'

25

Isobel woke from a dreamless sleep. She was on a single bed in a child's room lined with trophies and rosettes, a gabled window set into the far wall. Rain fell in a steady stream beyond primrose-yellow curtains. A digital alarm clock on the bedside table glowed in the afternoon storm. Outside it was almost dark.

She knew she was in Mary Mason's room, but for a moment she couldn't recall why. In the space before the memories returned there was only a sense of dread.

The door opened and Agnes came in.

'How are you feeling?'

OK. Isobel shrugged.

Thank you for playing with Mary.

A box of vinyl singles, now placed in order of Mary's preference. It had taken an hour and Mary had giggled the whole time. In the corner, under the eaves, was the blue record player.

It was Angie's, Agnes signed.

Isobel nodded. *I remember.*

Agnes sat down on the end of the bed and looked at Isobel.

Anything you would like to ask me?

Isobel stared at the woman who had known her since

she was four. The woman who had watched her grow up and seen the best and the worst of her for all those years at the Schoolhouse. Who knew her secret. Isobel felt the ache in her temple again, the deep curdling in her stomach. She couldn't understand how she had allowed herself to be here, in the same house, in the same room, with the one person left who knew the truth about what she had done. Her mother had never fully understood what happened the night of the accident. Her father knew and it had killed him.

Your mother is worried about you.

Isobel could imagine how the conversation had gone. *She worries about everyone.*

Agnes frowned. *Yes, her job. But different with you. She protected you.*

Isobel tried to see how Clare's parenting could ever have been thought of as 'protective'. *OK,* she signed.

For the whole trial. Isobel blanched at the sign for 'trial' but Agnes continued. *She made sure you were not called as a witness but that your voice was heard. Your diary,* Agnes answered the question in Isobel's eyes. *They used your diary as evidence.*

The room started to shimmer and Isobel had to reach down and hold on to the bed frame. Her diary. They had read it, heard it. All this time, her mother had known.

We supported her. The three of us agreed.

Three of them.

Patricia, your mother, me.

Mrs Mason, Clare and Agnes. They had spoken to each other, worked together on the trial. Of course they had. There had been a trial, a big trial, because Angie was kidnapped and then Angie was dead. And Jason had gone to prison. Isobel knew the facts but she never went over them, never wanted to absorb the details of the process that had sent Jason away. It was enough that she had the memories of that night circling her mind as a zoetrope whenever she closed her eyes.

Agnes was wrong.

My father? she signed. It was her father who had been there for her all that time. Her father who had looked after her. Her father who had cared.

I know you miss him.

Of course she missed him.

He blamed himself to the end. Not being there for you and your mother. I'm so sorry.

Isobel looked away. Her father had been there, he had looked after her. Every day at the hospital. But not at the trial. Her mother had dealt with the trial, had helped to convict Jason. And before all of that? Her father had been with her all along. She thought of the arguments, of Clare shouting and her father giving up. That day in the Wimpy when she'd asked him if he ever got into trouble. 'Better ask your mother,' he'd said. Isobel knew the kind of trouble now.

Through the quilt, Isobel felt a hand on her knee. She looked back at Agnes.

Your mother forgave him, Agnes signed. *But he did not forgive himself.*

The hand squeezed her knee gently.

Not your fault. Nothing your fault.

Isobel forced herself to hold Agnes's gaze. She couldn't hide from her old teacher. Agnes Spill had seen her diary too. She knew what Isobel had done, how she had let her friend down, had led the brothers to her house and how she had stayed away when Angie needed her. She had not been brave, had not protected the girl who trusted her, had not stopped Jason. She shook her head.

You were eleven. A child. Not your job. Our job. Adults.

Isobel's hand was still on the bedframe. She held on to it to stop herself from falling. To stop herself from crying. Not her fault.

Agnes turned her head to the door. *Mary's waiting,* she signed. 'How about that walk?'

They both looked towards the window. Water cascaded from the roof.

'I have coats and boots. Mary loves the rain.'

For a moment Isobel thought she would have to tell Agnes that Jason and Steven had found her, that her letter had come too late. Her head ached and shimmers of pain still clouded at the edges of her vision.

Yes. I would like that.

She wanted to go outside and forget again. To kick through the mud with the wind rushing at her and nothing to think about except putting one foot in front of the other.

Agnes tapped her cheek with her forefinger. *Soft.*

'My sign,' she said.

Mary stood by the back door hopping from foot to foot. She was dressed in waterproofs, her face barely visible under the hood of a fuchsia anorak. A row of Wellington boots was lined up on the doormat, one navy-blue pair and two in shades of pink.

'Mary can wear her old ones. You take these.' Agnes handed Isobel the larger pink boots.

My new boots.

Mary stared as Isobel tried them on.

Thank you. Isobel signed. *I will take care of them.*

Isobel put on a heavy coat with a fleeced lining. She looked at the handbag she had brought down from the bedroom.

Safe here, Mary signed.

There was nothing in it. Her keys and thin wallet, the letter, her diary, and the vial. 'A lovely memory to have,' Agnes had said. She pushed the bag to the wall with one foot.

I know your sign. Mary crooked her forefinger to her nose. *Sister.*

Outside, the afternoon seemed brighter. Yellowed light touched the edges of the storm clouds as they rolled apart. The wind whipped them from all directions. Agnes walked to the end of the garden and opened a small gate.

We will walk along the railway path. She indicated beyond the bridge Isobel had seen earlier. *Not too far.*

They set off across the marshes. Ahead of them was an expanse of rough grass and gorse. A thin line of trees stood on the brow of the hill, their bony branches distended with crows' nests. Isobel felt the wind press into her eyes and body, tugging at her hair. She could almost hear it, like the pump of her heart at night. Whoosh. A memory of sound.

Mary had overtaken her and was skipping beside Agnes. They came to the bridge over the railway tracks. At the top, Isobel turned to look back at the solitary house. Seen from that angle, it reminded her of the houses she had drawn with her father as a child. One building with many extensions as Isobel had thought of new rooms for the family she imagined living there. Her father had stopped imagining. He had left them. She pressed her hands into the pockets of the heavy coat and walked across the bridge.

From the other side, she could see canal boats fringing the edges of a canal, clots of woodsmoke hanging above the flues. Ahead of her was a crop of outbuildings. As the rain eased the evening light travelled through the sheds and barns and out into a yard, reflecting pinkly in the windows and standing pools of water. Her head felt lighter now, the shadows behind her eyes fainter.

Agnes pointed out a paddock. *We like to feed the horses.* She produced a couple of apples from her coat, 'But I think they've already gone in for the night.'

Isobel stared at her. *Horses?*

Yes, Mary nodded. *Riding school.*

A flash of lightning sliced the horizon.

Let's go. Let's go. Mary signed with great sweeping motions.

'Five minutes,' said Agnes, putting the apples back in her pocket. 'Then we have to get back.'

Mary grabbed both women by the hand and pulled.

They let themselves be dragged for a few steps but had to steady their pace on the muddy track at the bottom. Isobel watched Mary charging ahead and remembered the day she went to the ski slope with Angie. Angie was the brave one, even then.

The track narrowed and followed a hedge that ran alongside what looked like another field. Isobel could see faded jump poles and sodden bales of straw. To one side, a light shone from the tinselled window of an office. Across the yard stood a large barn, its corrugated iron roof funnelling rainwater onto the mud below. The barn doors were open and Isobel could see all the equipment for the horses hanging inside. Old riding hats and saddles. Bridles and lead reins. A door in the back wall opened on to stables.

'They're not inside.' Agnes waved at the office window.

The last of the sun's light was dipping behind the barn, shadowing the yard. They followed Mary along a path to a small paddock. Two shaggy brown horses looked up as the group approached.

Mary took the apples from Agnes's pocket and stepped up to the fence.

Isobel stood quite still. The horses ambled over, their breath steaming around them. If she moved they might disappear. She saw the muddied animals shining in the fading light and she was eleven again, walking with Turpin through Bethnal Green, standing on a bench in Victoria Park to climb on his sturdy back.

The horses were chocolate-brown to Turpin's dark grey, with white patches on their noses and flanks, and long tails and manes where he had sported only a scruff. They each took an apple from Mary's outstretched palms. Isobel ventured one step closer. The horse nearest to her lifted his head and looked directly at her. She felt a tap on her shoulder and turned to see Agnes.

'Here.' She handed her a sugar lump. 'He's only allowed one of these.'

Isobel took the sugar and moved closer. Beside her, Mary's small hand still pressed against the other horse's neck.

'This is Flint,' Mary mouthed, 'and that's Brodie.'

The sugar was dissolving against Isobel's skin. She brought her hand up to the fence and tried to keep it from shaking. Brodie inched forward and thudded his nose down on to her palm. She closed her eyes and felt the rasp of his tongue, the blunt edges of his teeth, the slimy sweep of his top lip sucking the last grains of sugar from her fingers. When she opened her eyes the horse was watching her.

He wants a hug. Mary signed. *Hug the horse.*

Isobel glanced back at Agnes. She nodded.

Brodie pressed his whole body into the fence, straining forward. Isobel lifted her arms around the thick shoulders and squeezed, letting her head fall against his neck, the wet coat rub against her cheek. She inhaled the scent of grass and rain and the richer notes of manure and old hay. This horse smelled of all horses. He smelled of her horse. She sunk her head further against him and held on tight. Not her fault. From deep within her the sob rose up and pushed her closer to the horse's flank. She laid her face against the warm body and the damp pelt absorbed her tears.

After some minutes, Agnes touched her arm.

We need to go home.

The sun had set. It was still possible to see the faces around her but the fields beyond were disappearing into the night. Agnes switched on a torch and started back towards the path. With a sigh, Isobel gave Brodie one last stroke of his neck. She was tired again, her eyes and nose thick with salt, but the pain above her brows had lifted. She felt the shape of Mary beside her.

They walked together towards the big barn where Agnes was waiting and set off up the hill, Mary's hand in Isobel's.

'The storm's passed.' Agnes turned as they reached the top of the bridge. 'The stars will be out soon.'

They walked towards the house as briskly as they could in the dark and the wet, Isobel shifting her focus between the glow of the house and the ground in front of her. She felt the sharp new fears of the last few days and the older, familiar pain rubbing along together like a raw scab. Whatever her teacher knew about the past, she couldn't know everything. She would have to tell Agnes about Jason and Steven Ryall. She would have to tell her what she had done.

Mary pushed ahead and reached the garden first. She ran to the back door, tried the handle, and went inside. Standing at the garden gate, Isobel grabbed Agnes's arm.

'Isobel?'

You locked the door.

'I must have forgotten.'

Agnes took another step.

Isobel shrank back, pulling Agnes with her. She could see the door, the kitchen and beyond it the hallway.

'Isobel?'

There was a flash from one of the upstairs rooms. Agnes swung round. She had heard something. She ran straight to the house but staggered back as she reached the door. She turned quickly to Isobel.

'Help,' Agnes exaggerated the words, 'go and get help.'

Isobel stumbled back into the shadows. A man stepped outside. She could not see his face. But she knew who he was.

Islington Gazette

22 December 1975

Brave Schoolgirl Stops Robbery

Local schoolgirl Isobel Williams is in hospital today, after she interrupted an attempted robbery on Friday night.

Williams, who is 11 years old, was babysitting at the Islington house when the thieves entered. It is believed the girl slipped on the stairs while the thieves made their escape.

Police are waiting to interview Williams, who suffered a head injury in the fall.

'Isobel Williams is a brave little girl, who did her best to protect the child in her care,' Detective Sergeant Leonard Finch told the *Gazette*. 'Nothing was stolen from the property. Her parents should be very proud of her.'

The owner of the house, Patricia Mason, was unavailable for comment.

26

Valerie Jenkins' flat was on the ground floor of a three-storey Victorian house. This was the address that matched Jenkins' car number plate. The address Fry had confirmed. He'd given them a description of the flat while they waited for his lawyer. After that, Atherton had pulled Carter out of the interview and delivered a lecture about codes of practice.

'He wants to make a complaint against you. Says you have some sort of female vendetta.'

Carter had heard many variations on this theme over the years. She wished it didn't surprise her when her own colleagues listened.

'Valerie Jenkins was a pupil of Robert Fry's over ten years ago.' She kept her tone even. 'He claims she's obsessed with him. But if he's the father of her child, she was a minor, and he was her teacher.'

'They are searching his place right now, and so far there is nothing to implicate him. You better not have cocked this up if all we have to go on is his statement to you, without a caution or a lawyer.'

Neither of them mentioned Brecon. He wasn't Atherton's problem.

She parked two streets away and pulled out her radio. 'Dispatch. Latest on Fry?'

'Atherton's in there with the lawyer. Brecon's joined Lafferty at Fry's house with the search team. Still nothing.'

'I'm at Valerie Jenkins' place. Ambulance and child services standing by.' Carter turned down the volume and put the PR in her pocket. Rebecca Hill knocked on the window.

Carter waved her in. The light was fading and a thin squall of rain rattled against the car as Hill slid into the passenger seat.

'So Fry said she's crazy.'

Carter nodded. 'Yeah, all these crazy women. They ruin everything.'

'That's pretty much what the DCI said to me. But he wasn't talking about Jenkins. I said I'd been chasing up Isobel Williams on my own orders but . . . ' Hill took a breath. 'You going to be ok, Sally?'

'I'm going to talk to Valerie Jenkins and make an assessment. If the girls are in there, get them out safely.'

The two women stared at the fogged windscreen.

'Rebecca . . . ' Carter said.

Hill sighed. 'It's fine.'

'Yeah,' Carter said. 'Those files you found on Angela Mason. We need to trace Jason Ryall.'

'I'm on it, Sarge.'

'Crazy women. What are we like?'

They got out of the car. Carter buttoned up her jacket and grabbed the radio.

'Two minutes away. All radios silent until further notice.'

Dawson and Marshall had pulled up on the next road with the officers from Finsbury Park. She could see the bonnet of Dawson's Ford as she rounded the corner. She turned to thank Hill but she'd already started back. Carter walked past the uniforms and on to Dartington Street.

A two-bedroom, ground-floor flat, with a communal hallway and a small garden that backed on to the railway tracks. Carter had the map in her head. There was no exit out of the garden, officers would stand by on the street if she went inside. Atherton would have taken the job on himself, but even he could see that it would be better if Carter took it. Less chance of spooking Valerie Jenkins. And Carter's fault if the girls were not found safe.

She stood on the doorstep and tried to forget about Atherton. She was here to get Caitlin. Fry had told them she was here, but he couldn't, or wouldn't, say what had happened.

The front door opened. Valerie wedged her body in the doorway, a gaping dressing gown revealing the creased work clothes of the day before. She was nervous, her face tense with exhaustion and her lips grey. Carter was reminded how young she seemed. About the same age as her own mum had been, the last time she'd seen her.

'Hello, Valerie?' There was no obvious movement or noise from the hallway. 'Detective Sergeant Sally Carter. Leabrook police station. We met yesterday. May I come in?'

Valerie didn't move. 'What do you want?'

Carter glanced down the street, making sure no one was out of position.

'It would be better if I could come inside and talk with you, Miss Jenkins.'

'Better for whom?'

'Is your daughter here? Rowena, isn't it? Is Rowena here?'

Valerie Jenkins sighed. 'She's not been well. I called the school.'

'And you're staying at home to take care of her?' Carter nodded sympathetically. 'It's hard, being a single parent.'

'What do you know about it?'

Carter kept nodding but her expression became serious. 'Look, I need to come in and talk to Rowena.'

'I told you, she's not well. She's in bed. You'll have to come back another day.' Valerie started to move away from the door. Carter blocked her with one arm.

'Valerie, you know why I'm here. We were at the library.' She was going to have to take a chance. 'Isobel Williams saw your daughter with the missing girl, Caitlin. You need to let me in or I will have to come in anyway and search the house.'

Valerie Jenkins sharpened. 'You need a warrant, Sally.'

'The thing is, right now it's just you and me having a talk. You make me a cup of tea and we can decide where we take it from there.' She held back from discussing the alternative. All Jenkins had to do was shut the door in her face and the game would change. Carter had the strength, she could charge in with all the backup at her disposal, but Jenkins had the power. 'What do you say?'

A gust of wind blew down the street, rolling sodden debris along the pavement. Carter's shoulders hunched against the cold. She thought she heard the hiss of a police radio under the breeze and wondered how long she had before someone made a mistake.

Jenkins' face grew slack again. She looked at the floor. Flakes of ash lay on the carpet at her feet.

'He's not coming, is he?' Her eyes were almost closed.

Carter only hesitated for a second. 'He's at the station right now, helping us with our enquiries. Would you like to speak to him?'

She shook her head. Carter shivered, her mind racing. Valerie was waiting for Fry. He had admitted to knowing she had the girls but maybe he was playing for time, thinking that the police would be too late.

'It's bloody cold out here. Can I come in? Valerie?'

Jenkins stood aside.

Carter held the radio steady in her pocket as she stepped into the communal hallway. Jenkins shut the front door and followed her down the narrow corridor. The door to the flat was ajar. As Jenkins squeezed past her into the living room, Carter noticed a red rubber band holding back her unbrushed hair.

She could see straight into the kitchen to the back door beyond. She forced herself to take a breath and think clearly. As they walked into the living room she saw two closed doors. One was Valerie's bedroom, the other one Rowena's.

'You can talk to me. I'm not waking her up. She's not been well.' Jenkins jerked her head in the direction of Rowena's bedroom.

There wasn't a sound from behind the door. Carter raised her voice.

'I'd like to have a quick check on her, if that's OK. She's on her own, is she?'

Jenkins immediately shifted closer to the door, completely barring her way.

'Leave her out of it. It's not her fault Rob's in trouble.'

Carter glanced down as Valerie unclenched her fist. They both stared at a small pair of scissors in her palm.

'I promised Rowena. When she's done her homework, we'll decorate the tree together.'

'Sounds like fun.' Carter shook her head. 'Couldn't do all that myself, homework, entertainment, all the responsibility.

Not patient enough. I expect it's different when they're your own though.'

Valerie looked up at Carter from under her half-lowered eyelids. 'I like all kids.'

'You help out at the school, don't you? You were there last week.' Carter forced herself to move away from Rowena's room. 'In Robert's office. When Caitlin came in.'

'She said she needed a hairband.'

'Yes?'

'I think it was just an excuse so she could come to see Rob.'

Carter stood by a low table. A box of Christmas decorations spilled onto the surface.

'We had a party. Something fun for the girls.'

Plural. 'Nice,' she said. 'How about that tea? We were going to have a chat. About Robert.'

Jenkins looked at Carter sharply.

'You have a dad?'

'Not any more.'

'I wanted Row to have one. A proper one.'

'I expect it's difficult for a headmaster. You're like everyone's dad, aren't you?'

'How did you know?'

'Well, I think it's probably just what I've seen, over the years . . . '

'Caitlin told you, I bet.'

'Valerie. Caitlin hasn't told me anything.'

'She saw us together. Told Row. He went mad.' She patted at the dressing gown pockets for her cigarettes. 'Said it would ruin his career.'

'You got one of those for me?' Carter asked.

She waited for the woman to reach for her cigarettes. Lighter, cigarettes, scissors. Valerie put down the scissors.

As soon as she set them on the coffee table, Carter reached forward but Jenkins was faster and swung the scissors up in a wide arc. The top edge of a blade sliced through Carter's shirt. She felt the metal slip beneath her skin as she pulled away.

Carter didn't wait for the pain to hit. She punched Valerie's shoulder, hard, forcing her aside. She made for the girl's bedroom, yanked the door open and slammed it behind her. She clamped the wound on her chest and grabbed at the radio with her free hand.

'All units. I need assistance.' She pressed her back against the door as Jenkins banged on the other side. 'Hostile female perp. Backup required. Forcible home entry.' On the single bed, two unconscious girls lay side by side. 'Ambulance required. I have Caitlin Thompson and Rowena Jenkins. All units, I have both girls. Immediate assistance required.'

Valerie Jenkins was screaming. The bars on the window were visible through the blind. A child's wardrobe was propped up in one corner of the room, a desk in the other. The desk chair stood by the bed, a stack of books and a table lamp balanced on top. Carter managed to hook one foot around the chair legs and drag it over. She braced it against the door and reached for the girls.

Caitlin started to wake up as soon as Carter touched her hand, but Rowena remained unconscious. Her pulse was faint. She wasn't breathing. Under her eyelid, her pupil was constricted. Probably both the girls had been drugged. Removing her hand from her wound, she started CPR.

She was not too late. She was not too late. Carter repeated the words. Outside, she heard the doors to the flat being forced open. With her thumb on Rowena's chin, she pinched her nose closed and blew into her mouth. Four short puffs. On the fifth she felt a jolt. A breath. She was not too late.

It took a little over a minute before a team reached the bedroom door. Carter kicked the chair away and continued chest compressions while Dawson and Marshall cleared the scene for the medical team.

As soon as the tech verified a pulse rate and blood pressure, the assistant readied a stretcher. He noticed Carter's blood-stained shirt but Carter waved him off.

'It's nothing. I'll get it checked in a bit. We need to take care of . . . ' She turned to look for Caitlin.

Caitlin Thompson was standing in the far corner of the room, watching. Her face was swollen with narcotic sleep and she was using her hands to prop herself against the wall. She stared at the bed, her thin body cratered. Child services were waiting outside; but they could not enter an active crime scene.

Carter took a step towards her. Caitlin's back straightened and she looked at Carter, arms falling to her sides, fingers curled into her palms. Carter paused. She was expecting fear, a scared child who needed comfort and reassurance, but Caitlin's eyes were clouded. She looked emptied.

The ambulance crew were checking the oxygen mask and safety straps. They lifted the stretcher and the tech turned to Carter.

'You'll stay here with her? The next ambulance is on its way.'

The crewman nodded to his partner and they carried the stretcher out.

Caitlin watched their retreating figures.

'Caitlin?' Carter put out her hand, palm up.

The girl glanced at the dried blood smeared between Carter's fingers.

'It's my blood. Not Rowena's.'

'Sarge?' Dawson stared at Carter's wound.

'I'm fine. Go and secure the premises, the garden door, the windows. Don't touch anything else.' Carter looked back to the girl.

'Caitlin, you're going to ride in the ambulance.'

Carter heard Dawson leave the flat, ignoring her orders. She would have done the same in Dawson's place, an officer injured, no one attending.

Caitlin was fully awake now, upright and alert. She pointed at Carter's bloodied shirt.

'She did that?'

Outside the bedroom window, the next ambulance drew up. Soon, Caitlin would be in hospital, child services would be with her, the police would want her statement. Her parents would be the last in line to see her that night.

'She was trying . . . to protect you.'

Carter moved forward to take her hand.

'Come on,' Carter attempted a smile. 'Let's get you to the hospital so the doctors can look after you.'

The girl didn't move.

'No, she wasn't.'

The second ambulance crew were in the doorway with a wheelchair. Caitlin turned away from Carter.

'I'm not getting in that.'

Carter spoke to the crew. 'We'll be right out. See you up there.'

When they'd gone, she walked through to the living room, and waited for the girl to follow. Apart from the wrenched door lock the flat was oddly neat. The single cardboard box still lay on the coffee table; the lid pushed aside, strands of silver tinsel trailing over the edge. Marshall stood guard by the front door, his lanky frame energised by the emergency.

'Dawson said you might need some help.'

'Yeah, thanks. Could you . . . ' Carter willed Marshall not to stare as Caitlin emerged from the bedroom, 'Could you give us a moment?'

Marshall took the hint.

Carter wanted the girl to get to the hospital but she also knew hearing her account of the past few days might be her only chance of finding out what really happened. Nothing that would be admissible in court, but an important part of the puzzle. And more than that, she wanted to help. She knew a little of what might be headed the girl's way, and none of it was easy.

Caitlin was watching the living room as though it had betrayed her too.

'Is there anything you want to take with you?' Carter said. 'To the hospital?'

The girl looked Carter up and down.

Carter paused. 'Caitlin, can you tell me what happened?'

Caitlin stared at her.

Carter sighed. 'Let's get you wrapped up. It's freezing out there.'

She went into the bedroom to grab a jumper from Rowena's cupboard. She saw a soft toy on the floor, some kind of rabbit, and picked it up. When she came back into the living room, Caitlin was staring at the box of Christmas decorations. Carter held out a sweatshirt and a pair of trainers.

'We'd better go before they send that wheelchair back for you.'

The girl stepped towards Carter, her eyes on the toy rabbit.

'Here.' She walked over and gave it to the girl. 'What's its name?'

Caitlin shook her head. 'She's Rowena's.'

'Right, well we'd better get her to the hospital as well then.'

The girl held the rabbit with both hands.

'You look after her. Come on.' She put the trainers on the floor, the sweatshirt round the girl's shoulders and guided her out of the flat. As they walked towards the street, the blue light from the police cars flooded the hallway.

Carter saw what was left of the child's bravado fading in the glare.

'I'll come with you to the ambulance.' Carter said. 'They'll look after you.'

Caitlin stared at the floor.

'Spencer's waiting to see you.'

At the mention of the dog, Caitlin looked up. She whispered but Carter couldn't hear. Carter bent down on one knee and wrapped the sweatshirt tighter, tucking some of the girl's hair behind her ear. 'Sorry. What did you say?'

The girl's face crumpled. 'It was my fault.'

'Hey.' Carter held the child's shoulders. 'Nothing's your fault.'

'I wasn't going to tell.'

Carter thought about Isobel Williams' written statement. 'They had a secret.'

'Did you tell Rowena?'

Carter could feel Caitlin's hot breath in her ear.

'I wanted her to know. About her dad.'

She looked at the girl.

'Mr Fry?'

Caitlin nodded.

'They said I mustn't tell. They were going to take us out for chips. But she wouldn't let me go home . . . '

Caitlin folded into Carter.

Carter had always understood she would be there at the end of the story. That was her job. If she was lucky, she could save a life. But not a childhood. That was gone.

The air stung when they stepped outside. Carter pulled at her jacket and carried Caitlin to the remaining ambulance. The girl was heavy in her arms, almost asleep again. Marshall waited by the ambulance door while Carter helped the child in and tucked the toy rabbit under her arm.

'I'll come and see you at the hospital. Look after Rowena's rabbit.'

She gave Caitlin's hand a squeeze and left her with the paramedic. She sat in the ambulance doorway while the driver dressed her wound.

'What's the news?' Carter asked Marshall.

'Atherton's holding Fry. Hill and Dawson have taken Jenkins to the station. Lafferty's on his way to meet the girls at the hospital. Local force are securing the scene. What happened?' Marshall couldn't stop looking at Carter's wound while the tech irrigated and swabbed it.

'She was blocking the kids. I rushed it. She attacked.'

'Good thing you did.'

'Thanks.' Carter glanced at Marshall.

'Well, apart from . . .' He reddened slightly as he nodded at the blood on Carter's chest.

'Yeah.'

The tech finished taping the gauze. 'We can take you in now. Maybe get some stitches?'

Carter rebuttoned the bloodied shirt and pulled her jacket back on.

'I'll drive myself in. Thanks.' She stepped out of the ambulance and grabbed Marshall's arm to steady herself.

Marshall frowned. 'Sure I shouldn't drive you?'

Carter shook her head. 'No need. See you back at the station.'

At the end of the street Carter could see a television van pulling in.

'Sarge, I've got Brecon on the radio. He's asking for you.'

'Mine's on the blink. I'll check in later. Tell him I've gone to the hospital.' Carter looked back down the road. 'And for Christ's sake keep the vultures away.'

She walked back to her car, avoiding the gathering press. Someone local must have phoned it in. She was never sure why. Have the uniforms outside your house and the neighbours would be on to the papers before you'd answered the doorbell, but get knocked down in the street by a man twice your size and no one would call the police. As Carter knew well.

Turning on the engine she dialled the heat up full blast. It was early evening and pitch-dark. She'd been up most of the previous night and out at the river by seven that morning but she couldn't go back to the station until she'd found Isobel Williams. She pulled a can of Fanta and some paracetamol from her glove box and headed for the Whittington hospital.

27

Isobel pressed herself against the garden fence and watched as the man looked around. She was tucked behind the low hedge. She still felt exposed but dared not move. The garden gate was in full view of the door.

She could only see his outline but she knew who it was. Steven. Same height as his brother but grown heavier. He took a step forward out of the glare of the porch light, and she shrank further back. She didn't know how they had found her here but she knew what they had done to Dan. And she had other memories.

Rain saturated the ground. Isobel watched Steven turn back to the house to shelter. She searched the soil beside her for something solid. She unearthed a fist-sized stone and held it tight.

She tried to shout. Sound desiccated to dust in her throat, emerging as a hollow rasp, but it was enough to get his attention. He was with her in seconds flat, pulling her up from her hiding place. She swung round and hit his shoulder with the stone as hard as she could. He grabbed her wrist, smiled and pushed her towards the house.

28

Carter pulled into the car park, turned on her radio and immediately heard her call sign. Brecon wouldn't haul her back to the station while she was at the hospital. Marshall must have told him she was getting medical attention. Her DI didn't need to know she had other plans.

She checked her bandage. The wound ached when she moved, and she knew not to twist. Other than that, the paracetamol were taking care of her. She took a swig of Fanta and answered the radio.

'I have WPC Hill for you, Sarge.'

Carter winced as she got her notebook out.

'I found Jason Ryall's adult record. He was released two weeks ago.'

'Address?'

'Victoria Park area. No answer on the phone.'

'Get hold of Isobel Williams' mother. Clare Williams, she lives in Brighton, number's in the files from Melanie Harris. Isobel might have gone to hers. I'm going to visit Dan Nash while I'm here.'

'He's on the third floor. Forrester Ward. I've spoken to security who were on duty last night. Nash ID'ed Williams and we have a physical description of two men who were looking for her. He can't be sure but he thinks it was the same men who attacked him.'

Carter struggled as she undid her seat belt and opened the car door. Across the tarmac she could see the hospital entrance. A few smokers huddled under the edges of the canopy. To one side was a uniformed officer holding a dog lead. Carter recognised the dog on the other end.

'Right. Do you know . . . '

'Caitlin Thompson and Rowena Jenkins are in private rooms on the fourth floor by the paediatric ward.'

'Thanks.'

Carter found Susan and David Thompson on the sagging sofa in the family room. They had been allowed to see Caitlin after the medical staff had assessed her. Then DS Lafferty and social services had moved them out and told them to wait.

'We just want to take her home.' David looked at Carter as though she was the obstacle. Carter wondered what they had been told.

'Of course you do. The doctors need to make sure Caitlin is well. And there will be some questions.'

'We have questions, too.' David glanced at the door. 'Who's Valerie Jenkins? Why did Caitlin go off with her?

Lafferty would be here soon, ready to go over the protocol, to ask and answer what was necessary, but she struggled to imagine him actually taking care of the parents' needs at all.

'Her daughter and Caitlin are friends at school. She took the girls out for tea, and they went home with her. We don't know the whole story yet, but Caitlin is safe now.'

'They thought we'd hurt her.' Susan Thompson looked at Carter. 'They thought it was us. Are they going to give her back?'

Carter could see that the Thompsons had lumped the police, the social services, the press, Valerie Jenkins, and now the hospital, into one hostile entity. She thought about her parents, the last time she had seen them at the foster carer's. The police had come then. Taken her dad away and left her mum crying in the street. Her parents had never looked after her but that day, at least, they had fought for her. It was a matter of record that they'd tried again. Sally didn't see them, though, the court had protected her. She watched the Thompsons' exhausted faces under the fluorescent light. They loved their daughter, but the system still treated them the same way.

'Course they are, Susan.' Carter sat in the chair opposite and reached out for the mother's hand. 'She's going to come home.'

She stood up and breathed hard against the shooting pain.

'Detective Sergeant Lafferty will be through soon. He'll take care of the paperwork.'

She opened the door and turned back to say goodbye. Susan Thompson sat with her head against her husband's chest, shoulders hunched, and sobbed. Carter raised a hand to David Thompson and he nodded. In a few days she would go and see them at home. Caitlin was safe. It was enough.

The smell of shepherd's pie lingered in the hospital corridor. Carter wondered when she was going to eat.

She went down one flight of stairs to find Forrester Ward. Near the entrance a few of the staff clustered round a desk.

'Dan Nash?' Carter showed her badge.

One of the nurses moved forward. 'You are here about last night? The deaf woman who came to see Mr Nash?'

'Yes, Miss . . . ?'

'Pearl. Staff Nurse Jennifer Pearl. I was on duty.'

'Right.' Carter nodded. 'Did you get a good look at the men?'

'Same types, fair-skinned, average height, one skinnier than the other.' She looked at Carter. 'Don't you want to write this down?'

Carter had no intention of digging around in her jacket and revealing the bloodied shirt.

'It's fine, go on. And if we could walk and talk, that would be good too. I need to speak to Mr Nash.'

The nurse led her down the ward.

'Anything else you can tell me, Staff Nurse?'

They stopped in front of a closed curtain.

'The skinny one was in charge.' She turned to Carter. 'But they were definitely a team.'

'You spoke to them?'

'When I went out to talk to them, they got in the lift without a word. Took the deaf lady's suitcase too.' She pulled back the curtain.

Dan Nash lay against the pillows with his eyes closed.

'She really didn't get a chance to visit with him. Poor thing ran off as soon as she saw them. Mr Nash, the police are here.' She stood back to look at Carter. 'Will that be it? We're discharging Mr Nash this evening. Minor concussion. Nothing broken.'

The nurse turned and left.

'Where's Isobel?'

A couple of nasty bruises.

'We don't know, Mr Nash. I was hoping you might be able to help me.' Carter moved closer to the bed. 'Whoever attacked you wants to find Miss Williams. We believe she's in danger.'

'No shit.'

'Can you think of anything from the evening you were attacked that could lead us to her?'

'A licence plate. G387 RFF.'

'I'm sorry?'

'On the way to the restaurant a car drove at us. I think it was the same guys.'

'You didn't remember this before?'

'It was just one of those driving things, you know, blokes in cars being pricks. But there was a guy in the restaurant too, who came up to me.'

Carter carefully got out her notebook.

'You all right?' Dan Nash stared at her.

'Oh, yeah. It's been a long day. The licence plate?'

'G387 RFF. Red convertible.'

'And you think the driver of this vehicle could be the same person who attacked you?'

Nash frowned. 'I didn't see them all. One of them came to the door, asked for Isobel. Then this other guy came up and started shouting. I told them to fuck off. They pushed the door in. I felt something smash into my head.'

'A third bloke?'

'I think so. But that's all I remember.'

'Except for the registration of the vehicle?'

'Three hundred and eighty-seven giraffes. It's a kid's game. GRFF.'

A tea trolley arrived just as a nurse called Carter's name. Carter looked down the ward to see the nurse waving a telephone receiver at her. She glanced at the tea lady and put her notebook away.

'May I?' She took a cup of tea. 'Will you excuse me, Mr Nash?'

The Staff Nurse had mentioned a suitcase. Williams had planned to go away.

'DS Carter.'

'Sally? It's me.' Hill sounded rushed. 'I've spoken to Melanie Harris, she confirmed Clare Williams is Isobel's mother, in Brighton.'

'That was where Isobel spent last weekend. She's probably there now. We need to get a car over.'

'There's no need, the police are already there.'

Carter took a swig of tea. The Brighton police could pick both women up and be on the alert for the car Nash had identified. A uniform on duty at Williams' house as a precaution, and she could go back to Leabrook.

'Nice work.'

'No, it wasn't me. I called the mother at home but a SOCO answered. Clare Williams is dead, Sally. She was murdered this afternoon.'

29

It was bright in the sitting room. Isobel squinted as she looked around. To one side she could see Jason, and behind him Agnes's legs sticking out from an armchair. She was still wearing the blue Wellington boots. There was no sign of Mary.

'Cat got your tongue?' It was a question he used to ask Lucy. She remembered how he said it to her. Clever Lucy who had made herself scarce.

He waited for Isobel to make eye contact and then stepped to the side.

Agnes lay slumped in the chair with a striped plastic bag draped over her head.

Steven said. 'She was making a fuss.'

Isobel lurched forward but Jason grabbed her by the coat collar, pushed her to the centre of the room and held her there.

'What are you doing here, Izzy? You used to whine about old Spill at school.' Isobel could see his lips moving.

She thought her legs were going to give way. Jason had pulled this trick before, at school. Drew had pissed him off and he'd taken a plastic bag, put it over Drew's head and made him walk around until he fell over and started to panic. Isobel looked at Agnes; she was still breathing.

Jason nodded. 'She's fine. Come here,' he pulled Isobel onto the sofa, 'let's warm you up. I expect you're wondering where the girl is. She's upstairs in her bedroom, having a rest.'

Isobel watched him. Mary might be shouting for help. The men's faces told her nothing. She half-hoped the girl was unconscious. Just for now. So she wouldn't have to remember what was coming.

Jason was sizing her up, working out what he wanted and how to get it. That was what he'd always done. So friendly, so interested. Isobel had never felt so much attention focused on her. Even now, she blushed to think how quickly she had trusted him and what that trust had bought him.

'Thanks for helping me find her.'

He wanted her to understand what he was saying.

Isobel had to force herself to watch his mouth. He knew she hadn't told anybody what happened at the party fifteen years ago. If she had, none of them would be here. She had stopped talking. But that wasn't enough for Jason. He wanted her to know that whatever happened, that night or this, was her fault.

She shrugged her shoulders.

'Don't be like that. Don't pretend you don't care. We used to be a team, remember? We belonged together.'

He was quoting their old headmaster. Mr Sanders was fond of telling the children that they should be happy at the Schoolhouse because it was a place where they belonged. As though nowhere else wanted them. Which in Jason's case was true. Not even the Schoolhouse in the end.

'Little Angie wanted to hang out too. We went away for a week together after I found out about her . . . condition. Tried to sort it out. But she promised me she'd never tell. And I do believe she kept that promise.'

Her thoughts were beads on an abacus, stacking together as she examined them. He'd got to Angie again, after that night. Six months later Angie was dead. Jason was capable of anything. She knew that. Mary was upstairs, Agnes was in the chair, Dan was in the hospital. Jason had put them all there.

'Look what we brought for you.' Jason nodded at his brother.

Steven dropped her suitcase at Jason's feet.

Isobel kept very still. The games Jason played were all about reactions. She was falling into a trap, just as she had with the kissing, the funeral for Turpin, the party. She would fight him and finally relent and his satisfaction would be all the greater for her resistance. He was smiling at her now.

'Load of old junk you carry around with you. Can't believe you still have this.' He rubbed the sole of his trainer along the top of the bag. 'Remember when we all went to the sea? Stupid Kathy Binks. Lucky no one believed her.'

Isobel remembered Kathy on the school trip. Miss Peden's face as they got on the bus home. 'Have you been a naughty girl?' The police had come to the school, but nothing really changed. Jason was moved to the other side of the playground fence. Kathy was Steven's girlfriend. They still had a party at Angie's house.

Jason bent down to the suitcase and took something out. She forced herself to concentrate. There were clothes and photos, letters and paperwork but no mention of Agnes Spill or this house. She had hardly known she was coming here herself, but they had found her. She put the beads together, one by one. This house. Agnes Spill. Her mother. She stared at the figure in the chair. Agnes had called Clare to tell her she was safe.

'There you go.' Jason held out his hand. In his palm was a glass vial filled with sand and orange liquid. A companion to the lavender container in her handbag. 'Bit morbid I thought. Your dad's ashes all over the place.'

Isobel looked at the vial. 'It's important to me,' Clare had said, 'and it should be to you.'

She stood up. Steven pulled her back.

'We got your mum's address from those letters in the suitcase.' Steven said.

Some noise escaped from deep within her, tearing her stomach, her throat, her jaw. She saw Jason look up, surprised, felt the crack of Steven's knuckles under her chin. Her teeth clamped down on her tongue and blood flowed into the back of her throat. Steven stood over her, fist clenched. She fell back into the sofa, clutching her mouth.

'Look who's woken up,' Jason pushed past her. She didn't want to watch him. She looked down at the floor and focused on Mary's pink boots. After a moment, Steven's hand closed over her shoulder and she looked up.

Jason perched on the arm of the chair in which Agnes sat, the bag stretching tighter around her mouth as she gasped for air. Her hands were bound by another plastic bag, twisted around her wrists.

'It's no good trying to speak. Isobel can't read lips through plastic, can she?'

She could see Agnes's open mouth through the blue and white stripes of the bag.

'Scabby Spill. Wouldn't let things be.'

Isobel tried to understand what Jason was saying. Her jaw ached and her tongue throbbed where she had bitten it.

'I've had plenty of time to think about what you all did. She gave evidence against me, the three of them did, her,

your old lady, and Angie's mother. And you, of course.' He
held up the cloth-bound book with the girl on the cover. Her
diary from her handbag in the hall.

Jason had gone to prison while she was in the rehabilitation unit. She hadn't asked how. She had her own reasons for
knowing he belonged there. Angie would never have told,
and in the end, she couldn't. But her mother had made sure.

Jason stood up and walked towards her. His face inches
from hers.

'Your mum had me put away, and you never even had to
come to court. You and your diaries. Well she's paid for it
now. You all will.'

What had they done to her mother?

His smirk faded. 'She's a fighter, though. Poor old Bish.
You remember Bishop? It was thanks to him we found you.
Went everywhere in Fortis Green looking for you and there
you were, outside the newsagents. In the flesh. And guess
what? Your name and address in a book behind the counter.
Nice and tidy.'

He sat on the sofa.

'Why did you cut your hair? Makes you seem older.'

Instinctively, her hand went to the back of her head.
Jason's lips curled up in delight.

'You haven't changed where it matters, Isobel Williams.'
He shifted closer to her.

She tried not to back away, to focus on his lips.

He put a hand up to her cheek. 'You always thought you
were better than us, didn't you? Turns out you're the worst.'

His face drew closer but she could still see the words.

'Guess that's what your dad knew too.'

His fingers were rough. She felt the calluses catch in the
fine hair around her temples. His touch was amplified, his

breath hot on her face. She remembered letting him lick her neck, after she stopped charging for kisses and before the party. His tongue was like his fingertips, coarse as sandpaper.

The bones of her resistance crumbled. Her life had been spent trying to close the gap between her old self and the person she wanted to be, hoping for a way out. Even as she'd faced Steven in the garden she had accepted there was a penance to be paid and that then, finally, she might be free. But when she had woken up in the bedroom with the prim-rose curtains, she had known what the night would bring. It was the same feeling she had the day of the party at Angie's house. There was no escape and there never had been. She started to scream.

I am at Angie's house and everything has gone wrong and I don't know what to do.

I came over to play with Angie like Mrs Mason asked me to. It was teatime and the lady who works here was doing some cleaning and Mrs Mason went out for Christmas shopping with a friend. She said she would be back at 6 o'clock. I don't know what time it is now. It is dark and the lady has gone. She left when they came for the party. Kathy and Bishop and Steven and Jason. I don't know what they said to her. She didn't say goodbye.

Jason brought beer in cans and he found some other drinks that Mrs Mason has in a cupboard. I had a glass of something yellow and it was hot in my mouth. They played records and it was too loud for Angie so she went upstairs. The yellow drink made me feel giddy.

Bishop broke one of the china animals that was on a shelf and Steven smashed another one on purpose. I tried to clear it up and I told them to go home but Jason said the party was only just getting started and we should take it upstairs and find Angie.

Kathy said they were disgusting. She told me it was time to go and when Steven grabbed her arm she told him to fuck off and she ran out the door and into the street. Steven was angry but Jason sent Bishop after her. He said there are two girls left and they could share. I wanted to go home. Everything is a mess and Jason was scaring me but he told me to cook some pizzas and I stayed in the kitchen. The boys went upstairs and shouted for Angie. I could hear her and she was crying. Maybe I should call the police but it is my fault they are having a party here and I will be in trouble. I think Mrs Mason will be home soon.

It's quiet now. I should go and check on Angie.

30

Carter took a deep breath and eased the seat belt across her chest with her right hand. It hurt less to lean back. Static crackled from the police radio. The dashboard clock showed 7.38. On the passenger seat lay Isobel Williams' juvenile file. With both parents accounted for, the only other names from the original file were a teacher from her old school and the mother of Angela Mason. There was no guarantee either of them was still alive or that they had anything to do with Williams.

In the dark of the Whittington Hospital car park a single overhead lamp lit a family huddled round the ticket machine a few feet ahead. At the edge of the group a boy in Batman pyjamas dripped green liquid from a carton onto the tarmac. Carter stared at the dirty pools of liquid in the gravel and listened to Brecon shouting at her on the radio.

'Carter?'

'Yes, sir.'

'I've got Hill in the office. She's been doing background checks on Isobel Williams.'

Carter looked back at the file on the seat beside her. She scanned the names again. Clare Williams. Julian Williams. Patricia Mason. Agnes Spill.

'Yes, sir.'

Brecon sighed. 'She's traced the licence plate to a Mark Bishop. Brighton police confirm they detained a Mark Bishop at the scene of Clare Williams' murder. He is currently receiving medical treatment.'

The child by the ticket machine put one foot in the puddle he had made.

'Bishop's name is in the system.' Brecon read from the print out in front of him. 'He's done time for assault. Sealed juvenile record. This is now a murder investigation.'

'I need an address, sir.'

'There's no point going to Brighton now, Carter.'

'Yes . . . No, sir. I need an address for a Mrs Patricia Mason, date of birth 11.03.1919 and for a Miss Agnes Spill, date of birth 12.09.1922.'

'Atherton's waiting for you to be discharged from hospital. You are there now?'

Carter looked down at her shirt. There was no fresh blood through the bandage but the dull ache had returned. She reached into the glovebox for the emergency light. 'I'll be at the station as soon as I've located Williams . . . '

Brecon cut her off, the blast of noise that returned indistinguishable from the static.

Carter opened the car door and tried to attach the light to the roof. She felt a pull in her chest and the seep of the wound opening. The boy at the ticket machine stuck out his tongue.

Brecon's radio crackled back to life.

'It's in Walthamstow. Home of Patricia Mason, deceased. The same address listed for Agnes Spill. I'll have to let Brighton know you have a lead.'

'Yes, sir.'

Brighton wouldn't get there before she did, and she'd

need backup. Walthamstow wasn't far from the marshes where they'd found Moffatt's body. With a grunt, Carter made one more attempt to stick the blue light to the roof of the Astra without getting out of the car. The boy watched her. His tongue retreated into his mouth as he saw the object in Carter's hand. He detached himself from the family and moved towards her.

'And what do I tell Atherton?' Brecon's voice skittered around the car park.

'Tell him to be ready to take the collar on a murder.' Carter held the light out to the boy, who looked at it for a moment before he handed the policewoman his drink carton, put one foot up on the doorway and lifted the globe into place.

'He'll want to be there.'

The boy took his drink back and Carter nodded. Wind whipped the thin fabric of the Batman pyjamas around the boy's body. He returned the nod and swung the door shut.

'Of course, sir. And some local force in Walthamstow standing by. They are not to proceed. And if you can spare anyone from the station . . .'

Blue light flooded the car park as Carter turned on the car engine. The boy turned around as his mother walked towards him. Carter reversed the car out of the parking space and headed to the exit.

'Carter?'

'Yes, sir.'

In her rear-view mirror, she saw the boy lift off the ground as a hand swiped across the seat of the pyjamas. The radio hissed.

'Sir?'

'You'll need the fucking address.'

31

Alive.

The thought came to her in sign. She was back in Mary's room. The overhead light was on and the curtains were drawn. The clock by the bed flashed 19:37. Her hands and bare feet were tied to the small bedframe and something was knotted around her mouth. She twisted and pulled but she was bound tight. Four pink Wellington boots lay in a heap on the floor.

Mary where?

She ran her tongue along the inside of her lip and tasted blood. Rage and panic overwhelmed her again. She needed to steady her thoughts and feelings, the way she had learned to calm herself after the accident. The nights in hospital beds, immobile. The months spent in wards after operations, not daring to close her eyes for fear of who would be there when she opened them. She had focused then on the things she could control.

Concentrate.

She tried to get a sense of the house. The walls were thin, the floors mostly bare boards. When she lay very still and held on to the metal bedframe, she could feel vibrations from the rooms below.

Music.

She let the sounds of the house travel through her body. There was a rhythm, the regular beat of music, and another, closer, vibration. Someone was on the stairs.

The door opened and Steven walked in. His body filled the room. He stood under the light and looked at her. For a moment, Isobel allowed his eyes to meet hers.

'You're awake.'

He stepped closer and Isobel fell back. In his hand was a kitchen knife. Isobel felt herself separate from her body. She watched from far away as he brought the knife up and trailed an edge along her outstretched arm.

She thought, both hands out, finger and thumb extended. *Stay still.*

He pressed the blade into her skin and she saw the turquoise artery bloom beneath the metal. She focused on the room. She focused on what she could do to save Mary.

He cut the rope from her nearest wrist.

She let it drop and lay still as he went to the end of the bed and cut one of the cords. Her foot fell and she waited for him to reach the other ankle.

Kick.

She knocked his skull against the iron bedpost.

Kick.

Under his jaw.

He staggered, losing his balance in the small space under the eaves. The back of his head caught the slope of the ceiling. He looked surprised. After a moment, he stopped and Isobel saw him drop to the ground.

She waited. She could feel the music downstairs but no movement from the end of the bed. When she had caught her breath she rolled over and untied her other hand. She pulled the gag from her mouth and leaned over.

The tops of his knees were visible where his legs had folded beneath him. She climbed off the bed. Steven's mouth was open and she didn't know if he had shouted or how loud his fall had been.

She stood still, hands shaking. She could feel the snap of Steven's jaw underfoot. She had kicked at him with everything she had.

Get knife.

She pressed the top of her foot against the nearest leg. He didn't stir.

She knelt down and felt for the knife, trying not to look at the body. Her fingers brushed against his jacket and she pulled back with a shudder. A slick of grease beneath her knuckles. She glanced down. Blood. From the underside of his neck she saw the knife handle and more blood still pooling under his head.

Jason would be up any minute. There was no time to think. She bent forward for the knife, pulled the handle from the heavy hand that still held it, and backed away from the body. As she straightened up she saw the shelves under the window where Mary stored her possessions. The record player had gone. Isobel looked around. On the shelf behind her was a photo in a frame. She had never seen the frame before but she recognised the picture. Angie and Isobel, an arm each around Turpin.

Mary get.

The skirt that Agnes had given her was stained. Her tongue was still swollen from where she had bitten it. Her chin grazed from Steven's blow. She wiped the blade and her hands on the bedclothes.

She tugged on the Wellingtons and threw a blanket over him. She tucked the knife tight into her waistband, turned out the light and went downstairs.

At the bottom of the stairs she stopped. A draught swept through the house from the back door. Jason might not notice she was gone for a few minutes. She could get help.

Don't run.

The hallway was dark but shafts of light spilled from under the sitting room and kitchen doors. She gripped the door handle and went into the sitting room.

Mary stood by the record player. She turned when she saw Jason look up from the sofa. She was still in her dancing dress with her coat over the top. She ran to Isobel.

Jason stared at them. 'Where's my baby brother?'

Mary clung to her, damp with sweat. An electric heater in the old fireplace was pumping out stale air. The room smelled of hospital incinerators, burned blood and dirt. There was no sign of Agnes. She took hold of Mary's hands.

'Time for a dance.' Jason jumped up.

She kept hold of Mary. The girl looked up at her. Isobel touched the tip of Mary's ring finger. *O.* Then she pressed her folded index finger against the girl's. *K.* She nodded and Mary nodded back.

Jason hadn't noticed anything. He was by the record player, flipping through Mary's records, announcing the name of each one. Mary was not wearing her hearing aid. Isobel squeezed Mary's hand and walked over to the record player. She tapped the top of the pile.

In a minute he would look for Steven.

'You'll dance to this? Go on then. Give us a preview.' Jason stared at her, his head to one side.

She tried to remember the song. She had never heard the tune but she knew the rhythm from watching Mary.

'Abra-abra-cadabra,' Isobel mouthed the words and swung her hips in time to the song in her head. The knife in her waistband dug into her with each movement. She focused on the feeling of it scraping against her skin.

She continued to sway as she placed the single on the stereo and turned the volume up. When the needle was in place, she turned to check on Mary and saw the room clearly for the first time. She had to stop herself from crying out. Behind the sofa lay Agnes Spill.

Mary took Isobel's hands but she was shaking. She needed to give Mary the best chance she could. They would have to leave Agnes. She turned her back to Jason.

'Show me the song again,' she mouthed to Mary.

A faint smile crossed Mary's face.

Dance. Isobel thought.

'Dance,' she mouthed.

Jason was getting restless. He glanced at the door and back at Isobel.

'Don't stop,' Isobel mouthed to Mary as though singing to the music. 'Until I say "run".'

Mary frowned.

'When I say "run", run to the bridge,' Isobel repeated.

She willed Mary to understand. The light in Mary's eyes seemed to return.

'Abra-abra-cadabra,' they sang. 'Abracadabra.'

Isobel felt Jason close to her. She could sense him getting ready for his next move.

'You done?' He stood by her side. 'Where's Steve?'

She glanced up at the ceiling.

Wait. She thought.

Jason jabbed at Isobel's chest. 'Come with me.' He pushed Mary away and grabbed Isobel's arm. Isobel held her body against his. She could see Mary stagger back and turn to Isobel.

Now.

'Run,' she mouthed to Mary. 'Run, now.'

Isobel lifted the knife as Jason turned to see Mary dart away.

The blade slid into his stomach and Jason doubled over. She let go and pulled back. In the hallway, she saw the outline of Mary as she ran through the gate. Isobel didn't turn around.

Run.

12 February 1977

Crown Prosecution Service vs Jason Ryall
Court Summary

Jason Ryall was accused of 1. abduction of a minor 2. child sexual abuse 3. common assault 4. burglary 5. ABH and was found guilty of charges 1, 3 and 4. The principal evidence against the defendant was supplied by Patricia Mason, Agnes Spill and Clare Williams, who were not witnesses to the crimes, and this is reflected in the decision of the court. The victim was not called upon to testify and neither was the principal witness, also a minor, whose written testimony was included in the prosecution's evidence. This case has challenged current legal definitions of consent and it is the recommendation of the court that an independent tribunal should be established to investigate the parameters of sexual consent and capacity as presented here.

32

Carter took the direct route, though the traffic was heavy even with her light on. The roads were familiar at least and she could get Leabrook on the radio for directions on the approach.

Carter thought about the three women whose testimonies had sent Jason Ryall to prison. Two of them were dead. Ryall might already have got to the third.

She had read the paperwork, the files from Islington and the ones Hill had retrieved. Carter understood why Williams wanted to help find Caitlin Thompson. Some memories glow in your mind, waiting for the chance to burn you again.

One night, that's what goes in the records. The night they take you to the pub, and the park afterwards. The night they introduce you to their friends, at a private club, or a penthouse flat. The night they knock on your bedroom door to check on you. One night. But it never is just one night. Carter had recognised it in Isobel Williams. The rest of your life.

33

Isobel could not see an exit to the main road. The only route she knew was straight ahead, towards the riding school. She held on to Mary and they ran towards the bridge.

At the top of the bridge they paused and looked back. Jason's outline was visible by the light of the porch. He walked stiffly to the gate and disappeared from view. A beam of white light shone into the garden. Jason had Agnes's torch.

They crouched down.

The light from the torch passed overhead, hitting the bricks on the far side of the bridge, and then the light went out.

With the torch off, Jason was invisible, but a blue light flashed into the cloud. Mary tapped her on the shoulder.

Hear police. She signed. *For us?*

Isobel tried to think who could have called for help. Maybe her mother had got to the phone. She glanced back at the houses. They had no choice but to go on.

They kept low across the bridge and down the steps. They ran to the paddock. Light from the canal boats was visible across the field. Between the canal and the path a steep bank led into bracken and hedging without any clear way through.

Mary was staring at something behind them.

'The man, the man, he fell,' Mary mouthed and surged ahead, dragging Isobel with her.

Mary sped along the path to the riding school, her bare feet sure of the ground. The office light was out.

They ran across the open yard. The barn gates were shut but Mary brushed past her and tipped a nearby plant pot. She had the keys.

They only had to hide until the police came. If they came.

Inside, they locked the doors. Hay bales, some harnesses and halters nailed to the walls, and doors to the stables at the back. The air smelled of horses and woodchip. Isobel felt a muffled vibration through the soles of her rubber boots. She turned to Mary. The barn gates were shaking.

They moved further inside, feeling their way through the darkness until they reached a wooden wall. Isobel swept along it until her hand hit a large metal ring. She turned the ring and felt the latch give. If they could find the path up to the house without Jason seeing them, they might reach the police.

Mary was jabbing her in the shoulder with urgent punches. Isobel gave the handle another twist. The door to the stable opened. She reached for Mary and pulled her through the gap.

Strong, thumping jolts shook the ground. In front of them a horse stamped at the straw-covered concrete. Mary's mouth opened in delight.

'Brodie!' She dashed forward, an arm outstretched to steady him.

Isobel watched as thin ribbons of light landed across Mary's body, shining through the battens in the wall. Jason was in the barn.

She put her hand beside Mary's on the horse. Brodie was

level with her head, no taller than Turpin. They moved closer, feeling the steady thump of the horse's heart as they pressed their faces to his flank.

Mary crooked her finger to her nose. *Sister.*

Isobel could not bring back Angie. But she could stop it happening again.

Sister.

Isobel took a step, one hand on Brodie's shoulder, and with all the effort in her body she threw herself across him. The horse shuddered. Mary held him and Isobel swung her leg over his back, just as she had always done.

Ahead of them the door was pulled open. Light flooded into the stable. Isobel closed her eyes against the whiteness, and clung to Brodie's neck.

'Yar!' she shouted, squeezing the horse's sides.

At the sound of Isobel's voice, Brodie reared up and Isobel held on tighter. For a moment, they were all held in the light from the barn. Isobel leaning forward on the rearing horse, Mary at their side. The silhouette of Jason in the doorway. Then Mary put a hand out to Brodie and shouted.

'Yar!' she yelled and jumped out of the way.

Isobel opened her eyes as she felt the doorway scrape her legs. Below her, Jason raised his arm as they passed. Brodie reared back up. Ahead of them a constellation shone through broken gates. Isobel lost her grip. She fell with the momentum of the horse, into the night around her. She felt the rush of cold, saw the marionette body of Jason as Brodie kicked out, saw Mary run towards her. She thought of Christopher and of her mother. She lay on the ground, her heart rising and falling with the hooves beside her.

34

Carter looked out at the yard, now illuminated by Scene of Crime lights. The riding school was crowded with police. Dawson and Marshall mixed with Walthamstow uniforms, and DCI Atherton was supervising it all. Mounted Branch officers had been called, and the SIO from Brighton had arrived in full uniform. Carter guessed there might be some sort of stand-off between him and Atherton. She didn't know the man but it hardly seemed a fair fight. Standing by the tinsel-draped office, taking notes from the two women who owned the riding school, Rebecca Hill returned Carter's gaze.

Atherton walked towards Carter with a PC from Brighton in tow. She guessed he'd already been co-opted.

'Quite a mess, DS Carter.'

'Yes, guv.'

'Who even knew this was here? Impossible to bloody find.'

They watched the Mounted Branch officers lead the horse away.

'Dangerous bloody animals.' Atherton shook his head.

'Yes, guv.' She had never seen a horse kick out like that, but the animal had calmed quickly enough when she had led him away from Jason Ryall. Ryall was on his way to hospital and if he ever left he wouldn't be going home.

'The man Brighton has in custody isn't cooperating, so we're lucky to have this wrapped up so quickly.'

Carter saw that it was wrapped up from a policing point of view. She looked at Isobel Williams and the young girl across the yard and wondered if they would see it the same way.

'Why were they after these three? An old woman, a child and a deaf girl? Not exactly a threat.'

Carter nodded. 'Turns out they were, though.'

She looked at the DCI.

'I suppose, on this occasion, they were.' He cleared his throat.

Carter wondered if he would ever notice that in the end the women could fight back. Maybe not as quickly as these three, but one day, somehow, their voices would be heard.

'No one has informed the victim's daughter yet, guv. I'd like to speak to her, if I may.'

Atherton frowned. 'She's your witness. But she's also a suspect now. Careful what you say.'

'Yes, guv.'

'Then I think it's time you went and had that seen to properly.'

He waved at Carter's wound. Grappling with a horse had caused it to bleed again, but the wave was both an official nod, and a dismissal. The press would be on their way. No need for an injured female Sergeant in the background.

'Yes, guv.'

Carter walked towards the isolated figures sitting arm in arm on a railway sleeper, draped in high-vis jackets. She thought of the photo she had seen in the files from the Schoolhouse. Angela Mason and Isobel Williams. For the second time that day Carter wondered how any woman could be a mother.

She lowered herself onto the sleeper beside them. Her chest felt wet and cold, and she pulled at her jacket for warmth.

'Is she dead?' Mary didn't take her eyes off her as she wiped her cheeks with her sleeve.

Carter was grateful to give the good news first.

'Agnes?'

The girl nodded.

'No, Mary. She told me where to find you. She . . . she's had a shock. But she wants to see you.'

Mary nodded again.

Isobel watched them, but even in the shadows, Carter could see a change. Carter knew what it was to have to leave the past behind and learn again to put one foot in front of the other. As though you had a right to move on. She hoped Isobel had that chance.

'Isobel?' Carter made sure her face was in the light. 'We found Caitlin. And her friend. They're safe. Thanks to you.'

Isobel looked into Carter's eyes.

Thank you, she signed.

Carter could see the next question, could read it as clearly as Williams had read her lips.

'I'm sorry,' Carter said. 'Your mother was attacked earlier today. She fought back but she died before they could get her to hospital. We have the man in custody.'

'Mark Bishop,' Isobel mouthed the words.

'Yes.' Carter heard the sob catch in the woman's throat. 'The brothers left him in Brighton. We found a man's body at Mary's house. We believe it to be Steven Ryall.'

Isobel struggled to breathe.

'I killed him,' she said, her voice barely a whisper.

Carter had seen the body on the bedroom floor, the knife entry wound and the blood from the back of the head.

'You saved yourself, Isobel. And probably saved Agnes and Mary too. Don't say anything more until you have a lawyer and an interpreter. Don't talk to anyone.'

Mary put her arms around Isobel and held her tight.

Carter called Dawson and Marshall over. They would look after Isobel Williams and the girl until social services came. She made sure they knew not to let anyone interview them that night.

It had started to rain. She ran through the investigation in her head. SOCO would take pictures but there were plenty of witnesses to the event. They could clear the barn quickly. The house along the railway was a different matter. That would take all night.

'You need to get back.' Rebecca Hill put a hand on Carter's shoulder.

'Don't push me. I'm about ready to fall.' Carter shook her head.

'I'm using you as a prop,' Hill said. 'I can barely stand myself.'

'How's it gone?'

'Jenkins has been charged with child abduction and attempted murder. Sleeping pills. Fry is still helping with enquiries. Obstruction, assisting an offender, not to mention historic sexual abuse of a minor. DI reckoned you might want to charge him yourself.'

'And the girls?'

Hill sighed. 'The Thompsons are waiting with Caitlin. And Rowena Jenkins' grandparents are on their way to the hospital now.'

Carter tipped her head back. The steady drizzle felt good on her tired eyes. Caitlin Thompson and Rowena Jenkins were safe. She let a few of the tears she had held back slide down her temples and hoped Rebecca wouldn't notice.

'You're raining, Sally. Time to go.'

Carter doubted she could walk to the car, let alone drive it home.

'We've got a lift back.'

She followed the sweep of Hill's arm to the top of the lane. DS Lafferty stood by his car, in conversation with a local uniform.

'Is that how you got here?' Carter accepted Hill's elbow as they walked to the car.

'I would have waited at yours but I don't have a key.'

Carter blinked at her girlfriend. She still couldn't imagine how it would all work out. She shook her head and handed Rebecca the hamburger keyring.

Saturday

Mary was waiting on the doorstep when I got there. Agnes bought her the right-sized hat for her birthday and she was wearing it with the strap hanging down and a grin on her face.

She put her hands up.

'Riding?'

Yes, riding today, I signed back. She ran ahead and I followed her.

As soon as we got to the riding school, Mary found the stall. We put the bridle on Brodie together but I left the saddle behind.

We walked up to the top field and into the woods. The sunlight moved through the trees and you could smell the earth. We put a blanket on the ground and ate our picnic. Brodie had an apple and we had bread and chocolate and milk in cartons.

I showed Mary how to fasten the strap on her new riding hat. I think she already knew but she never ties laces either. Not like her mum. Angie loved to practise on the clothes frames in kindergarten; bows, buttons and zips. She would do them up and ask me to undo them again. I will try and find some of those frames for Mary. Angie wouldn't want her going around with her shoes undone.

We mounted Brodie and walked through the woods to the flat pasture on the other side. I had the song in my head from when I used to take Turpin to the park, the white horses song. Mary held me and I turned around to make sure she was ready. I nudged Brodie into a canter. Mary squeezed tight but after a minute I felt her relax her body against my back. She was laughing. I let the sound of her laughter rumble through me and up to the blue-and-white sky.

'Wooooooooooo!' Mary's breath rushed past my cheek as we both shouted at the top of our lungs.

'Wooooooohooooooo.'

Acknowledgements

This book was inspired by the many extraordinary children I have met, and by the teachings of Maria Montessori and the dignity and independence of the pupils for whom she worked her whole life. I am grateful for all I learned in my seven years as a pupil at a Montessori school, and for my training as a teacher in the Montessori method. I would like to thank the teachers who taught me the point of learning and gave me a desire to continue studying long after my early education: Miss Beatrice Deveaux, Anna Scher, Mrs Wright (née Clay), and George Leith.

I have been incredibly lucky to have had the kind and clever Sarah Castleton as my editor, in addition to early support from Nicola Monaghan, Richard Beard and the writers of the National Academy of Writing. Caroline Knight, Phoebe Carney and Gesche Ipsen helped to guide me through the later drafts and any remaining errors are entirely my own. I write about flaws and frailties and guilt from my own continued familiarity with those conditions.

Thank you to James Gurbutt, Zoe Hood, Celeste Ward-Best, Sophie Harris, and all at the great Corsair. And thank you to my friend and agent Laura Macdougall and United Agents, to Sarah Ballard for standing in when Thea

Macdougall was being published, and to Christina Shepherd, my acting agent of many years, who gave me a place to rewrite when I really needed it.

Much thanks to my BSL teacher Deborah Lush, who was also an early reader of the book and provided valuable advice. And thank you to other early readers, Mary Brannan, Claudia Devlin, Leah Dunthorne, Josh Hobson, Katie McCrum, Linda Riley, Abi Shapiro and Cathryn Wright, and to Molly Macleod.

Thanks to my mum, Alexandra, and my mother-in-law, Kyong Sue, and to all my family and friends who listened to the story and helped me to let it grow.

Lastly, firstly, and always, thank you to Rena for going to school with me every day.